The Masters Of The Peaks
A Story Of The Great North Woods

by
Joseph A. Altsheler

The Masters Of The Peaks
A Story Of The Great North Woods
by Joseph A. Altsheler

Copyright © 2023

All Rights reserved.
No part of this publication may be reproduced, stored in a retrieval system, or transmitted in any form or by any means, electronic, mechanical, photocopying or Otherwise, without the written permission of the publisher.

The author/editor asserts the moral right to be identified as the author/editor of this work.

ISBN: 978-93-57485-57-9

Published by

DOUBLE 9 BOOKS
2/13-B, Ansari Road
Daryaganj, New Delhi – 110002
info@double9books.com
www.double9books.com
Tel. 011-40042856

This book is under public domain

ABOUT THE AUTHOR

Joseph A. Altsheler was born on April 29, 1862, in Three Springs, Hart County, Kentucky, to Joseph and Louise Altsheler. He was a newspaper reporter, editor, and author of popular juvenile historical fiction. He wrote fifty novels and at least fifty-three short stories. Seven of his novels were in sequence. He worked as an editor at the Louisville Courier-Journal in 1885. In 1892, he started to work for New York World and then as the editor of the World's tri-weekly magazine. He wrote children's stories due to a lack of suitable stories. On May 30, 1880; Altsheler married Sarah Boles and had a son named Sidney. In 1914, during World War I Altsheler and his family were in Germany and they were forced to remain there. Altsheler died at the age of 57, on June 5, 1919, in New York. His wife, Sarah Boles died after 30 years. Their bodies are buried at the Cave Hill Cemetery in Louisville, Kentucky. Although each of the thirty-two novels constitutes an independent story, Altsheler suggested reading in sequence for each series (that is, he numbered the volumes). You can read the remaining eighteen novels in any order.

CONTENTS

CHAPTER I.
IN THE DEEP WOODS 7

CHAPTER II.
ON THE RIDGES 23

CHAPTER III.
THE BRAVE DEFENSE 38

CHAPTER IV.
THE GODS AT PLAY 53

CHAPTER V.
TAMING A SPY 70

CHAPTER VI.
PUPILS OF THE BEAR 84

CHAPTER VII.
THE SLEEPING SENTINELS 98

CHAPTER VIII.
BEFORE MONTCALM 112

CHAPTER IX.
THE SIGN OF THE BEAR 128

CHAPTER X.
THE FLIGHT OF THE TWO 141

CHAPTER XI.
THE MYSTIC VOYAGE 155

CHAPTER XII.
THE MARVELOUS TRAILER 170

CHAPTER XIII.
READING THE SIGNS 186

CHAPTER XIV.
ST. LUC'S REVENGE 200

CHAPTER I.
IN THE DEEP WOODS

A light wind sang through the foliage, turned to varying and vivid hues now by the touch of autumn, and it had an edge of cold that made Robert Lennox shiver a little, despite a hardy life in wilderness and open. But it was only a passing feeling. A moment or two later he forgot it, and, turning his eyes to the west, watched the vast terraces of blazing color piled one above another by the sinking sun.

Often as he had seen it the wonderful late glow over the mighty forest never failed to stir him, and to make his pulse beat a little faster. His sensitive mind, akin in quality to that of a poet, responded with eagerness and joy to the beauty and majesty of nature. Forgetting danger and the great task they had set for themselves, he watched the banks of color, red and pink, salmon and blue, purple and yellow, shift and change, while in the very heart of the vast panorama the huge, red orb, too strong for human sight, glittered and flamed.

The air, instinct with life, intoxicated him and he became rapt as in a vision. People whom he had met in his few but eventful years passed before him again in all the seeming of reality, and then his spirit leaped into the future, dreaming of the great things he would see, and in which perhaps he would have a share.

Tayoga, the young Onondaga, looked at his comrade and he understood. The same imaginative thread had been woven into the warp of which he was made, and his nostrils and lips quivered as he drank in the splendor of a world that appealed with such peculiar force to him, a son of the woods.

"The spirit of Areskoui (the Sun God) is upon Dagaeoga, and he has left us to dwell for a little while upon the seas of color heaped against the western horizon," he said.

Willet, the hunter, smiled. The two lads were very dear to him. He knew that they were uncommon types, raised by the gift of God far above the normal.

"Let him rest there, Tayoga," he said, "while those brilliant banks last, which won't be long. All things change, and the glorious hues will soon give way to the dark."

"True, Great Bear, but if the night comes it, in turn, must yield to the dawn. All things change, as you say, but nothing perishes. The sun tomorrow will be the same sun that we see today. Black night will not take a single ray from its glory."

"It's so, Tayoga, but you talk like a book or a prophet. I'm wondering if our lives are not like the going and coming of the sun. Maybe we pass on from one to another, forever and forever, without ending."

"Great Bear himself feels the spell of Areskoui also."

"I do, but we'd better stop rhapsodizing and think about our needs. Here, Robert, wake up and come back to earth! It's no time to sing a song to the sun with the forest full of our red enemies and the white too, perhaps."

Robert awoke with a start.

"You dragged me out of a beautiful world," he said.

"A world in which you were the central star," rejoined the hunter.

"So I was, but isn't that the case with all the imaginary worlds a man creates? He's their sun or he wouldn't create 'em."

"We're getting too deep into the unknown. Plant your feet on the solid earth, Robert, and let's think about the problems a dark night is going to bring us in the Indian country, not far south of the St. Lawrence."

Young Lennox shivered again. The terraces in the west suddenly began to fade and the wind took on a fresh and sharper edge.

"I know one thing," he said. "I know the night's going to be cold. It always is in the late autumn, up here among the high hills, and I'd like to see a fire, before which we could bask and upon which we could warm our food."

The hunter glanced at the Onondaga.

"That tells the state of my mind, too," he said, "but I doubt whether it would be safe. If we're to be good scouts, fit to discover the plans of the French and Indians, we won't get ourselves cut off by some rash act in the very beginning."

"It may not be a great danger or any at all," said Tayoga. "There is much rough and rocky ground to our right, cut by deep chasms, and we might find in there a protected recess in which we could build a smothered fire."

"You're a friend at the right time, Tayoga," said Robert. "I feel that I must have warmth. Lead on and find the stony hollow for us."

The Onondaga turned without a word, and started into the maze of lofty hills and narrow valleys, where the shadows of the night that was coming so swiftly already lay thick and heavy.

The three had gone north after the great victory at Lake George, a triumph that was not followed up as they had hoped. They had waited to see Johnson's host pursue the enemy and strike him hard again, but there were bickerings among the provinces which were jealous of one another, and the army remained in camp until the lateness of the season indicated a delay of all operations, save those of the scouts and roving bands that never rested. But Robert, Willet and Tayoga hoped, nevertheless, that they could achieve some deed of importance during the coming cold weather, and they were willing to undergo great risks in the effort.

They were soon in the heavy forest that clothed all the hills, and passed up a narrow ravine leading into the depths of the maze. The wind followed them into the cleft and steadily grew colder. The glowing terraces in the west broke up, faded quite away, and night, as yet without stars, spread over the earth.

Tayoga was in front, the other two following him in single file, stepping where he stepped, and leaving to him without question the selection of a place where they could stay. The Onondaga, guided by long practice and the inheritance from countless ancestors who had lived all their lives in the forest, moved forward with confidence. His instinct told him they would soon come to such a refuge as they desired, the rocky uplift about him indicating the proximity of many hollows.

The darkness increased, and the wind swept through the chasms with alternate moan and whistle, but the red youth held on his course for a full two miles, and his comrades followed without a word. When the cliffs about them rose to a height of two or three hundred feet, he stopped, and, pointing with a long forefinger, said he had found what they wished.

Robert at first could see nothing but a pit of blackness, but gradually as he gazed the shadows passed away, and he traced a deep recess in the stone of the cliff, not much of a shelter to those unused to the woods, but sufficient for hardy forest runners.

"I think we may build a little fire in there," said Tayoga, "and no one can see it unless he is here in the ravine within ten feet of us."

Willet nodded and Robert joyfully began to prepare for the blaze. The night was turning even colder than he had expected, and the chill was creeping into his frame. The fire would be most welcome for its warmth, and also because of the good cheer it would bring. He swept dry leaves into a heap within the recess, put upon them dead wood, which was abundant everywhere, and then Tayoga with artful use of flint and steel lighted the spark.

"It is good," admitted the hunter as he sat Turkish fashion on the leaves, and spread out his hands before the growing flames. "The nights grow cold mighty soon here in the high hills of the north, and the heat not only loosens up your muscles, but gives you new courage."

"I intend to make myself as comfortable as possible," said Robert. "You and Tayoga are always telling me to do so and I know the advice is good."

He gathered great quantities of the dry leaves, making of them what was in reality a couch, upon which he could recline in halfway fashion like a Roman at a feast, and warm at the fire before him the food he carried in a deerskin knapsack. An appetizing odor soon arose, and, as he ate, a pleasant warmth pervaded all his body, giving him a feeling of great content. They had venison, the tender meat of the young bear which, like the Indians, they loved, and they also allowed themselves a slice apiece of precious bread. Water was never distant in the northern wilderness, and Tayoga found a brook not a hundred yards away, flowing down a ravine that cut across their own. They drank at it in turn, and, then, the three lay down on the leaves in the recess, grateful to the Supreme Power which provided so well for them, even in the wild forest.

They let the flames die, but a comfortable little bed of coals remained, glowing within the shelter of the rocks. Young Lennox heaped up the leaves until they formed a pillow under his head, and then half dreaming, gazed into the heart of the fire, while his comrades reclined near him, each silent but with his mind turned to that which concerned him most.

Robert's thoughts were of St. Luc, of the romantic figure he had seen in the wilderness after the battle of Lake George, the knightly chevalier, singing his gay little song of mingled sentiment and defiance. An unconscious smile passed over his face. He and St. Luc could never be enemies. In very truth, the French leader, though an official enemy, had proved more than once the best of friends, ready even to risk his life in the service of the American lad. What was the reason? What could be the tie between them? There must be some connection. What was the mystery of his origin? The events of the last year indicated to him very clearly that there was such a mystery. Adrian Van Zoon and Master Benjamin Hardy surely knew something about it, and Willet too. Was it possible that a thread lay in the hand of St. Luc also?

He turned his eyes from the coals and gazed at the impassive face of the hunter. Once the question trembled on his lips, but he was sure the Great Bear would evade the answer, and the lad thought too much of the man who had long stood to him in the place of father to cause him annoyance. Beyond a doubt Willet had his interests at heart, and, when the time came for him to speak, speak he would, but not before.

His mind passed from the subject to dwell upon the task they had set for themselves, a thought which did not exclude St. Luc, though the chevalier now appeared in the guise of a bold and skillful foe, with whom they must match their wisdom and courage. Doubtless he had formed a new band, and, at the head of it, was already roaming the country south of the St. Lawrence. Well, if that were the case perhaps they would meet once more, and he would have given much to penetrate the future.

"Why don't you go to sleep, Robert?" asked the hunter.

"For the best of reasons. Because I can't," replied the lad.

"Perhaps it's well to stay awake," said the Onondaga gravely.

"Why, Tayoga?"

"Someone comes."

"Here in the ravine?"

"No, not in the ravine but on the cliff opposite us."

Robert strained both eye and ear, but he could neither see nor hear any human being. The wall on the far side of the ravine rose to a considerable height, its edge making a black line against the sky, but nothing there moved.

"Your fancy is too much for you, Tayoga," he said. "Thinking that someone might come, it creates a man out of air and mist."

"No, Dagaeoga, my fancy sleeps. Instead, my ear, which speaks only the truth, tells me a man is walking along the crest of the cliff, and coming on a course parallel with our ravine. My eye does not yet see him, but soon it will confirm what my ear has already told me. This deep cleft acts as a trumpet and brings the sound to me."

"How far away, then, would you say is this being, who, I fear, is mythical?"

"He is not mythical. He is reality. He is yet about three hundred yards distant. I might not have heard him, even with the aid of the cleft, but tonight Areskoui has given uncommon power to my ear, perhaps to aid us, and I know he is walking among thick bushes. I can hear the branches swish as they fly back into place, after his body has passed. Ah, a small stick popped as it broke under his foot!"

"I heard nothing."

"That is not my fault, O Dagaeoga. It is a heavy man, because I now hear his footsteps, even when they do not break anything. He walks with some uncertainty. Perhaps he fears lest he should make a false step, and tumble into the ravine."

"Since you can tell so much through hearing, at such a great distance, perhaps you know what kind of a man the stranger is. A warrior, I suppose?"

"No, he is not of our race. He would not walk so heavily. It is a white man."

"One of Rogers' rangers, then? Or maybe it is Rogers himself, or perhaps Black Rifle."

"It is none of those. They would advance with less noise. It is one not so much used to the forest, but who knows the way, nevertheless, and who doubtless has gone by this trail before."

"Then it must be a Frenchman!"

"I think so too."

"It won't be St. Luc?"

"No, Dagaeoga, though your tone showed that for a moment you hoped it was. Sharp Sword is too skillful in the forest to walk with so heavy a step. Nor can it be either of the leaders, De Courcelles or Jumonville. They also are too much at home in the woods. The right name of the man forms itself on my lips, but I will wait to be sure. In another minute he will enter the bare space almost opposite us and then we can see."

The three waited in silence. Although Robert had expressed doubt he felt none. He had a supreme belief in the Onondaga's uncanny powers, and he was quite sure that a man was moving upon the bluff. A stranger at such a time was to be watched, because white men came but little into this dangerous wilderness.

A dark figure appeared within the prescribed minute upon the crest and stopped there, as if the man, whoever he might be, wished to rest and draw fresh breath. The sky had lightened and he was outlined clearly against it. Robert gazed intently and then he uttered a little cry.

"I know him!" he said. "I can't be mistaken. It's Achille Garay, the one whose name we found written on a fragment of a letter in Albany."

"It's the man who tried to kill you, none other," said Tayoga gravely, "and Areskoui whispered in my ear that it would be he."

"What on earth can he be doing here in this lone wilderness at such a time?" asked Robert.

"Likely he's on his way to a French camp with information about our forces," said Willet. "We frightened Mynheer Hendrik Martinus, when we were in Albany, but I suppose that once a spy and traitor always a spy and traitor. Since the immediate danger has moved from Albany, Martinus and Garay may have begun work again."

"Then we'd better stop him," said Robert.

"No, let him go on," said Willet. "He can't carry any information about us that the French leaders won't find out for themselves. The fact that he's traveling in the night indicates a French camp somewhere near. We'll put him to use. Suppose we follow him and discover what we can about our enemies."

Robert looked at the cheerful bed of coals and sighed. They were seeking the French and Indians, and Garay was almost sure to lead straight to them. It was their duty to stalk him.

"I wish he had passed in the daytime," he said ruefully.

Tayoga laughed softly.

"You have lived long enough in the wilderness, O Dagaeoga," he said, "to know that you cannot choose when and where you will do your work."

"That's true, Tayoga, but while my feet are unwilling to go my will moves me on. So I'm entitled to more credit than you who take an actual physical de light in trailing anybody at any time."

The Onondaga smiled, but did not reply. Then the three took up their arms, returned their packs to their backs and without noise left the alcove. Robert cast one more reluctant glance at the bed of coals, but it was a farewell, not any weakening of the will to go.

Garay, after his brief rest on the summit, had passed the open space and was out of sight in the bushes, but Robert knew that both Tayoga and Willet could easily pick up his trail, and now he was all eagerness to pursue him and see what the chase might disclose. A little farther down, the cliff sloped back to such an extent that they could climb it without trouble, and, when they surmounted the crest, they entered the bushes at the point where Garay had disappeared.

"Can you hear him now, Tayoga?" asked Robert.

"My ears are as good as they were when I was in the ravine," replied the Onondaga, "but they do not catch any sounds from the Frenchman. It is, as we wish, because we do not care to come so near him that he will hear."

"Give him a half mile start," said Willet. "The ground is soft here, and it won't be any sort of work to follow him. See, here are the traces of his footsteps now, and there is where he has pushed his way among the little boughs. Notice the two broken twigs, Robert."

They followed at ease, the trail being a clear one, and the light of moon and stars now ample. Robert began to feel the ardor of the chase. He did not see Garay, but he believed that Tayoga at times heard him with those wonderful ears of his. He rejoiced too that chance had caused them to find the French spy in the wilderness. He remembered that foul attempt upon his life in Albany, and, burning with resentment, he was eager to thwart Garay in whatever he was now attempting to do. Tayoga saw his face and said softly:

"You hate this man Garay?"

"I don't like him."

"Do you wish me to go forward and kill him?"

"No! No, Tayoga! Why do you ask me such a cold-blooded question?"

The Onondaga laughed gently.

"I was merely testing you, Dagaeoga," he said. "We of the Hodenosaunee perhaps do not regard the taking of life as you do, but I would not shoot Garay from ambush, although I might slay him in open battle. Ah, there he is again on the crest of the ridge ahead!"

Robert once more saw the thick, strong figure of the spy outlined against the sky which was now luminous with a brilliant moon and countless clear stars, and the feeling of resentment was very powerful within him. Garay, without provocation, had attempted his life, and he could not forget it, and, for a moment or two, he felt that if the necessity should come in battle he was willing for a bullet from Tayoga to settle him. Then he rebuked himself for harboring rancor.

Garay paused, as if he needed another rest, and looked back, though it was only a casual glance, perhaps to measure the distance he had come, and the three, standing among the dense bushes, had no fear that he saw them or even suspected that anyone was on his traces. After a delay of a minute or so he passed over the crest and Robert, Willet and Tayoga moved on in pursuit. The Frenchman evidently knew his path, as the chase led for a long time over hills, down valleys and across small streams. Toward morning he put his fingers to his lips and blew a shrill whistle between them. Then the three drew swiftly near until they could see him, standing under the boughs of a great oak, obviously in an attitude of waiting.

"It is a signal to someone," said Robert.

"So it is," said Willet, "and it means that he and we have come to the end of our journey. I take it that we have arrived almost at the French and Indian camp, and that he whistles because he fears lest he should be shot by a sentinel through mistake. The reply should come soon."

As the hunter spoke they heard a whistle, a faint, clear note far ahead, and then Garay without hesitation resumed his journey. The three followed, but when they reached the crest of the next ridge they saw a light shining through the forest, a light that grew and finally divided into many lights, disclosing to them with certainty the presence of a camp. The figure of Garay appeared for a little while outlined against a fire, another figure came forward to meet him, and the two disappeared together.

From the direction of the fires came sounds subdued by the distance, and the aroma of food.

"It is a large camp," said Tayoga. "I have counted twelve fires which proves it, and the white men and the red men in it do not go hungry. They have deer, bear, fish and birds also. The pleasant odors of them all come to my nostrils, and make me hungry."

"That's too much for me," said Robert. "I can detect the blended savor, but I know not of what it consists. Now we go on, I suppose, and find out what this camp holds."

"We wouldn't dream of turning back," said the hunter. "Did you notice anything familiar, Robert, about the figure that came forward to meet Garay?"

"Now that you speak of it, I did, but I can't recall the identity of the man."

"Think again!"

"Ah, now I have him! It was the French officer, Colonel Auguste de Courcelles, who gave us so much trouble in Canada and elsewhere."

"That's the man," said Willet. "I knew him at once. Now, wherever De Courcelles is mischief is likely to be afoot, but he's not the only

Frenchman here. We'll spy out this camp to the full. There's time yet before the sunrise comes."

Now the three used all the skill in stalking with which they were endowed so plentifully, creeping forward without noise through the bushes, making so little stir among them that if a wary warrior had been looking he would have taken the slight movement of twig or leaf for the influence of a wandering breeze. Gradually the whole camp came into view, and Tayoga's prediction that it would be a large one proved true.

Robert lay on a little knoll among small bushes growing thick, where the keenest eye could not see him, but where his own vision swept the whole wide shallow dip, in which the French and Indian force was encamped. Twelve fires, all good and large, burned gayly, throwing out ruddy flames from great beds of glowing coals, while the aroma of food was now much stronger and very appetizing.

The force numbered at least three hundred men, of whom about one third were Frenchmen or Canadians, all in uniform. Robert recognized De Courcelles and near him Jumonville, his invariable comrade, and a little farther on a handsome and gallant young face.

"It's De Galissonnière of the Battalion Languedoc, whom we met in Québec," he whispered to Tayoga. "Now I wonder what he's doing here."

"He's come with the others on a projected foray," Tayoga whispered back. "But look beyond him, Dagaeoga, and you will see one more to be dreaded than De Courcelles or Jumonville."

Robert's gaze followed that of the young Onondaga and was intercepted by the huge figure of Tandakora, the Ojibway, who stood erect by one of the fires, bare save for a breech cloth and moccasins, his body painted in the most hideous designs, of which war paint was possible, his brow lowering.

"Tandakora is not happy," said Tayoga.

"No," said Robert. "He is thinking of the battle at Lake George that he did not win, and of all the scalps he did not take. He is thinking of his lost warriors, and the rout of his people and the French."

"Even so, Dagaeoga. Now Tandakora and De Courcelles talk with the spy, Garay. They want his news. They rejoice when he tells them Waraiyageh and his soldiers still make no preparations to advance after their victory by the lake. The long delay, the postponement of a big campaign until next spring will give the French and Indians time to breathe anew and renew their strength. Tandakora and De Courcelles consider themselves fortunate, and they are pleased with the spy, Garay. But look, Dagaeoga! Behold who comes now!"

Robert's heart began to throb as the handsomest and most gallant figure of them all walked into the red glow of the firelight, a tall man, young, lithe, athletic, fair of hair and countenance, his manner at once graceful and proud, a man to whom the others turned with deference, and perhaps in the case of De Courcelles and Jumonville with a little fear. He wore a white uniform with gold facings, and a small gold hilted sword swung upon his thigh. Even in the forest, dress impresses, and Robert was quite sure that St. Luc was in his finest attire, not from vanity, but because he wished to create an effect. It would be like him, when his fortunes were lowest, to assume his highest manner before both friend and foe.

"You'd think from his looks that he had nothing but a string of victories and never knew defeat," whispered Willet. "Anyway, his is the finest spirit in all that crowd, and he's the greatest leader and soldier, too. Notice how they give way to him, and how they stop asking questions of Garay, leaving it to him. And now Garay himself bows low before him, while De Courcelles, Jumonville and Tandakora stand aside. I wish we could hear what they say; then we might learn something worth all our risk in coming here."

But their voices did not reach so great a distance, though the three, eager to use eye even if ear was of no use, still lay in the bushes and watched the flow of life in the great camp. Many of the French and Indians who had been asleep awoke, sat up and began to cook breakfast for themselves, holding strips of game on sharp sticks over the coals. St. Luc talked a long while with Garay, afterward with the French officers and Tandakora, and then withdrew to a little knoll, where he leaned against a tree, his face expressing intense thought. A dark, powerfully built man, the Canadian, Dubois, brought him food which he ate mechanically.

The dusk floated away, and the sun came up, great and brilliant. The three stirred in their covert, and Willet whispered that it was time for them to be going.

"Only the most marvelous luck could save us from detection in the daylight," he said, "because presently the Indians, growing restless, will wander about the camp."

"I'm willing to go," Robert whispered back. "I know the danger is too great. Besides I'm starving to death, and the odors of all their good food will hasten my death, if I don't take an antidote."

They retreated with the utmost care and Robert drew an immense breath of relief when they were a full mile away. It was well to look upon the French and Indian camp, but it was better to be beyond the reach of those who made it.

"And now we make a camp of our own, don't we?" he said. "All my bones are stiff from so much bending and creeping. Moreover, my hunger has grown to such violent pitch that it is tearing at me, so to speak, with red hot pincers."

"Dagaeoga always has plenty of words," said Tayoga in a whimsical tone, "but he will have to endure his hunger a while longer. Let the pincers tear and burn. It is good for him. It will give him a chance to show how strong he is, and how a mighty warrior despises such little things as food and drink."

"I'm not anxious to show myself a mighty warrior just now," retorted young Lennox. "I'd be willing to sacrifice my pride in that respect if I could have carried off some of their bear steaks and venison."

"Come on," said Willet, "and I'll see that you're satisfied. I'm beginning to feel as you do, Robert."

Nevertheless he marshaled them forward pretty sternly and they pursued a westward course for many miles before he allowed a halt. Even then they hunted about among the rocks until they found a secluded place, no fire being permitted, at which it pleased Robert to grumble, although he did not mean it.

"We were better off last night when we had our little fire in the hollow," he said.

"So we were, as far as the body is concerned," rejoined Willet, "but we didn't know then where the Indian camp lay. We've at least increased our knowledge. Now, I'm thinking that you two lads, who have been awake nearly all night and also the half of the morning that has passed, ought to sleep. Time we have to spare, but you know we should practice all the economy we can with our strength. This place is pretty well hidden, and I'll do the watching. Spread your blankets on the leaves, Robert. It's not well even for foresters to sleep on the bare ground. Now draw the other half of it over you. Tayoga has done so already. I'm wondering which of you will get to sleep first. Whoever does will be the better man, a question I've long wanted to decide."

But the problem was still left for the future. They fell asleep so nearly at the same time that Willet could tell no difference. He noticed with pleasure their long, regular breathing, and he said to himself, as he had said so often before, that they were two good and brave lads.

Then he made a very comfortable cushion of fallen leaves to sit upon, and remained there a long time, his rifle across his knees.

His eyes were wide open, but no part of his body stirred. He had acquired the gift of infinite patience, and with it the difficult physical art of remaining absolutely motionless for a long time. So thorough was his mastery over himself that the small wild game began to believe by and by that he was not alive. Birds sang freely over his head and the hare hopped through the undergrowth. Yet the hunter saw everything and his very stillness enabled him to listen with all the more acuteness.

The sun which had arisen great and brilliant, remained so, flooding the world with golden lights and making it wonderfully alluring to Willet, whose eyes never grew weary of the forest's varying shades and aspects. They were all peaceful now, but he had no illusions. He knew that the hostile force would send out many hunters. So many men must have much game and presently they would be prowling through the woods, seeking deer and bear. The chief danger came from them.

The hours passed and noon arrived. Willet had not stirred. He did not sleep, but he rested nevertheless. His great body was relaxed thoroughly, and strength, after weariness, flowed back into his veins. Presently his head moved forward a little and his attitude grew more intent. A slight sound that was not a part of the wilderness had come to him. It was very faint, few would have noticed it, but he knew it was the report of a rifle. He knew also that it was not a shot fired in battle. The hunters, as he had surmised, were abroad, and they had started up a deer or a bear.

But Willet did not stir nor did his eyelids flicker. He was used to the proximity of foes, and the distant report did not cause his heart to miss a single beat. Instead, he felt a sort of dry amusement that they should be so near and yet know it not. How Tandakora would have rejoiced if there had been a whisper in his ear that Willet, Robert and Tayoga whom he hated so much were within sound of his rifle! And how he would have spread his nets to catch such precious game!

He heard a second shot presently from the other side, and then the hunter began to laugh softly to himself. His faint amusement was turning into actual and intense enjoyment. The Indian hunters were obviously on every side of them but did not dream that the finest game of all was at hand. They would continue to waste their time on deer and bear while the three formidable rangers were within hearing of their guns.

But the hunter was still silent. His laughter was wholly internal, and his lips did not even move. It showed only in his eye and the general expression of his countenance. A third shot and a fourth came, but no anxiety marred his sense of the humorous.

Then he heard the distant shouts of warriors in pursuit of a wounded bear and still he was motionless.

Willet knew that the French and Tandakora suspected no pursuit. They believed that no American rangers would come among the lofty peaks and ridges south of the border, and he and his comrades could lie in safe hiding while the hunt went on with unabated zeal. But he was sure one day would be sufficient for the task. That portion of the wilderness was full of game, and, since the coming of the war, deer and bear were increasing rapidly. Willet often noted how quickly game returned to regions abandoned by man, as if the wild animals promptly told one another the danger had passed.

Joyous shouts came now and then and he knew that they marked the taking of game, but about the middle of the afternoon the hunt drifted entirely away. A little later Tayoga awoke and sat up. Then Willet moved slightly and spoke.

"Tandakora's hunters have been all about us while you slept," he said, "but I knew they wouldn't find us."

"Dagaeoga and I were safe in the care of the Great Bear," said the Onondaga confidently. "Tandakora will rage if we tell him some day that we were here, to be taken if he had only seen us. Now Lennox awakes also! O Dagaeoga, you have slept and missed all the great jest."

"What do you mean, Tayoga?"

"Tandakora built his fire just beyond the big bush that grows ten feet away, and sat there two hours without suspecting our presence here."

"Now I know you are romancing, Tayoga, because I can see the twinkle in your eyes. But I suspect that what you say bears some remote relation to the truth."

"The hostile hunters passed while you slept, and while I slept also, but the Great Bear was all eyes and ears and he did not think it needful to awaken us."

"What are we going to do now, Dave?"

"Eat more venison. We must never fail to keep the body strong."

"And then?"

"I'm not sure. I thought once that we'd better go south to our army at Lake George with news of this big band, but it's a long distance down there, and it may be wiser to stay here and watch St. Luc. What do you say, Robert?"

"Stay here."

"And you, Tayoga?"

"Watch St. Luc."

"I was inclining to that view myself, and it's settled now. But we mustn't move from this place until dark; it would be too dangerous in the day."

The lads nodded and the three settled into another long period of waiting.

CHAPTER II.
ON THE RIDGES

Late in the afternoon Willet went to sleep and Robert and Tayoga watched, although, as the hunter had done, they depended more upon ear than eye. They too heard now and then the faint report of distant shots from the hunt, and Robert's heart beat very fast, but, if the young Onondaga felt emotion, he did not show it. At twilight, they ate a frugal supper, and when the night had fully come they rose and walked about a little to make their stiffened muscles elastic again.

"The hunters have all gone back to the camp now," said Tayoga, "since it is not easy to pursue the game by dusk, and we need not keep so close, like a bear in its den."

"And the danger of our being seen is reduced to almost nothing," said Robert.

"It is so, Dagaeoga, but we will have another fight to make. We must strive to keep ourselves from freezing. It turns very cold on the mountains! The wind is now blowing from the north, and do you not feel a keener edge to it?"

"I do," replied Robert, sensitive of body as well as mind, and he shivered as he spoke. "It's a most unfortunate change for us. But now that I think of it we've got to expect it up among the high mountains toward Canada. Shall we light another fire?"

"We'll talk of that later with the Great Bear when he comes out of his sleep. But it fast grows colder and colder, Dagaeoga!"

Weather was an enormous factor in the lives of the borderers. Wilderness storms and bitter cold often defeated their best plans, and shelterless men, they were in a continual struggle against them. And here in the far north, among the high peaks and ridges, there was much to be feared, even with official winter yet several weeks away.

Robert began to rub his cold hands, and, unfolding his blanket, he wrapped it about his body, drawing it well up over his neck and ears. Tayoga imitated him and Willet, who was soon awakened by the cold blast, protected himself in a similar manner.

"What does the Great Bear think?" asked the Onondaga.

The hunter, with his face to the wind, meditated a few moments before replying.

"I was testing that current of air on my face and eyes," he said, "and, speaking the truth, Tayoga, I don't like it. The wind seemed to grow colder as I waited to answer you. Listen to the leaves falling before it! Their rustle tells of a bitter night."

"And while we freeze in it," said Robert, whose imagination was already in full play, "the French and Indians build as many and big fires as they please, and cook before them the juicy game they killed today."

The hunter was again very thoughtful.

"It looks as if we would have to kindle a fire," he said, "and tomorrow we shall have to hunt bear or deer for ourselves, because we have food enough left for only one more meal."

"The face of Areskoui is turned from us," said Tayoga. "We have done something to anger him, or we have failed to do what he wished, and now he sends upon us a hard trial to test us and purify us! A great storm with fierce cold comes!"

The wind rose suddenly, and it began to make a sinister hissing among all the passes and gorges. Robert felt something damp upon his face, and he brushed away a melting flake of snow. But another and another took its place and the air was soon filled with white. And the flakes were most aggressive. Driven by the storm they whipped the cheeks and eyes of the three, and sought to insert themselves, often with success, under their collars, even under the edges of the protecting blankets, and down their backs. Robert, despite himself, shivered violently and even the hunter was forced to walk vigorously back and forth in the effort to keep warm. It was evident that the Onondaga had told the truth, and that the face of Areskoui was in very fact turned from them.

Robert awaited the word, looking now and then at Willet, but the hunter hung on for a long time. The leaves fell in showers before the storm, making a faint rustling like the last sigh of the departing, and the snow, driven with so much force, stung his face like hail when it struck. He was anxious for a fire, and its vital heat, but he was too proud to speak. He would endure without complaint as much as his comrades, and he knew that Tayoga, like himself, would wait for the older man to speak.

But he could not keep, meanwhile, from thinking of the French and Indians beside their vast heaps of glowing coals, fed and warmed to their hearts' content, while the three lay in the dark and bitter cold of the wilderness. An hour dragged by, then two, then three, but the storm showed no sign of abating. The sinister screaming of the wind did not cease and the snow accumulated upon their bodies. At last Willet said:

"We must do it."

"We have no other choice," said Tayoga. "We have waited as long as we could to see if Areskoui would turn a favoring face upon us, but his anger holds. It will not avail, if in our endeavor to escape the tomahawk of Tandakora, we freeze to death."

The fire decided upon, they took all risks and went about the task with eagerness. Ordinary men could not have lighted it under such circumstances, but the three had uncommon skill upon which to draw. They took the bark from dead wood, and shaved off many splinters, building up a little heap in the lee of a cliff, which they sheltered on the windward side with their bodies. Then Willet, working a long time with his flint and steel, set to it the sparks that grew into a blaze.

Robert did not stop with the fire. Noticing the vast amount of dead wood lying about, as was often the case in the wilderness, he dragged up many boughs and began to build a wall on the exposed side of the flames. Willet and Tayoga approving of the idea soon helped him, and three pairs of willing hands quickly raised the barrier of trunks and brush to a height of at least a yard.

"A happy idea of yours, Robert," said the hunter. "Now we achieve two ends at once. Our wall hides the glow of the fire and at the same time protects us in large measure from the snow and wind."

"I have bright thoughts now and then," said Robert, whose spirits had returned in full tide. "You needn't believe you and Tayoga have all of 'em. I don't believe either of you would have ever thought of this fine wooden wall. In truth, Dave, I don't know what would become of you and Tayoga if you didn't have me along with you most all the time! How good the fire feels! The warmth touches my fingers and goes stealing up my arms and into my body! It reaches my face too and goes stealing down to meet the fine heat that makes a channel of my fingers! A glorious fire, Tayoga! I tell you, a glorious fire, Dave! The finest fire that's burning anywhere in the world!"

"The quality of a fire depends on the service it gives," said the hunter.

"Dagaeoga has many words when he is happy," said the Onondaga. "His tongue runs on like the pleasant murmur of a brook, but he does it because Manitou made him that way. The world must have talkers as well as doers, and it can be said for Lennox that he acts as well as talks."

"Thanks, I'm glad you put in the saving clause," laughed Robert. "But it's a mighty good thing we built our wooden wall. That wind would cut to the bone if it could get at you."

"The wind at least will keep the warriors away," said Tayoga. "They will all stay close in the camp on such a night."

"And no blame to them," murmured the hunter. "If we weren't in the Indian country I'd build our own fire five times as big. Now, Robert, suppose you go to sleep."

"I can't, Dave. You know I slept all the morning, but I'm not suffering from dullness. I'm imagining things. I'm imagining how much worse off we'd be if we didn't have flint and steel. I can always find pleasure in making such contrasts."

But he crouched down lower against the cliff, drew his blanket closer and spread both hands over the fire, which had now died down into a glowing mass of coals. He was wondering what they would do on the morrow, when their food was exhausted. They had not only the storm to fight, but possible starvation in the days to come. He foresaw that instead of discovering all the plans of the enemy they would have a struggle merely to live.

"Areskoui must truly be against us, Tayoga," he said. "Who would have predicted such a storm so early in the season?"

"We are several thousand feet above the sea level," said Willet, "and that will account for the violent change. I think the wind and snow will last all tonight, and probably all tomorrow."

"Then," said Robert, "we'd better gather more wood, build our wall higher and save ample fuel for the fire."

The other two found the suggestion good, and all three acted upon it promptly, ranging through the forest about them in search of brushwood, which they brought back in great quantities. Robert's blood began to tingle with the activity, and his spirits rose. Now the snow, as it drove against his face, instead of making him shiver, whipped his blood. He was the most energetic of the three, and went the farthest, in the hunt for fallen timber.

One of his trips took him into the mouth of a little gorge, and, as he bent down to seize the end of a big stick, he heard just ahead a rustling that caused him with instinctive caution to straighten up and spring back, his hand, at the same time, flying to the butt of the pistol in his belt. A figure, tall and menacing, emerged from the darkness, and he retreated two or three steps.

It was his first thought that a warrior stood before him, but reason told him quickly no Indian was likely to be there, and, then, through the thick dusk and falling snow, he saw a huge black bear, erect on his hind legs, and looking at him with little red eyes. The animal was so near that the lad could see his expression, and it was not anger but surprise and inquiry. He divined at once that this particular bear had never seen a human being before, and, having been roused from some warm den by Robert's advance, he was asking what manner of creature the stranger and intruder might be.

Robert's first impulse was one of friendliness. It did not occur to him to shoot the bear, although the big fellow, fine and fat, would furnish all the meat they needed for a long time. Instead his large blue eyes gave back the curious gaze of the little red ones, and, for a little space, the two stood there, face to face, with no thought of danger or attack on the part of either.

"If you'll let me alone I'll let you alone," said the lad.

The bear growled, but it was a kindly, reassuring growl.

"I didn't mean to disturb you. I was looking for wood, not for bear."

Another growl, but of a thoroughly placid nature.

"Go wherever you please and I'll return to the camp with this fallen sapling."

A third growl, now ingratiating.

"It's a cold night, with fire and shelter the chief needs, and you and I wouldn't think of fighting."

A fourth growl which clearly disclosed the note of friendship and understanding.

"We're in agreement, I see. Good night, I wish you well."

A fifth growl, which had the tone of benevolent farewell, and the bear, dropping on all fours, disappeared in the brush. Robert, whose fancy had been alive and leaping, returned to the camp rather pleased with himself, despite the fact that about three hundred pounds of excellent food had walked away undisturbed.

"I ran upon a big bear," he said to the hunter and the Onondaga.

"I heard no shot," said Willet.

"No, I didn't fire. Neither my impulse nor my will told me to do so. The bear looked at me in such brotherly fashion that I could never have sent a bullet into him. I'd rather go hungry."

Neither Willet nor Tayoga had any rebuke for him.

"Doubtless the soul of a good warrior had gone into the bear and looked out at you," said the Onondaga with perfect sincerity. "It is sometimes so. It is well that you did not fire upon him or the face of Areskoui would have remained turned from us too long."

"That's just the way I felt about it," said Robert, who had great tolerance for Iroquois beliefs. "His eyes seemed fully human to me, and, although I had my pistol in my belt and my hand when I first saw him flew to its butt, I made no attempt to draw it. I have no regrets because I let him go."

"Nor have we," said Willet. "Now I think we can afford to rest again. We can build our wall six feet high if we want to and have wood enough left over to feed a fire for several days."

The two lads, the white and the red, crouched once more in the lee of the cliff, while the hunter put two fresh sticks on the coals. But little of the snow reached them where they lay, wrapped well in their blankets, and all care disappeared from Robert's mind. Inured to the wilderness he ignored what would have been discomfort to others. The trails they had left in the snow when they hunted wood would soon be covered up by the continued fall, and for the night, at least, there would be no danger from the warriors. He felt an immense comfort and security, and by-and-by fell asleep again. Tayoga soon followed him to slumberland, and Willet once more watched alone.

Tayoga relieved Willet about two o'clock in the morning, but they did not awaken Robert at all in the course of the night. They knew that he would upbraid them for not summoning him to do his share, but there would be abundant chance for him to serve later on as a sentinel.

The Onondaga did not arouse his comrades until long past daylight, and then they opened their eyes to a white world, clear and cold. The snow had ceased falling, but it lay several inches deep on the ground, and all the leaves had been stripped from the trees, on the high point where they lay. The coals still glowed, and they heated over them the last of their venison and bear meat, which they ate with keen appetite, and then considered what they must do, concluding at last to descend into the lower country and hunt game.

"We can do nothing at present so far as the war is concerned," said Willet. "An army must eat before it can fight, but it's likely that the snow and cold will stop the operations of the French and Indians also. While we're saving our own lives other operations will be delayed, and later on we may find Garay going back."

"It is best to go down the mountain and to the south," said Tayoga, in his precise school English. "It may be that the snow has fallen only on the high peaks and ridges. Then we'll be sure to find game, and perhaps other food which we can procure without bullets."

"Do you think we'd better move now?" asked Robert.

"We must send out a scout first," said Willet.

It was agreed that Tayoga should go, and in about two hours he returned with grave news. The warriors were out again, hunting in the snow, and although unconscious of it themselves they formed an almost complete ring about the three, a ring which they must undertake to break through now in full daylight, and with the snow ready to leave a broad trail of all who passed.

"They would be sure to see our path," said Tayoga. "Even the short trail I made when I went forth exposes us to danger, and we must trust to luck that they will not see it. There is nothing for us to do, but to remain hidden here, until the next night comes. It is quite certain that the face of Areskoui is still turned from us. What have we done that is displeasing to the Sun God?"

"I can't recall anything," said Robert.

"Perhaps it is not what we have done but what we have failed to do, though whatever it is Areskoui has willed that we lie close another day."

"And starve," said Robert ruefully.

"And starve," repeated the Onondaga.

The three crouched once more under the lee of the cliff, but toward noon they built their wooden wall another foot higher, driven to the work by the threatening aspect of the sky, which turned to a somber brown. The wind sprang up again, and it had an edge of damp.

"Soon it will rain," said Tayoga, "and it will be a bitter cold rain. Much of the snow will melt and then freeze again, coating the earth with ice. It will make it more difficult for us to travel and the hunting that we need so much must be delayed. Then we'll grow hungrier and hungrier."

"Stop it, Tayoga," exclaimed Robert. "I believe you're torturing me on purpose. I'm hungry now."

"But that is nothing to what Dagaeoga will be tonight, after he has gone many hours without food. Then he will think of the juicy venison, and of the tender steak of the young bear, and of the fine fish from the mountain streams, and he will remember how he has enjoyed them in the past, but it will be only a memory. The fish that he craves will be swimming in the clear waters, and the deer and the bear will be far away, safe from his bullet."

"I didn't know you had so much malice in your composition, Tayoga, but there's one consolation; if I suffer you suffer also."

The Onondaga laughed.

"It will give Dagaeoga a chance to test himself," he said. "We know already that he is brave in battle and skillful on the trail, and now we will see how he can sit for days and nights without anything to eat, and not complain. He will be a hero, he will draw in his belt notch by notch, and never say a word."

"That will do, Tayoga," interrupted the hunter. "While you play upon Robert's nerves you play upon mine also, and they tell me you've said enough. Actually I'm beginning to feel famished."

Tayoga laughed once more.

"While I jest with you I jest also with myself," he said. "Now we'll sleep, since there is nothing else to do."

He drew his blanket up to his eyes, leaned against the stony wall and slept. Robert could not imitate him. As the long afternoon, one of the longest he had ever known, trailed its slow length away, he studied the forest in front of them, where the cold and mournful rain was still falling, a rain that had at least one advantage, as it had long since obliterated all traces of a trail left by Tayoga on his scouting expedition, although search as he would he could find no other profit in it.

Night came, the rain ceased, and, as Tayoga had predicted, the intense cold that arrived with the dark, froze it quickly, covering the earth with a hard and polished glaze, smoother and more treacherous than glass. It was impossible for the present to undertake flight over such a surface, with a foe naturally vigilant at hand, and they made themselves as comfortable as they could, while they awaited another day. Now Robert began to draw in his belt, while a hunger that was almost too fierce to be endured assailed him. His was a strong body, demanding much nourishment, and it cried out to him for relief. He tried to forget in sleep that he was famished, but he only dozed a while to awaken to a hunger more poignant than ever.

Yet he said never a word, but, as the night with its illimitable hours passed, he grew defiant of difficulties and dangers, all of which became but little things in presence of his hunger. It was his impulse to storm the Indian camp itself and seize what he wanted of the supplies there, but his reason told him the thought was folly. Then he tried to forget about the steaks of bear and deer, and the delicate little fish from the mountain stream that Tayoga had mentioned, but they would return before his eyes with so much vividness that he almost believed he saw them in reality.

Dawn came again, and they had now been twenty-four hours without food. The pangs of hunger were assailing all three fiercely, but they did not yet dare go forth, as the morning was dark and gloomy, with a resumption of the fierce, driving rain, mingled with hail, which rattled now and then like bullets on their wooden wall.

Robert shivered in his blanket, not so much from actual cold as from the sinister aspect of the world, and his sensitive imagination, which always pictured both good and bad in vivid colors, foresaw the enormous difficulties that would confront them. Hunger tore at him, as with the talons of a dragon, and he felt himself growing weak, although his constitution was so strong that the time for a decline in vitality had not yet really come. He was all for going forth in the storm and seeking game in the slush and cold, ignoring the French and Indian danger. But he knew the hunter and the Onondaga would not hear to it, and so he waited in silence, hot anger swelling in his heart against the foes who kept him there. Unable to do anything else, he finally closed his eyes that he might shut from his view the gray and chilly world that was so hostile.

"Is Areskoui turning his face toward us, Tayoga?" he asked after a long wait.

"No, Dagaeoga. Our unknown sin is not yet expiated. The day grows blacker, colder and wetter."

"And I grow hungrier and hungrier. If we kill deer or bear we must kill three of each at the same time, because I intend to eat one all by myself, and I demand that he be large and fat, too. I suppose we'll go out of this place some time or other."

"Yes, Dagaeoga."

"Then we'd better make up our minds to do it before it's too late. I feel my nerves and tissues decaying already."

"It's only your fancy, Dagaeoga. You can exist a week without food."

"A week, Tayoga! I don't want to exist a week without food! I absolutely refuse to do so!"

"The choice is not yours, now, O Dagaeoga. The greatest gift you can have is patience. The warrior, Daatgadose, of the clan of the Bear, of the nation Onondaga, of the great League of the Hodenosaunee, even as I am, hemmed in by enemies in the forest, and with his powder and bullets gone, lay in hiding ten days without food once passing his lips, and took no lasting hurt from it. You, O Dagaeoga, will surely do as well, and I can give you many other examples for your emulation."

"Stop, Tayoga. Sometimes I'm sorry you speak such precise English. If you didn't you couldn't have so much sport with a bad situation."

The Onondaga laughed deeply and with unction. He knew that Robert was not complaining, that he merely talked to fill in the time, and he went on with stories of illustrious warriors and chiefs among his people who had literally defied hunger and thirst and who had lived incredible periods without either food or water. Willet listened in silence, but with approval. He knew that any kind of talk would cheer them and strengthen them for the coming test which was bound to be severe.

Feeling that no warriors would be within sight at such a time they built their fire anew and hovered over the flame and the coals, drawing a sort of sustenance from the warmth. But when the day was nearly gone and there was no change in the sodden skies Robert detected in himself signs of weakness that he knew were not the product of fancy. Every inch of his healthy young body cried out for food, and, not receiving it, began to rebel and lose vigor.

Again he was all for going forth and risking everything, and he noticed with pleasure that the hunter began to shift about and to peer into the forest as if some plan for action was turning in his mind. But he said nothing, resolved to leave it all to Tayoga and Willet, and by-and-by, in the dark, to which his eyes had grown accustomed, he saw the two exchanging glances. He was able to read these looks. The hunter said: "We must try it. The time has come." The Onondaga replied: "Yes, it is not wise to wait longer, lest we grow too feeble for a great effort." The hunter rejoined: "Then it is agreed," and the Onondaga said: "If our comrade thinks so too." Both turned their eyes to young Lennox who said aloud: "It's what I've been waiting for a long time. The sooner we leave the better pleased I'll be."

"Then," said Willet, "in an hour we'll start south, going down the trail between the high cliffs, and we'll trust that either we've expiated our sin, whatever it was, or that Areskoui has forgiven us. It will be terrible traveling, but we can't wait any longer."

They wrapped their blankets about their bodies as additional covering, and, at the time appointed, left their rude shelter. Yet when they were away from its protection it did not seem so rude. When their moccasins sank in the slush and the snow and rain beat upon their faces, it was remembered as the finest little shelter in the world. The bodies of all three regretted it, but their wills and dire necessity sent them on.

The hunter led, young Lennox followed and Tayoga came last, their feet making a slight sighing sound as they sank in the half-melted snow and ice now several inches deep. Robert wore fine high moccasins of tanned mooseskin, much stronger and better than ordinary deerskin, but before long he felt the water entering them and chilling him to the bone. Nevertheless, keeping his resolution in mind, and, knowing that the others were in the same plight, he made no complaint but trudged steadily on, three or four feet behind Willet, who chose the way that now led sharply downward. Once more he realized what an enormous factor changes in temperature were in the lives of borderers and how they could defeat supreme forethought and the greatest skill. Winter with its snow and sleet was now the silent but none the less potent ally of the French and Indians in preventing their escape.

They toiled on two or three miles, not one of the three speaking. The sleet and hail thickened. In spite of the blanket and the deerskin tunic it made its way along his neck and then down his shoulders and chest, the chill that went downward meeting the chill that came upward from his feet, now almost frozen. He could not recall ever before having been so miserable of both mind and body. He did not know it just then, but the lack of nourishment made him peculiarly susceptible to mental and physical depression. The fires of youth were not burning in his veins, and his vitality had been reduced at least one half.

Now, that terrible hunger, although he had striven to fight it, assailed him once more, and his will weakened slowly. What were those tales Tayoga had been telling about men going a week or ten days without food? They were clearly incredible. He had been less than two days without it, and his tortures were those of a man at the stake.

Willet's eyes, from natural keenness and long training, were able to pierce the dusk and he showed the way, steep and slippery though it was, with infallible certainty. They were on a lower slope, where by some freak of the weather there was snow instead of slush, when he bent down and examined the path with critical and anxious eyes. Robert and Tayoga waited in silence, until the hunter straightened up again. Then he said:

"A war party has gone down the pass ahead of us. There were about twenty men in it, and it's not more than two hours beyond us. Whether it's there to cut us off, or has moved by mere chance, I don't know, but the effect is just the same. If we keep on we'll run into it."

"Suppose we try the ascent and get out over the ridges," said Robert.

Willet looked up at the steep and lofty slopes on either side.

"It's tremendously bad footing," he replied, "and will take heavy toll of our strength, but I see no other way. It would be foolish for us to go on and walk straight into the hands of our enemies. What say you, Tayoga?"

"There is but a single choice and that a desperate one. We must try the summits."

They delayed no longer, and, Willet still leading, began the frightful climb, choosing the westward cliff which towered above them a full four hundred feet, and, like the one that faced it, almost precipitous. Luckily many evergreens grew along the slope and using them as supports they toiled slowly upward. Now and then, in spite of every precaution, they sent down heaps of snow that rumbled as it fell into the pass. Every time one of these miniature avalanches fell Robert shivered. His fancy, so vitally alive, pictured savages in the pass, attracted by the noise, and soon to fire at his helpless figure, outlined against the slope.

"Can't you go a little faster?" he said to Willet, who was just ahead.

"It wouldn't be wise," replied the hunter. "We mustn't risk a fall. But I know why you want to hurry on, Robert. It's the fear of being shot in the back as you climb. I feel it too, but it's only fancy with both of us."

Robert said no more, but, calling upon his will, bent his mind to their task. Above him was the dusky sky and the summit seemed to tower a mile away, but he knew that it was only sixty or seventy yards now, and he took his luxurious imagination severely in hand. At such a time he must deal only in realities and he subjected all that he saw to mathematical calculation. Sixty or seventy yards must be sixty or seventy yards only and not a mile.

After a time that seemed interminable Willet's figure disappeared over the cliff, and, with a gasp, Robert followed, Tayoga coming swiftly after. The three were so tired, their vitality was so reduced that they lay down in the snow, and drew long, painful breaths. When some measure of strength was restored they stood up and surveyed the place where they stood, a bleak summit over which the wind blew sharply. Nothing grew there but low bushes, and they felt that, while they may have escaped the war band, their own physical case was worse instead of better. Both cold and wind were more severe and a bitter hail beat upon them. It was obvious that Areskoui did not yet forgive, although it must surely be a sin of ignorance, of omission and not of commission, with the equal certainty that a sin of such type could not be unforgivable for all time.

"We seem to be on a ridge that runs for a great distance," said Tayoga. "Suppose we continue along the comb of it. At least we cannot make ourselves any worse off than we are now."

They toiled on, now and then falling on the slippery trail, their vitality sinking lower and lower. Occasionally they had glimpses of a vast desolate region under a somber sky, peaks and ridges and slopes over which clouds hovered, the whole seeming to resent the entry of man and to offer to him every kind of resistance.

Robert was now wet through and through. No part of his body had escaped and he knew that his vitality was at such a low ebb that at least seventy-five per cent, of it was gone. He wanted to stop, his cold and aching limbs cried out for rest, and he craved heat at the cost of every risk, but his will was still firm, and he would not be the first to speak. It was Willet who suggested when they came to a slight dip that they make an effort to build a fire.

"The human body, no matter how strong it may be naturally, and how much it may be toughened by experience, will stand only so much," he said.

They were constantly building fires in the wilderness, but the fire they built that morning was the hardest of them all to start. They selected, as usual, the lee of a rocky uplift, and, then by the patient use of flint and steel, and, after many failures, they kindled a blaze that would last. But in their reduced state the labor exhausted them, and it was some time before they drew any life from the warmth. When the circulation had been restored somewhat they piled on more wood, taking the chance of being seen. They even went so far as to build a second fire, that they might sit between the two and dry themselves more rapidly. Then they waited in silence the coming of the dawn.

CHAPTER III.
THE BRAVE DEFENSE

Robert hoped for a fair morning. Surely Areskoui would relent now! But the sun that crept languidly up the horizon was invisible to them, hidden by a dark curtain of clouds that might shed, at any moment, torrents of rain or hail or snow. The whole earth swam in chilly damp. Banks of cold fog filled the valleys and gorges, and shreds and patches of it floated along the peaks and ridges. The double fires had dried his clothing and had sent warmth into his veins, increasing his vitality somewhat, but it was far below normal nevertheless. He had an immense aversion to further movement. He wanted to stay there between the coals, awaiting passively whatever fate might have for him. Somehow, his will to make an effort and live seemed to have gone.

While weakness grew upon him and he drooped by the fire, he did not feel hunger, but it was only a passing phase. Presently the desire for food that had gnawed at him with sharp teeth came back, and with it his wish to do, like one stirred into action by pain. Hunger itself was a stimulus and his sinking vitality was arrested in its decline. He looked around eagerly at the sodden scene, but it certainly held out little promise of game. Deer and bear would avoid those steeps, and range in the valleys. But the will to action, stimulated back to life, remained. However comfortable it was between the fires they must not stay there to perish.

"Why don't we go on?" he said to Willet.

"I'm glad to hear you ask that question," replied the hunter.

"Why, Dave?"

"Because it shows that you haven't given up. If you've got the courage to leave such a warm and dry place you've got the courage also to make another fight for life. And you were the first to speak, too, Robert."

"We must go on," said Tayoga. "But it is best to throw slush over the fire and hide our traces."

The task finished they took up their vague journey, going they knew not where, but knowing that they must go somewhere, their uncertain way still leading along the crests of narrow ridges, across shallow dips and through drooping forests, where the wind moaned miserably. At intervals, it rained or snowed or hailed and once more they were wet through and through. The recrudescence of Robert's strength was a mere flare-up. His vitality ebbed again, and not even the fierce gnawing hunger that refused to depart could stimulate it. By-and-by he began to stumble, but Tayoga and Willet, who noticed it, said nothing—they staggered at times themselves. They toiled on for hours in silence, but, late in the afternoon, Robert turned suddenly to the Onondaga.

"Do you remember, Tayoga," he said, "something you said to me a couple of days since, or was it a week, or maybe a month ago? I seem to remember time very uncertainly, but you were talking about repasts, banquets, Lucullan banquets, more gorgeous banquets than old Nero had, and they say he was king of epicures. I think you spoke of tender venison, and juicy bear steaks, and perhaps of a delicate broiled trout from one of these clear mountain streams. Am I not right, Tayoga? Didn't you mention viands? And perhaps you may still be thinking of them?"

"I *am*, Dagaeoga. I am thinking of them all the time. I confess to you that I am so hungry I could gnaw the inside of the fresh bark upon a tree, and if I were turned loose upon a deer, slain and cooked, I could eat him all from the tip of his nose to the tip of his tail."

"Stop, you boys," said Willet sternly. "You only aggravate your sufferings. Isn't that a valley to the right, Tayoga, and don't you catch the gleam of a little lake among its trees?"

"It is a valley, Great Bear, and there *is* a small lake in the center. We will go there. Perhaps we can catch fish."

Hope sprang up in Robert's heart. Fish? Why, of course there were fish in all the mountain lakes! and they never failed to carry hooks and lines in their packs. Bait could be found easily under the rocks. He did not conceal his eagerness to descend into the valley and the others were not less forward than he.

The valley was about half a square mile in area, of which the lake in the center occupied one-fourth, the rest being in dense forest. The three soon had their lines in water, and they waited full of anticipation, but they waited in vain until long after night had come. Not one of the three received a bite. The lines floated idly.

"Every lake in the mountains except one is full of fish—except one!" exclaimed Robert bitterly, "and this is the one!"

"No, it is not that," said Tayoga gravely. "It means that the face of Areskoui is still turned from us, that the good Sun God does not relent for our unknown sin. We must have offended him deeply that he should remain angry with us so long. This lake is swarming with fish, like the others of the mountains, but he has willed that not one should hang upon our hooks. Why waste time?"

He drew his line from the water, wound it up carefully and replaced it in his pack. The others, after a fruitless wait, imitated him, convinced that he was right. Then, after infinite pains, as before, they built two fires again, and slept between them. But the next morning all three were weak. Their vitality had declined fast in the night, and the situation became critical in the extreme.

"We must find food or we die," said Willet. "We might linger a long time, but soon we won't have the strength to hunt, and then it would only be a question of when the wolves took us."

"I can hear them howling now on the slopes," said Tayoga. "They know we are here, and that our strength is declining. They will not face our rifles, but will wait until we are too weak to use them."

"What is your plan, Dave?" asked Robert.

"There must be game on the slopes. What say you, Tayoga?"

"If Areskoui has willed for game to be there it will be there. He will even send it to us. And perhaps he has decided that he has now punished us enough."

"It certainly won't hurt for us to try, and perhaps we'd better separate. Robert, you go west; Tayoga, you take the eastern slopes, and I'll hunt toward the north. By night we'll all be back at this spot, full-handed or empty-handed, as it may be, but full-handed, I hope."

He spoke cheerfully, and the others responded in like fashion. Action gave them a mental and physical tonic, and bracing their weak bodies they started in the direction allotted to each. Robert forgot, for a little while, the terrible hunger that seemed to be preying upon his very fiber, and, as he started away, showed an elasticity and buoyancy of which he could not have dreamed himself capable five minutes before.

Westward stretched forest, lofty in the valley, high on the slopes and everywhere dense. He plunged into it, and then looked back. Tayoga and Willet were already gone from his sight, seeking what he sought. Their experience in the wilderness was greater than his, and they were superior to him in trailing, but he was very hopeful that it would be his good fortune to find the game they needed so badly, the game they must have soon, in truth, or perish.

The valley was deep in slush and mire, and the water soaked through his leggings and moccasins again, but he paid no attention to it now. His new courage and strength lasted. Glancing up at the heavens he beheld a little rift in the western clouds. A bar of light was let through, and his mind, so imaginative, so susceptible to the influences of earth and air, at once saw it as an omen. It was a pillar of fire to him, and his faith was confirmed.

"Areskoui is turning back his face, and he smiles upon us," he said to himself. Then looking carefully to his rifle, he held it ready for an instant shot.

He came to the westward edge of the valley, and found the slope before him gentle but rocky. He paused there a while in indecision, and, then glancing up again at the bar of light that had grown broader, he murmured, so much had he imbibed the religion and philosophy of the Iroquois:

"O Areskoui, direct me which way to go."

The reply came, almost like a whisper in his ear:

"Try the rocks."

It always seemed to him that it was a real whisper, not his own mind prompting him, and he walked boldly among the rocks which stretched for a long distance along the slopes. Then, or for the time, at least, he felt sure that a powerful hand was directing him. He saw tracks in the soft soil between the strong uplifts and he believed that they were fresh. Hollows were numerous there, and game of a certain kind would seek them in bitter weather.

His heart began to pound hard, too heavily, in fact, for his weakened frame, and he was compelled to stop and steady himself. Then he resumed the hunt once more, looking here and there between the rocky uplifts and in the deep depressions. He lost the tracks and then he found them, apparently fresher than ever. Would he take what he sought? Was the face of Areskoui still inclining toward him? He looked up and the bar of light was steadily growing broader and longer. The smile of the Sun God was deeper, and his doubts went away, one by one.

He turned toward a tall rock and a black figure sprang up, stared at him a moment or two, and then undertook to run away. Robert's rifle leaped to his shoulder, and, at a range so short that he could not miss, he pulled the trigger. The animal went down, shot through the heart, and then, silently exulting, young Lennox stood over him.

Areskoui had, in truth, been most kind. It was a young bear, nearly grown, very fat, and, as Robert well knew, very tender also. Here was food, splendid food, enough to last them many days, and he rejoiced. Then he was in a quandary. He could not carry the bear away, and while he could cut him up, he was loath to leave any part of him there. The wolves would soon be coming, insisting upon their share, but he was resolved they should have none.

He put his fingers over his mouth and blew between them a whistle, long, shrill and piercing, a sound that penetrated farther than the rifle shot. It was answered presently in a faint note from the opposite slope, and, then sitting down, he waited patiently. He knew that Tayoga and Willet would come, and, after a while, they appeared, striding eagerly through the forest. Then Robert rose, his heart full of gratitude and pride, and, in a grand manner, he did the honors.

"Come, good comrades," he said. "Come to the banquet. Have a steak of a bear, the finest, juiciest, tenderest bear that was ever killed. Have two steaks, three steaks, four steaks, any number of them. Here is abundant food that Areskoui has sent us."

Then he reeled and would have fallen to the ground had not Willet caught him in his arms. His great effort, made in his weakened condition, had exhausted him and a sudden collapse came, but he revived almost instantly, and the three together dragged the body of the bear into the valley. Then they proceeded dextrously, but without undue haste, to clean it, to light a fire, and to cook strips. Nor did they eat rapidly, knowing it was not wise to do so, but took little pieces, masticating them long and well, and allowing a decent interval between. Their satisfaction was intense and enormous. Life, fresh and vigorous, poured back into their veins.

"I'm sorry our bear had to die," said Robert, "but he perished in a good cause. I think he was reserved for the especial purpose of saving our lives."

"It is so," said Tayoga with deep conviction. "The face of Areskoui is now turned toward us. Our unknown sin is expiated. We must cook all the bear, and hang the flesh in the trees."

"So we must," said the hunter. "It's not right that we three, who are engaged in the great service of our country, should be hindered by the danger of starvation. We ought now to be somewhere near the French and Indians, watching them."

"Tomorrow we will seek them, Great Bear," said Tayoga, "but do you not think that tonight we should rest?"

"So we should, Tayoga. You're right. We'll take all chances on being seen, keep a good fire going and enjoy our comfort."

"And eat a big black bear steak every hour or so," said Robert.

"If we feel like it that's just what we'll do," laughed Willet. "It's our night, now. Surely, Robert, you're the greatest hunter in the world! Neither Tayoga nor I saw a sign of game, but you walked straight to your bear."

"No irony," said Robert, who, nevertheless, was pleased. "It merely proves that Areskoui had forgiven me, while he had not forgiven you two. But don't you notice a tremendous change?"

"Change! Change in what?"

"Why, everything! The whole world is transformed! Around us a little while ago stretched a scrubby, gloomy forest, but it is now magnificent and cheerful. I never saw finer oaks and beeches. That sky which was black and sinister has all the gorgeous golds and reds and purples of a benevolent sunset. The wind, lately cold and wet, is actually growing soft, dry and warm. It's a grand world, a kind world, a friendly world!"

"Thus, O Dagaeoga," said Tayoga, "does the stomach rule man and the universe. It is empty and all is black, it is filled and all that was black turns to rose. But the rose will soon be gone, because the sunlight is fading and night is at hand."

"But it's a fine night," said Robert sincerely. "I think it about the finest night I ever saw coming."

"Have another of these beautiful broiled steaks," said Willet, "and you'll be sure it's the finest night that ever was or ever will be."

"I think I will," said Robert, as he held the steak on the end of a sharpened stick over the coals and listened to the pleasant sizzling sound, "and after this is finished and a respectable time has elapsed, I may take another."

The revulsion in all three was tremendous. Although they had hidden it from one another, the great decrease in physical vitality had made their minds sink into black despair, but now that strength was returning so fast they saw the world through different eyes. They lay back luxuriously and their satisfaction was so intense that they thought little of danger. Tandakora might be somewhere near, but it did not disturb men who were as happy as they. The night came down, heavy and dark, as had been predicted, and they smothered their fire, but they remained before the coals, sunk in content.

They talked for a while in low tones, but, at length, they became silent. The big hunter considered. He knew that, despite the revulsion in feeling, they were not yet strong enough to undertake a great campaign against their enemies, and it would be better to remain a while in the valley until they were restored fully.

Beside their fire was a good enough place for the time, and Robert kept the first watch. The night, in reality, had turned much warmer and the sky was luminous with stars. The immense sense of comfort remained with him, and he was not disturbed by the howling of the wolves, which he knew had been drawn by the odor of game, but which he knew also would be afraid to invade the camp and attack three men.

His spirits, high as they were already, rose steadily as he watched. Surely after the Supreme Power had cast them down into the depths, a miracle had been worked in their behalf to take them out again. It was no skill of his that had led him to the bear, but strength far greater than that of man was now acting in their behalf. As they had triumphed over starvation they would triumph over everything. His sanguine mind predicted it.

The next morning was crisp and cold, but not wet, and Robert ate the most savory breakfast he could recall. That bear must have been fed on the choicest of wild nuts, topped off with wild honey, to have been so juicy and tender, and the thought of nuts caused him to look under the big hickory trees, where he found many of them, large and ripe. They made a most welcome addition to their bill of fare, taking the place of bread. Then, they were so well pleased with themselves that they concluded to spend another day and night in the valley.

Tayoga about noon climbed the enclosing ridge to the north, and, when he returned, Willet noticed a sparkle in his eyes. But the hunter said nothing, knowing that the Onondaga would speak in his own good time.

"There is another valley beyond the ridge," said Tayoga, "and a war party is encamped in it. They sit by their fire and eat prodigiously of deer they have killed."

Robert was startled, but he kept silent, he, too, knowing that Tayoga would tell all he intended to tell without urging.

"They do not know we are here, I do not think they dream of our presence," continued the Onondaga, "Areskoui smiles on us now, and Tododaho on his star, which we cannot see by day, is watching over us. Their feet will not bring them this way."

"Then you wouldn't suggest our taking to flight?" said Willet. "You would favor hiding here in peace?"

"Even so. It will please us some day to remember that we rested and slept almost within hearing of our enemies, and yet they did not take us."

"That's grim humor, Tayoga, but if it's the way you feel, Robert and I are with you."

Later in the afternoon they saw smoke rising beyond the ridge and they knew the warriors had built a great fire before which they were probably lying and gorging themselves, after their fashion when they had plenty of food, and little else to do. Yet the three remained defiantly all that day and all through the following night. The next morning, with ample supplies in their packs, they turned their faces southward, and cautiously climbed the ridge in that direction, once more passing into the region of the peaks. To their surprise they struck several comparatively fresh trails in the passes, and they were soon forced to the conclusion that the hostile forces were still all about them. Near midday they stopped in a narrow gorge between high peaks and listened to calls of the inhabitants of the forest, the faint howls of wolves, and once or twice the yapping of a fox.

"The warriors signaling to one another!" said Willet.

"It is so," said Tayoga. "I think they have noticed our tracks in the earth, too slight, perhaps, to tell who we are, but they will undertake to see."

"I hear the call of a moose directly ahead," said Robert, "although I know it is no moose that makes it. Our way there is cut off."

"And there is the howl of the wolf behind us," said Tayoga. "We cannot go back."

"Then," said Robert, "I suppose we must climb the mountain. It's lucky we've got our strength again."

They scaled a lofty summit once more, fortunately being able to climb among rocks, where they left no trail, and, crouched at the crest in dense bushes, they saw two bands meet in the valley below, evidently searching for the fugitives. There was no white man among them, but Robert knew a gigantic figure to be that of Tandakora, seeking them with the most intense and bitter hatred. The muzzle of his rifle began to slide forward, but Willet put out a detaining hand.

"No, Robert, lad," he said. "He deserves it, but his time hasn't come yet. Besides your shot would bring the whole crowd up after us."

"And he belongs to me," added Tayoga. "When he falls it is to be by my hand."

"Yes, he belongs to you, Tayoga," said Willet "Now they've concluded that we continued toward the south, and they're going on that way."

As they felt the need of the utmost caution they spent the remainder of the day and the next night on the crest. Robert kept the late watch, and he saw the dawn come, red and misty, a huge sun shining over the eastern mountains, but shedding little warmth. He was hopeful that Tandakora and his warriors had passed on far into the south, but he heard a distant cry rising in the clear air east of the peak and then a reply to the west. His heart stood still for a moment. He knew that they were the whoops of the savages and he felt that they signified a discovery. Perhaps chance had disclosed their trail. He listened with great intentness, but the shouts did not come again. Nevertheless the omen was bad.

He awoke Willet and the Onondaga, who had been sleeping soundly, and told them what had happened, both agreeing that the shouts were charged with import.

"I think it likely that we will be attacked," said the hunter. "Now we must take another look at our position."

The peak, luckily for them, was precipitous, and its crest did not cover an area of more than twenty or thirty square yards. On the three sides the ascent was so steep that a man could not climb up except with extreme difficulty, but on the fourth, by which they had come, the slope was more gradual. The gentle climb faced the east, and it was here that the hunter and Robert watched, while Tayoga, for the sake of utmost precaution, kept an eye on the steep sides.

Knowing that it was wise to economize and even to increase their strength, they ate abundantly of the bear steaks, afterward craving water, which they were forced to do without—the one great flaw in their position, since the warriors might hold them there to perish of thirst.

Robert soon forgot the desire for water in the tenseness of watching and waiting. But even the anxiety and the peril to his life did not keep him from noticing the singularity of his situation, upon the slender peak of a high mountain far in the wilderness. The sun, full of splendor but still cold, touched with gold all the surrounding crests and ridges and filled with a yellow but luxurious haze every gorge and ravine. He was compelled to admire its wintry beauty, a beauty, though, that he knew to be treacherous, surcharged as it was with savage wile and stratagem, and a burning desire for their lives.

A time that seemed incredible passed without demonstration from the enemy. But he realized that it was only about two hours. He did not expect to see any of the warriors creeping up the slopes toward them, but too wise to watch for their faces he did expect to notice the bushes move ever so slightly under their advance. He and Willet remained crouched in the same positions in the shelter of high rocks. Tayoga, who had been moving about the far side, came to them and whispered:

"I am going down the northern face of the cliff!"

"Why, it's sheer insanity, Tayoga!" said the astonished hunter.

"But I'm going."

"What'll you achieve after you've gone? You'll merely walk into Tandakora's hands!"

"I go, Great Bear, and I will return in a half hour, alive and well."

"Is your mind upset, Tayoga?"

"I am quite sane. Remember, Great Bear, I will be back in a half hour unhurt."

Then he was gone, gliding away through the low vegetation that covered the crest, and Robert and the hunter looked at each other.

"There is more in this than the eye sees," said young Lennox. "I never knew Tayoga to speak with more confidence. I think he will be back just as he says, in half an hour."

"Maybe, though I don't understand it. But there are lots of things one doesn't understand. We must keep our eyes on the slope, and let Tayoga solve his own problem, whatever it is."

There was no wind at all, but once Robert thought he saw the shrubs halfway down the steep move, though he was not sure and nothing followed. But, intently watching the place where the motion had occurred, he caught a gleam of metal which he was quite sure came from a rifle barrel.

"Did you see it?" he whispered to the hunter.

"Aye, lad," replied Willet. "They're there in that dense clump, hoping we've relaxed the watch and that they can surprise us. But it may be two or three hours before they come any farther. Always remember in your dealings with Indians that they have more time than anything else, and so they know how to be patient. Now, I wonder what Tayoga is doing! That boy certainly had something unusual on his mind!"

"Here he is, ready to speak for himself, and back inside his promised half hour."

Tayoga parted the bushes without noise, and sat down between them behind the big rocks. He offered no explanation, but seemed very content with himself.

"Well, Tayoga," said Willet, "did you go down the side of the mountain?"

"As far as I wished."

"What do you mean by that?"

"I have been engaged in a very pleasant task, Great Bear."

"What pleasure can you find in scaling a steep and rocky slope?"

"I have been drinking, Great Bear, drinking the fresh, pure water of the mountains, and it was wonderfully cool and good to my dry throat."

The two gazed at him in astonishment, and he laughed low, but with deep enjoyment.

"I took one drink, two drinks, three drinks," he said, "and when the time comes I shall take more. The fountain also awaits the lips of the Great Bear and of Dagaeoga."

"Tell it all," said Robert.

"When I looked down the steep side a long time I thought I caught a gleam as of falling water in the bushes. It was only twenty or thirty yards below us, and, when I descended to it, I found a little fountain bursting from a crevice in the rock. It was but a thread, making a tiny pool a few inches across, before it dropped away among the bushes, but it is very cool, very clear, and there is always plenty of it for many men."

"Is the descent hard?" asked Willet.

"Not for one who is strong and cautious. There are thick vines and bushes to which to hold, and remember that the splendid water is at the end of the journey."

"Then, Robert, you go," said the hunter, "and mind, too, that you get back soon, because my throat is parching. I'd like to have one deep drink before the warriors attack."

Robert followed Tayoga, and, obeying his instructions, was soon at the fountain, where he drank once, twice, thrice, and then once more of the finest water he could recall. Then, deeply grateful for the Onondaga's observation, he climbed back, and the hunter took his turn.

"It was certainly good, Tayoga," he said, when he was back in position. "Some men don't think much of water, but none of us can live without it. You've saved our lives."

"Perhaps, O Great Bear," responded the Onondaga, "but if the bushes below continue to shake as they are doing we shall have to save them again. Ah!"

The exclamation, long drawn but low, was followed by the leap of his rifle to the shoulder, and the pressing of his finger on the trigger. A stream of fire sprang from the muzzle of the long barrel to be followed by a yell in one of the thickets clustering on the slope. A savage rose to his feet, threw up his arms and fell headlong, his body crashing far below on the rocks. Robert shut his eyes and shivered.

"He was dead before he touched earth, lad," said the hunter. "Now the others are ready to scramble back. Look how the bushes are shaking again!"

Robert had shut his eyes only for a moment, and now he saw the scrub shaking more violently than ever. Then he had a fleeting glimpse of brown bodies as all the warriors descended rapidly. Anyone of the three might have fired with good aim, but they did not raise their rifles. Since their enemies were retreating they would let them retreat.

"They're all back in the valley now," said the hunter after a little while, "and they'll think a lot before they try the steep ascent a second time. Now it's a question of patience, and they hope we'll become so weak from thirst that we'll fall into their hands."

"Tandakora and his warriors would be consumed with anger if they knew of our spring," said Tayoga.

"They'll find out about it soon," said Robert.

"I think not," said Tayoga. "I noticed when I was at the fountain that the rivulet ran back into the cliff about a hundred feet below, and one can see the water only from the crest. If Areskoui has allowed us to be besieged here, he at least has created much in our favor."

He looked toward the east, where the great red sun was shining, and worshiped silently. It seemed to Robert that his young comrade stared unwinking for a long time into the eye of the Sun God, though perhaps it was only a few seconds. But his form expanded and his face was illumined. Robert knew that the Onondaga's confidence had become supreme, and he shared in it.

The hunter and Tayoga kept the watch after a while, and young Lennox was free to wander about the crest as he wished. He examined carefully the three sides they had left unguarded, but was convinced that no warrior, no matter how skillful and tenacious, could climb up there. Then he wandered back toward the sentinels, and, sitting down under a tree, began to study the distant slopes across the gorge.

He saw the warriors gather by-and-by in a deep recess out of rifle shot, light a fire and begin to cook great quantities of game, as if they meant to stay there and keep the siege until doomsday, if necessary. He saw the gigantic figure of Tandakora approach the fire, eat voraciously for a while and then go away. After him came a white man in French uniform. He thought at first it was St. Luc and his heart beat hard, but he was able to discern presently that it was an officer not much older than himself, in a uniform of white faced with violet and a black, three-cornered hat. Finally he recognized young

De Galissonnière, whom he had met in Québec, and whom he had seen a few days since in the French camp.

As he looked De Galissonnière left the recess, descended into the valley and then began to climb their slope, a white handkerchief held aloft on the point of his small sword. Young Lennox immediately joined the two watchers at the brink.

"A flag of truce! Now what can he want!" he exclaimed.

"We'll soon see," replied Willet. "He's within good hearing now, and I'll hail him."

He shouted in powerful tones that echoed in the gorge:

"Below there! What is it?"

"I have something to say that will be of great importance to you," replied De Galissonnière.

"Then come forward, while we remain here. We don't trust your allies."

Robert saw the face of the young Frenchman flush, but De Galissonnière, as if knowing the truth, and resolved not to quibble over it, climbed steadily. When he was within twenty feet of the crest the hunter called to him to halt, and he did so, leaning easily against a strong bush, while the three waited eagerly to hear what he had to say.

CHAPTER IV.
THE GODS AT PLAY

De Galissonnière gazed at the three faces, peering at him over the brink, and then drew himself together jauntily. His position, perched on the face of the cliff, was picturesque, and he made the most of it.

"I am glad to see you again Mr. Willet, Mr. Lennox and Tayoga, the brave Onondaga," he said. "It's been a long time since we met in Québec and much water has flowed under that bridge of Avignon, of which we French sing, but I can't see that any one of you has changed much."

"Nor you," said Robert, catching his tone and acting as spokesman for the three. "The circumstances are unusual, Captain Louis de Galissonnière, and I'm sorry I can't invite you to come up on our crest, but it wouldn't be military to let you have a look at our fortifications."

"I understand, and I do very well where I am. I wish to say first that I am sorry to see you in such a plight."

"And we, Captain, regret to find you allied with such a savage as Tandakora."

A quick flush passed over the young Frenchman's face, but he made no other sign.

"In war one cannot always choose," he replied. "I have come to receive your surrender, and I warn you very earnestly that it will be wise for you to tender it. The Indians have lost one man already and they are inflamed. If they lose more I might not be able to control them."

"And if we yield ourselves you pledge us our lives, a transfer in safety to Canada where we are to remain as prisoners of war, until such time as we may be exchanged?"

"All that I promise, and gladly."

"You're sure, Captain de Galissonnière, that you can carry out the conditions?"

"Absolutely sure. You are surrounded here on the peak, and you cannot get away. All we have to do is to keep the siege."

"That is true, but while you can wait so can we."

"But we have plenty of water, and you have none."

"You would urge us again to surrender on the ground that it would be the utmost wisdom for us to do so?"

"It goes without saying, Mr. Lennox."

"Then, that being the case, we decline."

De Galissonnière looked up in astonishment at the young face that gazed down at him. The answer he had expected was quite the reverse.

"You mean that you refuse?" he exclaimed.

"It is just what I meant."

"May I ask why, when you are in such a hopeless position?"

"Tayoga, Mr. Willet and I wish to see how long we can endure the pangs of thirst without total collapse. We've had quite a difference on the subject. Tayoga says ten days, Mr. Willet twelve days, but I think we can stand it a full two weeks."

De Galissonnière frowned.

"You are frivolous, Mr. Lennox," he said, "and this is not a time for light talk. I don't know what you mean, but it seems to me you don't appreciate the dire nature of your peril. I liked you and your comrades when I met you in Québec and I do not wish to see you perish at the hands of the savages. That is why I have climbed up here to make you this offer, which I have wrung from the reluctant Tandakora. It was he who assured me that the besieged were you. It pains me that you see fit to reject it."

"I know it was made out of a good heart," said Robert, seriously, "and we thank you for the impulse that brought you here. Some day we may be able to repay it, but we decline because there are always chances. You know, Captain, that while we have life we always have hope. We may yet escape."

"I do not see wherein it is possible," said the young Frenchman, with actual reluctance in his tone. "But it is for you to decide what you wish to do. Farewell."

"Farewell, Captain de Galissonnière," said Robert, with the utmost sincerity. "I hope no bullet of ours will touch you."

The captain made a courteous gesture of good-by and slowly descended the slope, disappearing among the bushes in the gorge, whence came a fierce and joyous shout.

"That was the cry of the savages when he told them our answer," said Willet. "They don't want us to surrender. They think that by-and-by we'll fall into their hands through exhaustion, and then they can work their will upon us."

"They don't know about that fountain, that pure, blessed fountain," said Robert, "the finest fountain that gushes out anywhere in this northern wilderness, the fountain that Tayoga's Areskoui has put here for our especial benefit."

His heart had become very light and, as usual when his optimism was at its height, words gushed forth. Water, and their ability to get it whenever they wanted it, was the key to everything, and he painted their situation in such bright colors that his two comrades could not keep from sharing his enthusiasm.

"Truly, Dagaeoga did not receive the gift of words in vain," said Tayoga. "Golden speech flows from him, and it lifts up the minds of those who hear. Manitou finds a use for everybody, even for the orator."

"Though it was a hard task, even for Manitou," laughed Robert.

They watched the whole afternoon without any demonstration from the enemy—they expected none—and toward evening the Onondaga, who was gazing into the north, announced a dark shadow on the horizon.

"What is it?" asked Robert. "A cloud? I hope we won't have another storm."

"It is no cloud," replied Tayoga. "It is something else that moves very fast, and it comes in our direction. A little longer and I can tell what it is. Now I see; it is a flight of wild pigeons, a great flock, hundreds of thousands, and millions, going south to escape the winter."

"We've seen such flights often."

"So we have, but this is coming straight toward us, and I have a great thought, Dagaeoga. Areskoui has not only forgiven us for our unknown sin—perhaps of omission—but he has also decided to put help in our way, if we will use it. You see many dwarf trees at the southern edge of the crest, and I believe that by dark they will be covered with pigeons, stopping for the night."

"And some of them will stop for our benefit, though we have bear meat too! I see, Tayoga."

Robert watched the flying cloud, which had grown larger and blacker, and then he saw that Tayoga was right. It was an immense flock of wild pigeons, and, as the twilight fell, they covered the trees upon their crest so thickly that the boughs bent beneath them. Young Lennox and the Onondaga killed as many as they wished with sticks, and soon, fat and juicy, they were broiling over the coals.

"Tandakora will guess that the pigeons have fed us," said Robert, "and he will not like it, but he will yet know nothing about the water."

They climbed down in turn in the darkness and took a drink, and Robert, who explored a little, found many vines loaded with wild grapes, ripe and rich, which made a splendid dessert. Then he took a number of the smaller but very tough stems, and knotting them together, with the assistance of Tayoga ran a strong rope from the crest down to the fountain, thus greatly easing the descent for water and the return.

"Now we can take two drinks where we took one before," he said triumphantly when the task was finished. "If you have your water there is nothing like making it easy to be reached. Moreover, while it was safe for an agile fellow like me, you and Dave, Tayoga, being stiff and clumsy, might have tumbled down the mountain and then I should have been lonesome."

Willet, who had been keeping the watch alone, was inclined to the belief that they might expect an attack in the night, if it should prove to be very dark. He felt able, however, should such an attempt come, to detect the advance of the savages, either by sight or hearing, especially the latter, ear in such cases generally informing him earlier than eye. But as neither Robert nor Tayoga was busy they joined him, and all three sat near the brink with their rifles across their knees, and their pistols loosened in their belts, ready for their foes should they come in numbers.

They talked a while in low tones, and then fell silent. The night had come, starless and moonless, favorable to the designs of Tandakora, but they felt intense satisfaction, nevertheless. It was partly physical. Robert's making of an easy road to the water, the coming of the pigeons, to be eaten, apparently sent by Areskoui, and the ease with which they believed they could hold their lofty fortress, combined to produce a victorious state of mind. Robert looked over the brink once or twice at the steep slope, and he felt that the warriors would, in truth, be taking a mighty risk, if they came up that steep path against the three.

He and Tayoga, in the heavy darkness, depended, like Willet, chiefly on ear. It was impossible to see to the bottom of the valley, where the dusk had rolled up like a sea, but, as the night was still, they felt sure they could hear anyone climbing up the peak. In order to make themselves more comfortable they spread their blankets at the very brink, and lay down upon them, thus being able to repose, and at the same time watch without the risk of inviting a shot.

Young Lennox knew that the attack, if it came at all, would not come until late, and restraining his naturally eager and impatient temper, he used all the patience that his strong will could summon, never ceasing meanwhile to lend an attentive ear to every sound of the night. He heard the wind rise, moan a little while in the gorge and then die; he heard a fitful breeze rustle the boughs on the slopes and then grow still, and he heard his comrades move once or twice to ease their positions, but no other sound came to him until nearly midnight, and then he heard the fall of a pebble on the slope, absolute proof to one experienced as he that it had been displaced by the incautious foot of a climbing enemy.

The rattling of the pebble was succeeded by a long interval of silence, and the lad understood that too. The warriors, to whom time was nothing, fearing that suspicion had been aroused by the fall of the pebble, would wait until it had been lulled before resuming their advance. They would flatten themselves like lizards against the slope, not stirring an inch. But the three were as patient as they, and while a full hour passed after the slip of the stone before the slightest sound came from the slope, they did not relax their vigilance a particle. Then all three heard a slight rustle among the bushes and they peered cautiously over.

They were able to discern the dim outline of figures among the bushes about twenty feet below, and Wilier, who directed the defense, whispered that Tayoga and he would take aim, while Robert held his fire in reserve. Then the Onondaga and he picked their targets in the darkness and pulled trigger. Shouts, the fall of bodies and the crackling of rifles came back. A half dozen bullets, fired almost at random, whistled over their heads and then Robert sent his own lead at a shadow which appeared very clearly among the bushes, a crashing fall following at once.

Then the three, not waiting to reload, snatched out their pistols and held themselves ready for a further attack, if it should come. But it did not come. Even the rage of Tandakora had had enough. His second repulse had been bloodier than the first, and it had been proved with the lives of his warriors that they could not storm that terrible steep, in the face of three such redoubtable marksmen.

Robert heard a number of pebbles rolling now, but they were made by men descending, and the three, certain of abundant leisure, reloaded their rifles. Their eyes told them nothing, but they were as sure as if they had seen them that the warriors had disappeared in the sea of darkness with which the gulf was filled. The lad breathed a long sigh of relief.

"You're justified in your satisfaction," said Willet. "I think it's the last direct attack they'll make upon us. Now they'll try the slow methods of siege and our exhaustion by thirst, and how it would make their venom rise if they knew anything about that glorious fountain of ours! Since it's to be a test of patience, we'd better make things easy for ourselves. I'll sit here and watch the slope, and, as the night is turning cold, you and Tayoga, Robert, can build a fire."

There was a dip in the center of the crest, and in this they heaped the fallen wood, which here as elsewhere in the wilderness was abundant. Wood and water, two great requisites of primitive man, they had in plenty, and had it not been for their eagerness to go forward with their work they would have been content to stay indefinitely on the peak.

The fire was soon blazing cheerfully. Warriors on the opposing peaks or crest might see it, but they did not care. No bullets from rival heights could reach them and the light would appear to their enemies as a beacon of defiance, a sort of challenge that was very pleasing to Robert's soul. He basked in the glow and heat of the coals, ate bear meat and wild pigeon for a late supper, and discoursed on the strength of their natural fortress.

"The peak was reared here by Areskoui for our especial benefit," he said. "It is in every sense a tower of strength, water even being placed in its side that we might not die of thirst."

"And yet we cannot stay here always," said the Onondaga. "Tomorrow we must think of a way of escape."

"Let tomorrow take care of itself. Tayoga, you're too serious! You're missing the pleasure of the night."

"Dagaeoga loves to talk and he talks well. His voice is pleasant in my ear like to the murmur of a silver brook. Perhaps he is right. Lo! the clouds have gone, and I can see Tododaho on his star. Areskoui watches over us by day and Tododaho by night. We are once more the favorites of the Sun God and of the great Onondaga who went away to his everlasting star more than four centuries ago. Again I say Dagaeoga is right; I will enjoy the night, and let the morrow care for itself."

He drew the folds of his blanket to his chin and stretched his length before the fire. Having made up his mind to be satisfied, Tayoga would let nothing interfere with such a laudable purpose. Soon he slept peacefully.

"You might follow him," said Willet.

"I don't think I can do it now," said Robert. "I've a restless spirit."

"Then wander about the peak, and I'll take up my old place at the edge of the slope."

Robert went back to the far side, where he had stretched his rope of grape vines down to the spring, and, craving their cool, fresh taste, he ate more of the grapes. He noticed then that they were uncommonly plentiful. All along the cliff they trailed in great, rich clusters, black and glossy, fairly asking to be eaten. In places the vines hung in perfect mazes, and he looked at them questioningly. Then the thought came to him and he wondered why it had been so slow of arrival. He returned to Willet and said:

"I don't think you need watch any longer here, Dave."

"Why?" was the hunter's astonished reply.

"Because we're going to leave the mountain."

"Leave the mountain! It's more likely, Robert, that your prudence has left you. If we went down the slope we'd go squarely into the horde, and then it would be a painful and lingering end for us."

"I don't mean the slope. We're to go down the other side of the cliff."

"Except here and near the bottom the mountain is as steep everywhere as the side of a house. The only way for us to get down is to fall down and then we'd stop too quick."

"We don't have to fall down, we'll climb down."

"Can't be done, Robert, my boy. There's not enough bushes."

"We don't need bushes, there are miles of grape vines as strong as leather. All we have to do is to knot them together securely and our rope is ready. If we eased our way to the spring with vines then we can finish the journey to the bottom of the cliff with them."

The hunter's gaze met that of the lad, and it was full of approval.

"I believe you've found the way, Robert," said Willet. "Wake Tayoga and see what he thinks."

The Onondaga received the proposal with enthusiasm, and he made the further suggestion that they build high the fire for the sake of deceiving the besiegers.

"And suppose we prop up two or three pieces of fallen tree trunk before it," added Robert. "Warriors watching on the opposite slopes will take them for our figures and will not dream that we're attempting to escape."

That idea, too, was adopted, and in a few minutes the fire was blazing and roaring, while a stream of sparks drifted up merrily from it to be lost in the dusk. Near it the fragments of tree trunks set erect would pass easily, at a great distance and in the dark, for human beings. Then, while Willet watched, Robert and Tayoga knotted the vines with quick and dextrous hands, throwing the cable over a bough, and trying every knot with their double weight. A full two hours they toiled and then they exulted.

"It will reach from the clump of bushes about the fountain to the next clump below, which is low down," said Robert, "and from there we can descend without help."

They called Willet, and the three, leaving the crest which had been such a refuge for them and which they had defended so well, descended to the fountain. At that point they secured their cable with infinite care to the largest of the dwarf trees and let it drop over across a bare space to the next clump of bushes below, a distance that seemed very great, it was so steep. Robert claimed the honor of the first descent, but it was finally conceded to Tayoga, who was a trifle lighter.

The Onondaga fastened securely upon his back his rifle and his pack containing food, and then, grasping the cable firmly with both hands, he began to go down, while his friends watched with great anxiety. He was not obliged to swing clear his whole weight, but was able to brace his feet against the cliff. Thus he steadied the vines, but Robert and Willet nevertheless breathed great sighs of relief, when he reached the bushes below, and detached himself from the cable.

"It is safe," he called back.

Robert went next and Willet followed. When the three were in the bushes, clinging to their tough and wiry strength, they found that the difficulties, as they invariably do, had decreased. Below them the slope was not so steep by any means, and, by holding to the rocky outcrops and scant bushes, they could make the full descent of the mountain. While they rested for a little space where they were, Robert suddenly began to laugh.

"Is Dagaeoga rejoicing so soon?" asked Tayoga

"Why shouldn't I laugh," replied Robert, "when we have such a good jest?"

"What jest? I see none."

"Why, to think of Tandakora sitting at the foot of our peak and watching there three or four days, waiting all the time for us to die of hunger and thirst, and we far to the south. At least he'll see that the mountain doesn't get away, and Tandakora, I take it, has small sense of humor. When he penetrates the full measure of the joke he'll love us none the less. Perhaps, though, De Galissonnière will not mourn, because he knows that if we were taken after a siege he could not save us from the cruelty of the savages."

The hunter and the Onondaga were forced to laugh a little with him, and then, rested thoroughly, they resumed the descent, leaving their cable to tell its own tale, later on. The rest of the slope, although possible, was slow and painful, testing their strength and skill to the utmost, but they triumphed over everything and before day were in a gorge, with the entire height of the peak towering above them and directly between them and their enemies. Here they flung themselves on the ground and rested until day, when they began a rapid flight southward, curving about among the peaks, as the easiest way led them.

The air rapidly grew warmer, showing that the sudden winter had come only on the high mountains, and that autumn yet lingered on the lower levels. The gorgeous reds and yellows and browns and vivid shades between returned, but there was a haze in the air and the west was dusky.

"Storm will come again before night," said Tayoga.

"I think so too," said Willet, "and as I've no mind to be beaten about by it, suppose we build a spruce shelter in the gorge here and wait until it passes."

The two lads were more than willing, feeling that the chance of pursuit had passed for a long time at least, and they set to work with their sharp hatchets, rapidly making a crude but secure wickiup, as usual against the rocky side of a hill. Before the task was done the sky darkened much more, and far in the west thunder muttered.

"It's rolling down a gorge," said Robert, "and hark! you can hear it also in the south."

From a point, far distant from the first, came a like rumble, and, after a few moments of silence, a third rumble was heard to the east. Silence again and then the far rumble came from the south.

"That's odd," said Robert. "It isn't often that you hear thunder on all sides of you."

"Listen!" exclaimed Tayoga, whose face bore a rapt and extraordinary look. The four rumbles again went around the horizon, coming from one point after the other in turn.

"It is no ordinary thunder," said the Onondaga in a tone of deep conviction.

"What is it, then?" asked Robert.

"It is Manitou, Areskoui, Tododaho and Hayowentha talking together. That is why we have the thunder north, east, south and west. Hear their voices carrying all through the heavens!"

"Which is Manitou?"

"That I cannot tell. But the great gods talk, one with another, though what they say is not for us to know. It is not right that mere mortals like ourselves should understand them, when they speak across infinite space."

"It may be that you're right, Tayoga," said Willet.

The three did not yet go into the spruce shelter, because, contrary to the signs, there was no rain. The wind moaned heavily and thick black clouds swept up in an almost continuous procession from the western horizon, but they did not let a drop fall. The thunder at the four points of the horizon went on, the reports moving from north to east, and thence to south and west, and then around and around, always in the same direction. After every crash there was a long rumble in the gorges until the next crash came again. Now and then lightning flared.

"It is not a storm after all," said the Onondaga, "or, at least, if a storm should come it will not be until after night is at hand, when the great gods are through talking. Listen to the heavy booming, always like the sound of a thousand big guns at one time. Now the lightning grows and burns until it is at a white heat. The great gods not only talk, but they are at play. They hurl thunderbolts through infinite space, and watch them fall. Then they send thunder rumbling through our mountains, and the sound is as soft to them as a whisper to us."

"Your idea is pretty sound, Tayoga," said Willet, who had imbibed more than a little of the Iroquois philosophy, "and it does look as if the gods were at play because there is so much thunder and lightning and no rain. Look at that flash on the mountain toward the east! I think it struck. Yes, there goes a tree! When the gods play among the peaks it's just as well for us to stay down here in the gorge."

"But the crashes still run regularly from north to east and on around," said Robert. "I suppose that when they finish talking, the rain will come, and we'll have plenty of need for our spruce shelter."

The deep rumbling continued all through the rest of the afternoon. A dusk as of twilight arrived long before sunset, but it was of an unusually dull, grayish hue, and it affected Robert as if he were breathing an air surcharged with gunpowder. It colored and intensified everything. The peaks and ridges rose to greater heights, the gorges and valleys were deeper, the reports of the thunder, extremely heavy, in fact, were doubled and tripled in fancy; all that Tayoga had said about the play of the gods was true. Tododaho, the great Onondaga, spoke across the void to Hayowentha, the great Mohawk, and Areskoui, the Sun God, conversed with Manitou, the All Powerful, Himself.

The imaginative lad felt awe but no fear. The gods at play in the heavens would not condescend to harm a humble mortal like himself and it was an actual pleasure because he was there to hear them. Just before the invisible sun went over the rim of the horizon, a brilliant red light shot for a minute or two from the west through the gray haze, and fell on the faces of the three, sitting in silence before their spruce shelter.

"It is Areskoui throwing off his most brilliant beams before he goes," said Tayoga. "Now I think the play will soon be over, and we may look for the rain."

The crashes of thunder increased swiftly and greatly in violence, and then, as the Onondaga had predicted, ceased abruptly. The silence that followed was so heavy that it was oppressive. No current of air was moving anywhere. Not a leaf stirred. The grayish haze became thicker and every ridge and peak was hidden. Presently a sound like a sigh came down the gorge, but it soon grew.

"We'll go inside," said Tayoga, "because the deluge is at hand."

They crowded themselves into their crude little hut, and in five minutes the flood was upon them, pouring with such violence that some of it forced its way through the hasty thatch, but they were able to protect themselves with their blankets, and they slept the night through in a fair degree of comfort.

In the morning they saw a world washed clean, bright and shining, and they breathed an autumnal air wonderful in its purity. Feeling safe now from pursuit, they were no longer eager to flee. A brief council of three decided that they would hang once more on the French and Indian flank. It had been their purpose to discover what was intended by the formidable array they had seen, and it was their purpose yet.

They did not go back on their path, but they turned eastward into a land of little and beautiful lakes, through which one of the great Indian trails from the northwest passed, and made a hidden camp near the shore of a sheet of water about a mile square, set in the mountains like a gem. They had method in locating here, as the trail ran through a gorge less than half a mile to the east of their camp, and they had an idea that the spy, Garay, might pass that way, two of them always abiding by the trail, while the third remained in their secluded camp or hunted game. Willet shot a deer and Tayoga brought down a rare wild turkey, while Robert caught some wonderful lake trout. So they had plenty of food, and they were content to wait.

They were sure that Garay had not yet gone, as the storms that had threatened them would certainly have delayed his departure, and neither the hunter nor the Onondaga could discover any traces of footsteps. Fortunately the air continued to turn warmer and the lower country in which they now were had all the aspects of Indian summer. Robert, shaken a little perhaps by the great hardships and dangers through which he had passed, though he may not have realized at the time the weight upon his nerves, recovered quickly, and, as usual, passed, with the rebound, to the heights of optimism.

"What do you expect to get from Garay?" he asked Willet as he changed places with him on the trail.

"I'm not sure," replied the hunter, "but if we catch him we'll find something. We've got to take our bird first, and then we'll see. He went north and west with a message, and that being the case he's bound to take one back. I don't think Garay is a first-class woodsman and we may be able to seize him."

Robert was pleased with the idea of the hunted turning into the hunters, and he and Tayoga now did most of the watching along the trail, a watch that was not relaxed either by day or by night. On the sixth night the two youths were together, and Tayoga thought he discerned a faint light to the north.

"It may be a low star shining over a hill," said Robert.

"I think it is the glow from a small camp fire," said the Onondaga.

"It's a question that's decided easily."

"You mean we'll stalk it, star or fire, whichever it may be?"

"That is what we're here for, Tayoga."

They began an exceedingly cautious advance toward the light, and it soon became evident that it was a fire, though, as Tayoga had said, a small one, set in a little valley and almost hidden by the surrounding foliage. Now they redoubled their caution, using every forest art to make a silent approach, as they might find a band of warriors around the blaze, and they did not wish to walk with open eyes into any such deadly trap. Their delight was great when they saw only one man crouched over the coals in a sitting posture, his head bent over his knees; so that, in effect, only his back was visible, but they knew him at once. It was Garay.

The heart of young Lennox flamed with anger and triumph. Here was the fellow who had tried to take his life in Albany, and, if he wished revenge, the moment was full of opportunity. Yet he could never fire at a man's back, and it was their cue, moreover, to take him alive. Garay's rifle was leaning against a log, six or eight feet from him, and his attitude indicated that he might be asleep. His clothing was stained and torn, and he bore all the signs of a long journey and extreme weariness.

"See what it is to come into the forest and not be master of all its secrets," whispered Tayoga. "Garay is the messenger of Onontio (the Governor General of Canada) and Tandakora, and yet he sleeps, when those who oppose him are abroad."

"A man has to sleep some time or other," said Robert, "or at least a white man must. We're not all like an Iroquois; we can't stay awake forever if need be."

"If one goes to the land of Tarenyawagon when his enemies are at hand he must pay the price, Dagaeoga, and now the price that Garay is going to pay will be a high one. Surely Manitou has delivered him, helpless, into our hands. Come, we will go closer."

They crept through the bushes until they could have reached out and touched the spy with the muzzles of their rifles, and still he did not stir. Into that heavy and weary brain, plunged into dulled slumbers, entered no thought of a stalking foe. The fire sank and the bent back sagged a little lower. Garay had traveled hard and long. He was anxious to get back to Albany with what he knew, and he felt sure that the northern forests contained only friends. He had built his fire without apprehension, and sleep had overtaken him quickly.

A fox stirred in the thicket beyond the fire and looked suspiciously at the coals and the still figure beyond them. He did not see the other two figures in the bushes but his animosity as well as his suspicion was aroused. He edged a little nearer, and then a slight sound in the thicket caused him to creep back. But he was an inquiring fox, and, although he buried himself under a bush, he still looked, staring with sharp, intent eyes.

He saw a shadow glide from the thicket, pick up the rifle of Garay which leaned against the fallen log, and then glide back, soundless. The curiosity of the fox now prevailed over his suspicion. The shadow had not menaced him, and his vulpine intelligence told him that he was not concerned in the drama now about to unfold itself. He was merely a spectator, and, as he looked, he saw the shadow glide back and crouch beside the sleeping man. Then a second shadow came and crouched on the other side.

What the fox saw was the approach of Robert and Tayoga, whom some whimsical humor had seized. They intended to make the surprise complete and Robert, with a memory of the treacherous shot in Albany, was willing also to fill the soul of the spy with terror. Tayoga adroitly removed the pistol and knife from the belt of Garay, and Robert touched him lightly on the shoulder. Still he did not stir, and then the youth brought his hand down heavily.

Garay uttered the sigh of one who comes reluctantly from the land of sleep and who would have gone back through the portals which were only half opened, but Robert brought his hand down again, good and hard. Then his eyes flew open and he saw the calm face beside him, and the calm eyes less than a foot away, staring straight into his own. It must be an evil dream, he thought at first, but it had all the semblance of reality, and, when he turned his head in fear, he saw another face on the other side of him, carved in red bronze, it too only a foot away and staring at him in stern accusation.

Then all the faculties of Garay, spy and attempted assassin, leaped into life, and he uttered a yell of terror, springing to his feet, as if he had been propelled by a galvanic battery. Strong hands, seizing him on either side, pulled him down again and the voice of Tayoga, of the clan of the Bear, of the nation Onondaga, of the great League of the Hodenosaunee said insinuatingly in his ear:

"Sit down, Achille Garay! Here are two who wish to talk with you!"

He fell back heavily and his soul froze within him, as he recognized the faces. His figure sagged, his eyes puffed out, and he waited in silent terror.

"I see that you recognize us, Achille Garay," said Robert, whose whimsical humor was still upon him. "You'll recall that shot in Albany. Perhaps you did not expect to meet my friend and me here in the heart of the northern forests, but here we are. What have you to say for yourself?"

Garay strove to speak, but the half formed words died on his lips.

"We wish explanations about that little affair in Albany," continued his merciless interlocutor, "and perhaps there is no better time than the present. Again I repeat, what have you to say? And you have also been in the French and Indian camp. You bore a message to St. Luc and Tandakora and beyond a doubt you bear another back to somebody. We want to know about that too. Oh, we want to know about many things!"

"I have no message," stammered Garay.

"Your word is not good. We shall find methods of making you talk. You have been among the Indians and you ought to know something about these methods. But first I must lecture you on your lack of woodcraft. It is exceedingly unwise to build a fire in the wilderness and go to sleep beside it, unless there is someone with you to watch. I'm ashamed of you, Monsieur Garay, to have neglected such an elementary lesson. It made your capture easy, so ridiculously easy that it lacked piquancy and interest. Tayoga and I were not able to give our faculties and strength the healthy exercise they need. Come now, are you ready to walk?"

"What are you going to do with me?" asked Garay in French, which both of his captors understood and spoke.

"We haven't decided upon that," replied Robert maliciously, "but whatever it is we'll make it varied and lively. It may please you to know that we've been waiting several days for you, but we scarce thought you'd go to sleep squarely in the trail, just where we'd be sure to see you. Stand up now and march like a man, ready to meet any fate. Fortune has turned against you, but you still have the chance to show your Spartan courage and endurance."

"The warrior taken by his enemies meets torture and death with a heroic soul," said Tayoga solemnly.

Garay shivered.

"You'll save me from torture?" he said to Robert.

Young Lennox shook his head.

"I'd do so if it were left to me," he said, "but my friend, Tayoga, has a hard heart. In such matters as these he will not let me have my way. He insists upon the ancient practices of his nation. Also, David Willet, the hunter, is waiting for us, and he too is strong for extreme measures. You'll soon face him. Now, march straight to the right!"

Garay with a groan raised himself to his feet and walked unsteadily in the direction indicated. Close behind him came the avenging two.

CHAPTER V.
TAMING A SPY

Young Lennox undeniably felt exultation. It fairly permeated his system. The taking of Garay had been so easy that it seemed as if the greater powers had put him squarely in their path, and had deprived him of all vigilance, in order that he might fall like a ripe plum into their hands. Surely the face of Areskoui was still turned toward them, and the gods, having had their play, were benevolent of mood—that is, so far as Robert and Tayoga were concerned, although the spy might take a different view of the matter. The triumph, and the whimsical humor that yet possessed him, moved him to flowery speech.

"Monsieur Garay, Achille, my friend," he said. "You are surprised that we know you so well, but remember that you left a visiting card with us in Albany, the time you sent an evil bullet past my head, and then proved too swift for Tayoga. That's a little matter we must look into some time soon. I don't understand why you wished me to leave the world prematurely. It must surely have been in the interest of someone else, because I had never heard of you before in my life. But we'll pass over the incident now as something of greater importance is to the fore. It was really kind of you, Achille, to sit down there in the middle of the trail, beside a fire that was sure to serve as a beacon, and wait for us to come. It reflects little credit, however, on your skill as a woodsman, and, from sheer kindness of heart, we're not going to let you stay out in the forest after dark."

Garay turned a frightened look upon him. It was mention of the bullet in Albany that struck renewed terror to his soul. But Robert, ordinarily gentle and sympathetic, was not inclined to spare him.

"As I told you," he continued, "Tayoga and I are disposed to be easy with you, but Willet has a heart as cold as a stone. We saw you going to the French and Indian camp, and we laid an ambush for you on your way back. We were expecting to take you, and Willet has talked of you in merciless fashion. What he intends to do with you is more than I've been able to determine. Ah, he comes now!"

The parting bushes disclosed a tall figure, rifle ready, and Robert called cheerily:

"Here we are, Dave, back again, and we bring with us a welcome guest. Monsieur Achille Garay was lost in the forest, and, taking pity on him, we've brought him in to share our hospitality. Mr. David Willet, Monsieur Achille Garay of everywhere."

Willet smiled grimly and led the way back to the spruce shelter. To Garay's frightened eyes he bore out fully Robert's description.

"You lads seem to have taken him without trouble," he said. "You've done well. Sit down, Garay, on that log; we've business with you."

Garay obeyed.

"Now," said the hunter, "what message did you take to St. Luc and the French and Indian force?"

The man was silent. Evidently he was gathering together the shreds of his courage, as his back stiffened. Willet observed him shrewdly.

"You don't choose to answer," he said. "Well, we'll find a way to make you later on. But the message you carried was not so important as the message you're taking back. It's about you, somewhere. Hand over the dispatch."

"I've no dispatch," said Garay sullenly.

"Oh, yes, you have! A man like you wouldn't be making such a long and dangerous journey into the high mountains and back again for nothing. Come, Garay, your letter!"

The spy was silent.

"Search him, lads!" said Willet.

Garay recoiled, but when the hunter threatened him with his pistol he submitted to the dextrous hands of Robert and Tayoga. They went through all his pockets, and then they made him remove his clothing piece by piece, while they thrust the points of their knives through the lining for concealed documents. But the steel touched nothing. Then they searched his heavy moccasins, and even pulled the soles loose, but no papers were disclosed. There was nowhere else to look and the capture had brought no reward.

"He doesn't seem to have anything," said Robert.

"He must have! He is bound to have!" said the hunter.

"You have had your look," said Garay, a note of triumph showing in his voice, "and you have failed. I bear no message because I am no messenger. I am a Frenchman, it is true, but I have no part in this war. I am not a soldier or a scout. You should let me go."

"But that bullet in Albany."

"I did not fire it. It was someone else. You have made a mistake."

"We've made no mistake," said the hunter. "We know what you are. We know, too, that a dispatch of great importance is about you somewhere. It is foolish to think otherwise, and we mean to have it."

"I carry no dispatch," repeated Garay in his sullen, obstinate tones.

"We mean that you shall give it to us," said the hunter, "and soon you will be glad to do so."

Robert glanced at him, but Willet did not reveal his meaning. It was impossible to tell what course he meant to take, and the two lads were willing to let the event disclose itself. The same sardonic humor that had taken possession of Robert seemed to lay hold of the older man also.

"Since you're to be our guest for a while, Monsieur Garay," he said, "we'll give you our finest room. You'll sleep in the spruce shelter, while we spread our blankets outside. But lest you do harm to yourself, lest you take into your head some foolish notion to commit suicide, we'll have to bind you. Tayoga can do it in such a manner that the thongs will cause you no pain. You'll really admire his wonderful skill."

The Onondaga bound Garay securely with strips, cut from the prisoner's own clothing, and they left him lying within the spruce shelter. At dawn the next day Willet awoke the captive, who had fallen into a troubled slumber.

"Your letter," he said. "We want it."

"I have no letter," replied Garay stubbornly.

"We shall ask you for it once every two hours, and the time will come when you'll be glad to give it to us."

Then he turned to the lads and said they would have the finest breakfast in months to celebrate the good progress of their work.

Robert built up a splendid fire, and, taking their time about it, they broiled bear meat, strips of the deer they had killed and portions of wild pigeon and the rare wild turkey. Varied odors, all appetizing, and the keen, autumnal air gave them an appetite equal to anything. Yet Willet lingered long, seeing that everything was exactly right before he gave the word to partake, and then they remained yet another good while over the feast, getting the utmost relish out of everything. When they finally rose from their seats on the logs, two hours had passed since Willet had awakened Garay and he went back to him.

"Your letter?" he said.

"I have no letter," replied Garay, "but I'm very hungry. Let me have my breakfast."

"Your letter?"

"I've told you again and again that I've no letter."

"It's now about 8:30 o'clock; at half past ten I'll ask you for it again."

He went back to the two lads and helped them to put out the fire. Garay set up a cry for food, and then began to threaten them with the vengeance of the Indians, but they paid no attention to him. At half past ten as indicated by the sun, Willet returned to him.

"The letter?" he said.

"How many times am I to tell you that I have no letter?"

"Very well. At half past twelve I shall ask for it again."

At half past twelve Garay returned the same answer, and then the three ate their noonday meal, which, like the breakfast, was rich and luscious. Once more the savory odors of bear, deer, wild turkey and wild pigeon filled the forest, and Garay, lying in the doorway of the hut, where he could see, and where the splendid aroma reached his nostrils, writhed in his bonds, but still held fast to his resolution.

Robert said nothing, but the sardonic humor of both the Onondaga and the hunter was well to the fore. Holding a juicy bear steak in his hand, Tayoga walked over to the helpless spy and examined him critically.

"Too fat," he said judicially, "much too fat for those who would roam the forest. Woodsmen, scouts and runners should be lean. It burdens them to carry weight. And you, Achille Garay, will be much better off, if you drop twenty pounds."

"Twenty pounds, Tayoga!" exclaimed Willet, who had joined him, a whole roasted pigeon in his hands. "How can you make such an underestimate! Our rotund Monsieur would be far more graceful and far more healthy if he dropped forty pounds! And it behooves us, his trainers and physicians, to see that he drops 'em. Then he will go back to Albany and to his good friend, Mynheer Hendrik Martinus, a far handsomer man than he was when he left. It may be that he'll be so much improved that Mynheer Hendrik will not know him. Truly, Tayoga, this wild pigeon has a most savory taste! When wild pigeon is well cooked and the air of the forest has sharpened your appetite to a knife edge nothing is finer."

"But it is no better than the tender steak of young bear," said Tayoga, with all the inflections of a gourmand. "The people of my nation and of all the Indian nations have always loved bear. It is tenderer even than venison and it contains more juices. For the hungry man nothing is superior to the taste or for the building up of sinews and muscles than the steak of fat young bear."

Garay writhed again in his bonds, and closed his eyes that he might shut away the vision of the two. Robert was forced to smile. At half past two, as he judged it to be by the sun, Willet said to Garay once more:

"The papers, Monsieur Achille."

But Garay, sullen and obstinate, refused to reply. The hunter did not repeat the question then, but went back to the fire, whistling gayly a light tune. The three were spending the day in homely toil, polishing their weapons, cleaning their clothing, and making the numerous little repairs, necessary after a prolonged and arduous campaign. They were very cheerful about it, too. Why shouldn't they be? Both Tayoga and the hunter had scouted in wide circles about the camp, and had seen that there was no danger. For a vast distance they and their prisoner were alone in the forest. So, they luxuriated and with abundance of appetizing food made up for their long period of short commons.

At half past four Willet repeated his question, but the lips of the spy remained tightly closed.

"Remember that I'm not urging you," said the hunter, politely. "I'm a believer in personal independence and I like people to do what they want to do, as long as it doesn't interfere with anybody else. So I tell you to think it over. We've plenty of time. We can stay here a week, two weeks, if need be. We'd rather you felt sure you were right before you made up your mind. Then you wouldn't be remorseful about any mistake."

"A wise man meditates long before he speaks," said Tayoga, "and it follows then that our Achille Garay is very wise. He knows, too, that his figure is improving already. He has lost at least five pounds."

"Nearer eight I sum it up, Tayoga," said Willet. "The improvement is very marked."

"I think you are right, Great Bear. Eight it is and you also speak truly about the improvement. If our Monsieur Garay were able to stand up and walk he would be much more graceful than he was, when he so kindly marched into our guiding hands."

"Don't pay him too many compliments, Tayoga. They'll prove trying to a modest man. Come away, now. Monsieur Garay wishes to spend the next two hours with his own wise thoughts and who are we to break in upon such a communion?"

"The words of wisdom fall like precious beads from your lips, Great Bear. For two hours we will leave our guest to his great thoughts."

At half past six came the question, "Your papers?" once more, and Garay burst forth with an angry refusal, though his voice trembled. Willet shrugged his shoulders, turned away, and helped the lads prepare a most luxurious and abundant evening meal, Tayoga adding wild grapes and Robert nuts to their varied course of meats, the grapes being served on blazing red autumn leaves, the whole very pleasing to the eye as well as to the taste.

"I think," said Willet, in tones heard easily by Garay, "that I have in me just a trace of the epicure. I find, despite my years in the wilderness, that I enjoy a well spread board, and that bits of decoration appeal to me; in truth, give an added savor to the viands."

"In the vale of Onondaga when the fifty old and wise sachems make a banquet," said Tayoga, "the maidens bring fruit and wild flowers to it that the eye also may have its feast. It is not a weakness, but an excellence in Great Bear to like the decorations."

They lingered long over the board, protracting the feast far after the fall of night and interspersing it with pleasant conversation. The ruddy flames shone on their contented faces, and their light laughter came frequently to the ears of Garay. At half past eight the question, grown deadly by repetition, was asked, and, when only a curse came, Willet said:

"As it is night I'll ask you, Achille Garay, for your papers only once every four hours. That is the interval at which we'll change our guard, and we don't wish, either, to disturb you many times in your pleasant slumbers. It would not be right to call a man back too often from the land of Tarenyawagon, who, you may know, is the Iroquois sender of dreams."

Garay, whom they had now laid tenderly upon the floor of the hut, turned his face away, and Willet went back to the fire, humming in a pleased fashion to himself. At half past twelve he awoke Garay from his uneasy sleep and propounded to him his dreadful query, grown terrifying by its continual iteration. At half past four Tayoga asked it, and it was not necessary then to awake Garay. He had not slept since half past twelve. He snarled at the Iroquois, and then sank back on the blanket that they had kindly placed for him. Tayoga, his bronze face expressing nothing, went back to his watch by the fire.

Breakfast was cooked by Robert and Willet, and again it was luscious and varied. Robert had risen early and he caught several of the fine lake trout that he broiled delicately over the coals. He had also gathered grapes fresh with the morning dew, and wonderfully appetizing, and some of the best of the nuts were left over. Bear, deer, venison and turkey they still had in abundance.

The morning itself was the finest they had encountered so far. Much snow had fallen in the high mountains, but winter had not touched the earth here. The deep colors of the leaves, moved by the light wind, shifted and changed like a prism. The glorious haze of

Indian summer hung over everything like a veil of finest gauze. The air was surcharged with vitality and life. It was pleasant merely to sit and breathe at such a time.

"I've always claimed," said Robert, as he passed a beautifully broiled trout to Tayoga and another to the hunter, "that I can cook fish better than either of you. Dave, I freely admit, can surpass me in the matter of venison and Tayoga is a finer hand with bear than I am, but I'm a specialist with fish, be it salmon, or trout, or salmon trout, or perch or pickerel or what not."

"Your boast is justified, in very truth, Robert," said Willet. "I've known none other who can prepare a fish with as much tenderness and perfection as you. I suppose 'tis born in you, but you have a way of preserving the juices and savors which defies description and which is beyond praise. 'Tis worth going hungry a long while to put one's tooth into so delicate a morsel as this salmon trout, and 'tis a great pity, too, that our guest, Monsieur Achille Garay, will not join us, when we've an abundance so great and a variety so rich."

The wretched spy and intermediary could hear every word they said, and Robert fell silent, but the hunter and the Onondaga talked freely and with abounding zest.

"'Tis a painful thing," said Willet, "to offer hospitality and to have it refused. Monsieur Garay knows that he would be welcome at our board, and yet he will not come. I fear, Robert, that you have cooked too many of these superlative fish, and that they must even go to waste, which is a sin. They would make an admirable beginning for our guest's breakfast, if he would but consent to join us."

"It is told by the wise old sachems of the great League," said Tayoga, "that warriors have gone many days without food, when plenty of it was ready for their taking, merely to test their strength of body and will. Their sufferings were acute and terrible. Their flesh wasted away, their muscles became limp and weak, their sight failed, pain stabbed them with a thousand needles, but they would not yield and touch sustenance before the time appointed."

"I've heard of many such cases, Tayoga, and I've seen some, but it was always warriors who were doing the fasting. I doubt whether white men could stand it so long, and 'tis quite sure they would suffer more. About the third day 'twould be as bad as being tied to the stake in the middle of the flames."

"Great Bear speaks the truth, as he always does. No white man can stand it. If he tried it his sufferings would be beyond anything of which he might dream."

A groan burst suddenly from the wretched Garay. The hunter and the Onondaga looked at each other and their eyes expressed astonishment.

"Did you hear a sound in the thicket?" asked Willet.

"I think it came from the boughs overhead," said Tayoga.

"I could have sworn 'twas the growl of a bear."

"To me it sounded like the croak of a crow."

"After all, we may have heard nothing. Imagination plays strange tricks with us."

"It is true, Great Bear. We hear queer sounds when there are no sounds at all. The air is full of spirits, and now and then they have sport with us."

A second groan burst from Garay, now more wretched than ever.

"I heard it again!" exclaimed the hunter. "'Tis surely the growl of a bear in the bush! The sound was like that of an angry wild animal! But, we'll let it go. The sun tells meet's half past eight o'clock and I go to ask our guest the usual question."

"Enough!" exclaimed Garay. "I yield! I cannot bear this any longer!"

"Your papers, please!"

"Unbind me and give me food!"

"Your papers first, our fish next."

As he spoke the hunter leaned over, and with his keen hunting knife severed Garay's bonds. The man sat up, rubbed his wrists and ankles and breathed deeply.

"Your papers!" repeated Willet.

"Bring me my pistol, the one that the Indian filched from me while I slept," said Garay.

"Your pistol!" exclaimed the hunter, in surprise. "Now I'd certainly be foolish to hand you a deadly and loaded weapon!"

But Robert's quick intellect comprehended at once. He snatched the heavy pistol from the Onondaga's belt, drew forth the bullet and then drew the charge behind it, not powder at all, but a small, tightly folded paper of tough tissue, which he held aloft triumphantly.

"Very clever! very clever!" said Willet in admiration. "The pistol was loaded, but 'twould never be fired, and nobody would have thought of searching its barrel. Tayoga, give Monsieur Garay the two spare fish and anything else he wants, but see that he eats sparingly because a gorge will go ill with a famished man, and then we'll have a look at his precious document."

The Onondaga treated Garay as the honored guest they had been calling him, giving him the whole variety of their breakfast, but, at guarded intervals, which allowed him to relish to the full all the savors and juices that had been taunting him so long. Willet opened the letter, smoothed it out carefully on his knee, and holding it up to the light until the words stood out clearly, read:

"To Hendrik Martinus At Albany.

"The intermediary of whom you know, the bearer of this letter, has brought me word from you that the English Colonial troops, after the unfortunate battle at Lake George, have not pushed their victory. He also informs us that the governors of the English colonies do not agree, and that there is much ill feeling among the different Colonial forces. He says that Johnson still suffering from his wound, does not move, and that the spirit has gone out of our enemies. All of which is welcome news to us at this juncture, since it has given to us the time that we need.

"Our defeat but incites us to greater efforts. The Indian tribes who have cast their lot with us are loyal to our arms. All the forces of France and New France are being assembled to crush our foes. We have lost Dieskau, but a great soldier, Louis Joseph de Saint Véran, the Marquis de Montcalm-Gozon, is coming from France to lead our armies. He will be assisted by the incomparable chieftains, the Chevalier de Levis, the Chevalier Bourlamaque and others who understand the warfare of the wilderness. Even now we are preparing to move with a great power on Albany and we may surprise the town.

"Tell those of whom you know in Albany and New York to be ready with rifles and ammunition and other presents for the Indian warriors. Much depends upon their skill and promptness in delivering these valuable goods to the tribes. It seals them to our standard. They can be landed at the places of which we know, and then be carried swiftly across the wilderness. But I bid you once more to exercise exceeding caution. Let no name of those associated with us ever be entrusted to writing, as a single slip might bring our whole fabric crashing to the ground, and send to death those who serve us. After you have perused this letter destroy it. Do not tear it in pieces and throw them away but burn it to the last and least little fragment. In conclusion I say yet again, caution, caution, caution.

Raymond Louis de St. Luc."

The three looked at one another. Garay was in the third course of his breakfast, and no longer took notice of anything else.

"Those associated with us in Albany and New York," quoted Willet. "Now I wonder who they are. I might make a shrewd guess at one, but no names are given and as we have no proof we must keep silent about him for the present. Yet this paper is of vast importance and it must be put in hands that know how to value it."

"Then the hands must be those of Colonel William Johnson," said Robert.

"I fancy you're right, lad. Yet 'tis hard just now to decide upon the wisest policy."

"The colonel is the real leader of our forces," persisted the lad. "It's to him that we must go."

"It looks so, Robert, but for a few days we've got to consider ourselves. Now that we have his letter I wish we didn't have Garay."

"You wouldn't really have starved him, would you, Dave? Somehow it seemed pretty hard."

The hunter laughed heartily.

"Bless your heart, lad," he replied. "Don't you be troubled about the way we dealt with Garay. I knew all the while that he would never get to the starving point, or I wouldn't have tried it with him. I knew by looking at him that his isn't the fiber of which martyrs are made. I calculated that he would give up last night or this morning."

"Are we going to take him back with us a prisoner?"

The face of Garay paled again, and he gazed at Robert in a sort of dazed fashion. The imagination of young Lennox was alive and leaping. He had found what seemed to him a happy solution of a knotty problem, and, as usual in such cases, his speech became fluent and golden.

"Oh, you'll enjoy it, Monsieur Achille Garay," he said in his mellow, persuasive voice. "The forest is beautiful at this time of the year and the mountains are so magnificent always that they must appeal to anyone who has in his soul the strain of poetry that I know you have. The snow, too, I think has gone from the higher peaks and ridges and you will not be troubled by extreme cold. If you should wander from the path back to St. Luc you will have abundant leisure in which to find it again, because for quite a while to come time will be of no importance to you. And as you'll go unarmed, you'll be in no danger of shooting your friends by mistake."

"You're not going to turn me into the wilderness to starve?"

"Not at all. We'll give you plenty of food. Tayoga and I will see you well on your way. Now, since you've eaten enough, you start at once."

Tayoga and the hunter fell in readily with Robert's plan. The captive received enough food to last four days, which he carried in a pack fastened on his back, and then Robert and Tayoga accompanied him northward and back on the trail.

Much of Garay's courage returned as they marched steadily on through the forest. When he summed it up he found that he had fared well. His captors had really been soft-hearted. It was not usual for one serving as an intermediary and spy like himself to escape, when taken, with his life and even with freedom. Life! How precious it was! Young Lennox had said that the forest was beautiful, and it was! It was splendid, grand, glorious to one who had just come out of the jaws of death, and the air of late autumn was instinct with vitality. He drew himself up jauntily, and his step became strong and springy.

They walked on many miles and Robert, whose speech had been so fluent before, was silent now. Nor did the Onondaga speak either. Garay himself hazarded a few words, but meeting with no response his spirits fell a little. The trail led over a low ridge, and at its crest his two guards stopped.

"That's the trouble. As a spy, which he undoubtedly is, his li is forfeit, but we are not executioners. For scouts and messenger. such as we are he'd be a tremendous burden to take along with us. Moreover, I think that after his long fast he'd eat all the game we could kill, and we don't propose to spend our whole time feeding one of our enemies."

"Call Tayoga," said Robert.

The Onondaga came and then young Lennox said to his two comrades:

"Are you willing to trust me in the matter of Garay, our prisoner?"

"Yes," they replied together.

Robert went to the man, who was still immersed in his gross feeding, and tapped him on the shoulder.

"Listen, Garay," he said. "You're the bearer of secret and treacherous dispatches, and you're a spy. You must know that under all the rules of war your life is forfeit to your captors."

Garay's face became gray and ghastly.

"You—you wouldn't murder me?" he said.

"There could be no such thing as murder in your case, and we won't take your life, either."

The face of the intermediary recovered its lost color.

"You will spare me, then?" he exclaimed joyfully.

"In a way, yes, but we're not going to carry you back in luxury to Albany, nor are we thinking of making you an honored member of our band. You've quite a time before you."

"I don't understand you."

"You will soon. You're going back to the Chevalier de St. Luc wh has little patience with failure, and you'll find that the road to hir abounds in hard traveling. It may be, too, that the savage Tandako will ask you some difficult questions, but if so, Monsieur Achil Garay, it will be your task to answer them, and I take it that you ha a fertile mind. In any event, you will be equipped to meet him your journey, which will be full of variety and effort and which v strengthen and harden your mind."

"Here we bid you farewell, Monsieur Achille Garay," said Robert. "Doubtless you will wish to commune with your own thoughts and our presence will no longer disturb you. Our parting advice to you is to give up the trade in which you have been engaged. It is full perilous, and it may be cut short at any time by sudden death. Moreover, it is somewhat bare of honor, and even if it should be crowned by continued success 'tis success of a kind that's of little value. Farewell."

"Farewell," said Garay, and almost before he could realize it, the two figures had melted into the forest behind him. A weight was lifted from him with their going, and once more his spirits bounded upward. He was Achille Garay, bold and venturesome, and although he was without weapons he did not fear two lads.

Three miles farther on he turned. He did not care to face St. Luc, his letter lost, and the curious, dogged obstinacy that lay at the back of his character prevailed. He would go back. He would reach those for whom his letter had been intended, Martinus and the others, and he would win the rich rewards that had been promised to him. He had plenty of food, he would make a wide curve, advance at high speed and get to Albany ahead of the foolish three.

He turned his face southward and walked swiftly through the thickets. A rifle cracked and a twig overhead severed by a bullet fell upon his face. Garay shivered and stood still for a long time. Courage trickled back, and he resumed his advance, though it was slow. A second rifle cracked, and a bullet passed so close to his cheek that he felt its wind. He could not restrain a cry of terror, and turning again he fled northward to St. Luc.

CHAPTER VI.
PUPILS OF THE BEAR

When Robert and Tayoga returned to the camp and told Willet what they had done the hunter laughed a little.

"Garay doesn't want to face St. Luc," he said, "but he will do it anyhow. He won't dare to come back on the trail in face of bullets, and now we're sure to deliver his letter in ample time."

"Should we go direct to Albany?" asked Robert.

The hunter cupped his chin in his hand and meditated.

"I'm all for Colonel Johnson," he replied at last. "He understands the French and Indians and has more vigor than the authorities at Albany. It seems likely to me that he will still be at the head of Lake George where we left him, perhaps building the fort of which they were talking before we left there."

"His wound did not give promise of getting well so very early," said Robert, "and he would not move while he was in a weakened condition."

"Then it's almost sure that he's at the head of the lake and we'll turn our course toward that point. What do you say, Tayoga?"

"Waraiyageh is the man to have the letter, Great Bear. If it becomes necessary for him to march to the defense of Albany he will do it."

"Then the three of us are in unanimity and Lake George it is instead of Albany."

They started in an hour, and changing their course somewhat, began a journey across the maze of mountains toward Andiatarocte, the lake that men now call George, and Robert's heart throbbed at the thought that he would soon see it again in all its splendor and beauty. He had passed so much of his life near them that his fortunes seemed to him to be interwoven inseparably with George and Champlain.

They thought they would reach the lake in a few days, but in a wilderness and in war the plans of men often come to naught. Before the close of the day they came upon traces of a numerous band traveling on the great trail between east and west, and they also found among them footprints that turned out. These Willet and Tayoga examined with the greatest care and interest and they lingered longest over a pair uncommonly long and slender.

"I think they're his," the hunter finally said.

"So do I," said the Onondaga.

"Those long, slim feet could belong to nobody but the Owl."

"It can be only the Owl."

"Now, who under the sun is the Owl?" asked Robert, mystified.

"The Owl is, in truth, a most dangerous man," replied the hunter. "His name, which the Indians have given him, indicates he works by night, though he's no sloth in the day, either. But he has another name, also, the one by which he was christened. It's Charles Langlade, a young Frenchman who was a trader before the war. I've seen him more than once. He's mighty shrewd and alert, uncommon popular among the western Indians, who consider him as one of them because he married a good looking young Indian woman at Green Bay, and a great forester and wilderness fighter. It's wonderful how the French adapt themselves to the ways of the Indians and how they take wives among them. I suppose the marriage tie is one of their greatest sources of strength with the tribes. Now, Tayoga, why do you think the Owl is here so far to the eastward of his usual range?"

"He and his warriors are looking for scalps, Great Bear, and it may be that they have seen St. Luc. They were traveling fast and they are now between us and Andiatarocte. I like it but little."

"Not any less than I do. It upsets our plans. We must leave the trail, or like as not we'll run squarely into a big band. What a pity our troops didn't press on after the victory at the lake. Instead of driving the French and Indians out of the whole northern wilderness we've left it entirely to them."

They turned from the trail with reluctance, because, strong and enduring as they were, incessant hardships, long traveling and battle were beginning to tell upon all three, and they were unwilling to be climbing again among the high mountains. But there was no choice and night found them on a lofty ridge in a dense thicket. The hunter and the Onondaga were disturbed visibly over the advent of Langlade, and their uneasiness was soon communicated to the sympathetic mind of Robert.

The night being very clear, sown with shining stars, they saw rings of smoke rising toward the east, and outlined sharply against the dusky blue.

"That's Langlade sending up signals," said the hunter, anxiously, "and he wouldn't do it unless he had something to talk about."

"When one man speaks another man answers," said Tayoga. "Now from what point will come the reply?"

Robert felt excitement. These rings of smoke in the blue were full of significance for them, and the reply to the first signal would be vital. "Ah!" he exclaimed suddenly. The answer came from the west, directly behind them.

"I think they've discovered our trail," said Willet. "They didn't learn it from Garay, because Langlade passed before we sent him back, but they might have heard from St. Luc or Tandakora that we were somewhere in the forest. It's bad. If it weren't for the letter we could turn sharply to the north and stay in the woods till Christmas, if need be."

"We may have to do so, whether we wish it or not," said Tayoga. "The shortest way is not always the best."

Before morning they saw other smoke signals in the south, and it became quite evident then that the passage could not be tried, except at a risk perhaps too great to take.

"There's nothing for it but the north," said Willet, "and we'll trust to luck to get the letter to Waraiyageh in time. Perhaps we can find Rogers. He must be roaming with his rangers somewhere near Champlain."

At dawn they were up and away, but all through the forenoon they saw rings of smoke rising from the peaks and ridges, and the last lingering hope that they were not followed disappeared. It became quite evident to their trained observation and the powers of inference from circumstances which had become almost a sixth sense with them that there was a vigorous pursuit, closing in from three points of the compass, south, east and west. They slept again the next night in the forest without fire and arose the following morning cold, stiff and out of temper. While they eased their muscles and prepared for the day's flight they resolved upon a desperate expedient.

It was vital now to carry the letter to Johnson and then to Albany, which they considered more important than their own escape, and they could not afford to be driven farther and farther into the recesses of the north, while St. Luc might be marching with a formidable force on Albany itself.

"With us it's unite to fight and divide for flight," said Robert, divining what was in the mind of the others.

"The decision is forced upon us," said Willet, regretfully.

Tayoga nodded.

"We'll read the letter again several times, until all of us know it by heart," said the hunter.

The precious document was produced, and they went over it until each could repeat it from memory. Then Willet said:

"I'm the oldest and I'll take the letter and go south past their bands. One can slip through where three can't."

He spoke with such decision that the others, although Tayoga wanted the task of risk and honor, said nothing.

"And do you, Robert and Tayoga," resumed the hunter, "continue your flight to the northward. You can keep ahead of these bands, and, when you discover the chase has stopped, curve back for Lake George. If by any chance I should fall by the way, though it's not likely, you can repeat the letter to Colonel Johnson, and let's hope you'll be in time. Now good-by, and God bless you both."

Willet never displayed emotion, but his feeling was very deep as he wrung the outstretched hand of each. Then he turned at an angle to the east and south and disappeared in the undergrowth.

"He has been more than a father to me," said Robert.

"The Great Bear is a man, a man who is pleasing to Areskoui himself," said Tayoga with emphasis.

"Do you think he will get safely through?"

"There is no warrior, not even of the Clan of the Bear, of the Nation Onondaga, of the great League of the Hodenosaunee, who can surpass the Great Bear in forest skill and cunning. In the night he will creep by Tandakora himself, with such stealth, that not a leaf will stir, and there will be not the slightest whisper in the grass. His step, too, will be so light that his trail will be no more than a bird's in the air."

Robert laughed and felt better.

"You don't stint the praise of a friend, Tayoga," he said, "but I know that at least three-fourths of what you say is true. Now, I take it that you and I are to play the hare to Langlade's hounds, and that in doing so we'll be of great help to Dave."

"Aye," agreed the Onondaga, and they swung into their gait. Robert had received Garay's pistol which, being of the same bore as his own, was now loaded with bullet and powder, instead of bullet and paper, and it swung at his belt, while Tayoga carried the intermediary's rifle, a fine piece. It made an extra burden, but they had been unwilling to throw it away—a rifle was far too valuable on the border to be abandoned.

They maintained a good pace until noon, and, as they heard no sound behind them, less experienced foresters than they might have thought the pursuit had ceased, but they knew better. It had merely settled into that tenacious kind which was a characteristic of the Indian mind, and unless they could hide their trail it would continue in the same determined manner for days. At noon, they paused a half hour in a dense grove and ate bear and deer meat, sauced with some fine, black wild grapes, the vines hanging thick on one of the trees.

"Think of those splendid banquets we enjoyed when Garay was sitting looking at us, though not sharing with us," said Robert.

Tayoga smiled at the memory and said:

"If he had been able to hold out a little longer he would have had plenty of food, and we would not have had the letter. The Great Bear would never have starved him."

"I know that now, Tayoga, and I learn from it that we're to hold out too, long after we think we're lost, if we're to be the victors."

They came in the afternoon to a creek, flowing in their chosen course, and despite the coldness of its waters, which rose almost to their knees, they waded a long time in its bed. When they went out on the bank they took off their leggings and moccasins, wrung or beat out of them as much of the water as they could, and then let them dry for a space in the sun, while they rubbed vigorously their ankles and feet to create warmth. They knew that Langlade's men would follow on either side of the creek until they picked up the trail again, but their maneuver would create a long delay, and give them a rest needed badly.

"Have you anything in mind, Tayoga?" asked Robert. "You know that the farther north and higher we go the colder it will become, and our flight may take us again into the very heart of a great snow storm."

"It is so, Dagaeoga, but it is also so that I do have a plan. I think I know the country into which we are coming, and that tells me what to do. The people of my race, living from the beginning of the world in the great forest, have not been too proud to learn from the animals, and of all the animals we know perhaps the wisest is the bear."

"The bear is scarcely an animal, Tayoga. He is almost a human being. He has as good a sense of humor as we have, and he is more careful about minding his own business, and letting alone that of other people."

"Dagaeoga is not without wisdom. We will even learn from the bear. A hundred miles to the north of us there is a vast rocky region containing many caves, where the bears go in great numbers to sleep the long winters through. It is not much disturbed, because it is a dangerous country, lying between the Hodenosaunee and the Indian nations to the north, with which we have been at war for centuries. There we will go."

"And hole up until our peril passes! Your plan appeals to me, Tayoga! I will imitate the bear! I will even be a bear!"

"We will take the home of one of them before he comes for it himself, and we will do him no injustice, because the wise bear can always find another somewhere else."

"They're fine caves, of course!" exclaimed Robert, buoyantly, his imagination, which was such a powerful asset with him, flaming up as usual. "Dry and clean, with plenty of leaves for beds, and with nice little natural shelves for food, and a pleasant little brook just outside the door. It will be pleasant to lie in our own cave, the best one of course, and hear the snow and sleet storms whistle by, while we're warm and comfortable. If we only had complete assurance that Dave was through with the letter I'd be willing to stay there until spring."

Tayoga smiled indulgently.

"Dagaeoga is always dreaming," he said, "but bright dreams hurt nobody."

When night came, they were many more miles on their way, but it was a very cold darkness that fell upon them and they shivered in their blankets. Robert made no complaint, but he longed for the caves, of which he was making such splendid pictures. Shortly before morning, a light snow fell and the dawn was chill and discouraging, so much so that Tayoga risked a fire for the sake of brightness and warmth.

"Langlade's men will come upon the coals we leave," he said, "but since we have not shaken them off it will make no difference. How much food have we left, Dagaeoga?"

"Not more than enough for three days."

"Then it is for us to find more soon. It is another risk that we must take. I wish I had with me now my bow and arrows which I left at the lake, instead of Garay's rifle. But Areskoui will provide."

The day turned much colder, and the streams to which they came were frozen over. By night, the ice was thick enough to sustain their weight and they traveled on it for a long time, their thick moosehide moccasins keeping their feet warm, and saving them from falling. Before they returned to the land it began to snow again, and Tayoga rejoiced openly.

"Now a white blanket will lie over the trail we have left on the ice," he said, "hiding it from the keenest eyes that ever were in a man's head."

Then they crossed a ridge and came upon a lake, by the side of which they saw through the snow and darkness a large fire burning. Creeping nearer, they discerned dusky forms before the flames and made out a band of at least twenty warriors, many of them sound asleep, wrapped to the eyes in their blankets.

"Have they passed ahead of us and are they here meaning to guard the way against us?" whispered Robert.

"No, it is not one of the bands that has been following us," replied the Onondaga. "This is a war party going south, and not much stained as yet by time and travel. They are Montagnais, come from Montreal. They seek scalps, but not ours, because they do not know of us."

Robert shuddered. These savages, like as not, would fall at midnight upon some lone settlement, and his intense imagination depicted the hideous scenes to follow.

"Come away," he whispered. "Since they don't know anything about us we'll keep them in ignorance. I'm longing more than ever for my warm bear cave."

They disappeared in the falling snow, which would soon hide their trail here, as it had hidden it elsewhere, and left the lake behind them, not stopping until they came to a deep and narrow gorge in the mountains, so well sheltered by overhanging bushes that no snow fell there. They raked up great quantities of dry leaves, after the usual fashion, and spread their blankets upon them, poor enough quarters save for the hardiest, but made endurable for them by custom and intense weariness. Both fell asleep almost at once, and both awoke about the same time far after dawn.

Robert moved his stiff fingers in his blanket and sat up, feeling cold and dismal. Tayoga was sitting up also, and the two looked at each other.

"In very truth those bear caves never seemed more inviting to me," said young Lennox, solemnly, "and yet I only see them from afar."

"Dagaeoga has fallen in love with bear caves," said the Onondaga, in a whimsical tone. "The time is not so far back when he never talked about them at all, and now words in their praise fall from his lips in a stream."

"It's because I've experienced enlightenment, Tayoga. It is only in the last two or three days that I've learned the vast superiority of a cave to any other form of human habitation. Our remote ancestors lived in them two or three hundred thousand years, and we've been living in houses of wood or brick or stone only six or seven thousand years, I suppose, and so the cave, if you judge by the length of time, is our true home. Hence I'm filled with a just enthusiasm at the thought of going back speedily to the good old ways and the good old days. It's possible, Tayoga, that our remote grandfathers knew best."

"When Dagaeoga comes to his death bed, seventy or eighty years from now, and the medicine man tells him but little more breath is left in his body, what then do you think he will do?"

"What will I do, Tayoga?"

"You will say to the medicine man, 'Tell me exactly how long I have to live,' and the medicine man will reply: 'Ten minutes, O Dagaeoga, venerable chief and great orator.' Then you will say: 'Let all the people be summoned and let them crowd into the wigwam in which I lie,' and when they have all come and stand thick about your bed, you will say, 'Now raise me into a sitting position and put the pillows thick behind my back and head that I may lean against them.' Then you will speak to the people. The words will flow from your lips in a continuous and golden stream. It will be the finest speech of your life. It will be filled with magnificent words, many of them, eight or ten syllables long. It will be mellow like the call of a trumpet. It will be armed with force, and it will be beautiful with imagery; it will be suffused and charged with color, it will be the very essence of poetry and power, and as the aged Dagaeoga draws his very last breath so he will speak his very last word, and thus, in a golden cloud, his soul will go away into infinite space, to dwell forever in the bosom of Manitou, with the immortal sachems, Tododaho and Hayowentha!"

"Do you know, Tayoga, I think that would be a happy death," said Robert earnestly.

The Onondaga laughed heartily.

"Thus does Dagaeoga show his true nature," he said. "He was born with the spirit and soul of the orator, and the fact is disclosed often. It is well. The orator, be he white or red, will lose himself sometimes in his own words, but he is a gift from the gods, sent to lift up the souls, and cheer the rest of us. He is the bugle that calls us to the chase and we must not forget that his value is great."

"And having said a whole cargo of words yourself Tayoga, now what do you propose that we do?"

"Push on with all our strength for the caves. I know now we are on the right path, because I recall the country through which we are passing. At noon we will reach a small lake, in which the fish are so numerous that there is not room for them all at the same time in the water. They have to take turns in getting the air above the surface on top of the others. For that reason the fish of this lake are different from all other fish. They will live a full hour on the bank after they are caught."

"Tayoga, in very truth, you've learned our ways well. You've become a prince of romancers yourself."

At the appointed time they reached the lake. There were no fish above its surface, but the Onondaga claimed it was due to the fact that the lake was covered with ice which of course kept them down, and which crowded them excessively, and very uncomfortably. They broke two big holes in the ice, let down the lines which they always carried, the hooks baited with fragments of meat, and were soon rewarded with splendid fish, as much as they needed.

Tayoga with his usual skill lighted a fire, despite the driving snow, and they had a banquet, taking with them afterward a supply of the cooked fish, though they knew they could not rely upon fish alone in the winter days that were coming. But fortune was with them. Before dark, Robert shot a deer, a great buck, fine and fat. They had so little fear of pursuit now that they cut up the body, saving the skin whole for tanning, and hung the pieces in the trees, there to freeze. Although it would make quite a burden they intended to carry practically all of it with them.

Many mountain wolves were drawn that night by the odor of the spoils, but they lay between twin fires and had no fear of an attack. Yet the time might come when they would be assailed by fierce wild animals, and now they were glad that Tayoga had kept Garay's rifle, and also his ammunition, a good supply of powder and bullets. It was possible that the question of ammunition might become vital with them, but they did not yet talk of it.

On the second day thereafter, bearing their burdens of what had been the deer, they reached the stony valley Tayoga had in mind, and Robert saw at once that its formation indicated many caves.

"Now, I wonder if the bears have come," he said, putting down his pack and resting. "The cold has been premature and perhaps they're still roaming through the forest. I shouldn't want to put an interloper out of my own particular cave, but, if I have to do it, I will."

"The bears haven't arrived yet," said Tayoga, "and we can choose. I do not know, but I do not think a bear always occupies the same winter home, so we will not have to fight over our place."

It was a really wonderful valley, where the decaying stone had made a rich assortment of small caves, many of them showing signs of former occupancy by large wild animals, and, after long searching, they found one that they could make habitable for themselves. Its entrance was several feet above the floor of the valley, so that neither storm nor winter flood could send water into it, and its own floor was fairly smooth, with a roof eight or ten feet high. It could be easily defended with their three rifles, the aperture being narrow, and they expected, with skins and pelts, to make it warm.

It was but a cold and bleak refuge for all save the hardiest, and for a little while Robert had to use his last ounce of will to save himself from discouragement. But vigorous exertion and keen interest in the future brought back his optimism. The hide of the deer they had slain was spread at once upon the cave floor and made a serviceable rug. They spoke hopefully of soon adding to it.

A brook flowed less than a hundred yards away, and they would have no trouble about their water supply, while the country about seemed highly favorable for game. But on their first day there they did not do any hunting. They rolled several large stones before the door of their new home, making it secure against any prying wild animals, and then, after a hearty meal, they wrapped themselves in their blankets and slept prodigiously.

Tayoga went into the forest the next day and set traps and snares, while Robert worked in the valley, breaking up fallen wood to be used for fires, and doing other chores. The Onondaga in the next three or four days shot a large panther, a little bear, and caught in the traps and snares a quantity of small game. The big pelts and the little pelts, after proper treatment, were spread upon the floor or hung against the walls of the cave, which now began to assume a much more inviting aspect, and the flesh of the animals that were eatable, cured after the primitive but effective processes, was stored there also.

Providence granted them a period of good weather, days and nights alike being clear and cold. The game, evidently not molested for a long time, fairly walked into their traps, and they were compelled to draw but little upon their precious supply of ammunition. Food for the future accumulated rapidly, and the floor and walls of the cave were soon covered entirely with furs.

Not one of the numerous caves and hollows about them contained an occupant and Robert wondered if their presence would frighten away the wild animals, so many of which had hibernated there so often. Yet he had a belief that the bears would come. His present mode of life and his isolation from the world gave him a feeling almost of kinship with them, and in some strange way, and through some medium unknown to him, they might reciprocate. He and Tayoga had killed several bears, it was true, but far from the cave, and they made up their minds to molest nothing in the valley or just about it.

It was a land of many waters and they caught with ease numerous fish, drying all the surplus and storing it with the other food in the cave. They also made soft beds for themselves of the little branches of the evergreen, over which they spread their blankets, and when they rolled the stone before the doorway at night they never failed to sleep soundly.

They did their cooking in front of the cave door, but it was always a smothered fire. While they felt safe from wandering bands in that lofty and remote region, they took no unnecessary risks. The valley itself, though deep, was much broken up into separate little valleys, and most of the caves were hidden from their own. It was this fact that made Robert still think the bears would come, despite coals and flame. In the evenings they would talk of Willet, and both were firm in the opinion that the hunter had got through to Lake George and that Johnson and Albany had been warned in time. Each was confirmed in his opinion by the other and in a few days it became certainty.

"I think Tododaho on his star whispered in my ear while I slept that Great Bear has passed the hostile lines," said Tayoga with conviction, "because I know it, just as if the Great Bear himself had told it to me, though I do not know how I know it."

"It's some sort of mysterious information," said Robert in the same tone of absolute belief, "and I don't worry any more about Dave and the letter. The men of the Hodenosaunee seem to have a special gift. You know the old chief, Hendrik, foretold that he would die on the shores of Andiatarocte, and it came to pass just as he had said."

"It was a glorious death, Dagaeoga, and it was, perhaps, he who saved our army, and made the victory possible."

"So it was. There's not a doubt of it, but, here, I don't feel much like taking part in a war. The great struggle seems to have passed around us for a while, at least. I appear to myself as a man of peace, occupied wholly with the struggle for existence and with preparations for a hard winter. I don't want to harm anything."

"Perhaps it's because nothing we know of wants to harm us. But, Dagaeoga, if the bears come at all they will come quickly, because in a few days winter will be roaring down upon us."

"Then, Tayoga, we must hurry our labors, and since the mysterious message brought in some manner through the air has told us that Dave has reached the lake, I'm rather anxious for it to rush down. While it keeps us here it will also hold back the forces of St. Luc."

"That's true, Dagaeoga. It's a poor snow that doesn't help somebody. Now, I will make a bow and arrow to take the place of my great bow and quiver, which await me elsewhere, because we must draw but little upon our powder and bullets."

The Onondaga had hatchet and knife and he worked with great rapidity and skill, cutting and bending a bow in two or three days, and making a string of strong sinews, after which he fashioned many arrows and tipped them with sharp bone. Then he contemplated his handiwork with pride.

"Hasty work is never the best of work," he said, "and these are not as good as those I left behind me, but I know they will serve. The game here, hunted but little, is not very wary and I can approach near."

His skill both in construction and use was soon proved, as he slew with his new weapons a great moose, two ordinary deer, and much smaller game, while the traps caught beaver, otter, fox, wolf and other animals, with fine pelts. Many splendid furs were soon drying in the air and were taken later into the cave, while they accumulated dried and jerked game enough to last them until the next spring.

Both worked night and day with such application and intensity that their hands became stiff and sore, and every bone in them ached. Nevertheless Robert took time now and then to examine the little caves in the other sections of the valley, only to find them still empty.

He thought, for a while, that the presence of Tayoga and himself and their operations with the game might have frightened the bears away, but the feeling that they would come returned and was strong upon him. As for Tayoga he never doubted. It had been decreed by Tododaho.

"The animals have souls," he said. "Often when great warriors die or fall in battle their souls go into the bodies of bear, or deer, or wolf, but oftenest into that of bear. For that reason the bear, saving only the dog which lives with us, is nearest to man, and now and then, because of the warrior soul in him, he is a man himself, although he walks on four legs—and he does not always walk on four legs, sometimes he stands on two. Doubt not, Dagaeoga, that when the stormy winter sweeps down the bears will come to their ancient homes, whether or not we be here."

The winds grew increasingly chill, coming from the vast lakes beyond the Great Lakes, those that lay in the far Canadian north, and the skies were invariably leaden in hue and gloomy. But in the cave it was cozy and warm. Furs and skins were so numerous that there was no longer room on the floor and walls for them all, many being stored in glossy heaps in the corners.

"Some day these will bring a good price from the Dutch traders at Albany," said Robert, "and it may be, Tayoga, that you and I will need the money. I've been a scout and warrior for a long time, and now I've suddenly turned fur hunter. Well, that spirit of peace and of a friendly feeling toward all mankind grows upon me. Why shouldn't I be full of brotherly love when your patron saint, Tododaho, has been so kind to us?"

He swept the cave once more with a glance of approval. It furnished shelter, warmth, food in abundance, and with its furs even a certain velvety richness for the eye, and Tayoga nodded assent. Meanwhile they waited for the fierce blasts of the mountain winter.

CHAPTER VII.
THE SLEEPING SENTINELS

A singular day came when it seemed to Robert that the wind alternately blew hot and cold, at least by contrast, and the deep, leaden skies were suffused with a peculiar mist that made him see all objects in a distorted fashion. Everything was out of proportion. Some were too large and some too small. Either the world was awry or his own faculties had become discolored and disjointed. While his interest in his daily toil decreased and his thoughts were vague and distant, his curiosity, nevertheless, was keen and concentrated. He knew that something unusual was going to happen and nature was preparing him for it.

The occult quality in the air did not depart with the coming of night, though the winds no longer alternated, the warm blasts ceasing to blow, while the cold came steadily and with increasing fierceness. Yet it was warm and close in the cave, and the two went outside for air, wandering up the face of the ridge that enclosed the northern side of their particular valley in the chain of little valleys. Upon the summit they stood erect, and the face of Tayoga became rapt like that of a seer. When Robert looked at him his own blood tingled. The Onondaga shut his eyes, and he spoke not so much to Robert as to the air itself:

"O Tododaho," he said, "when mine eyes are open I do not see you because of the vast clouds that Manitou has heaped between, but when I close them the inner light makes me behold you sitting upon your star and looking down with kindness upon this, the humblest and least of your servants. O Tododaho, you have given my valiant comrade and myself a safe home in the wilderness in our great need, and I beseech you that you will always hold your protecting shield between us and our enemies."

He paused, his eyes still closed, and stood tense and erect, the north wind blowing on his face. A shiver ran through Robert, not a shiver of fear, but a shiver caused by the mysterious and the unknown. His own eyes were open, and he gazed steadily into the northern heavens. The occult quality in the air deepened, and now his nerves began to tingle. His soul thrilled with a coming event. Suddenly the deep, leaden clouds parted for a few moments, and in the clear space between he could have sworn that he saw a great dancing star, from which a mighty, benevolent face looked down upon them.

"I saw him! I saw him!" he exclaimed in excitement. "It was Tododaho himself!"

"I did not see him with my eyes, but I saw him with my soul," said the Onondaga, opening his eyes, "and he whispered to me that his favor was with us. We cannot fail in what we wish to do."

"Look in the next valley, Tayoga. What do you behold now?"

"It is the bears, Dagaeoga. They come to their long winter sleep."

Rolling figures, enlarged and fantastic, emerged from the mist. Robert saw great, red eyes, sharp teeth and claws, and yet he felt neither fear nor hostility. Tayoga's statement that they were bears, into which the souls of great warriors had gone, was strong in his mind, and he believed. They looked up at him, but they did not pause, moving on to the little caves.

"They see us," he said.

"So they do," said Tayoga, "but they do not fear us. The spirits of mighty warriors look out of their eyes at us, and knowing that they were once as we are they know also that we will not harm them."

"Have you ever seen the like of this before, Tayoga?"

"No! But a few of the old men of the Hodenosaunee have told of their grandfathers who have seen it. I think it is a mark of favor to us that we are permitted to behold such a sight. Now I am sure Tododaho has looked upon us with great approval. Lo, Dagaeoga, more of them come out of the mist! Before morning every cave, save those in our own little corner of the valley, will be filled. All of them gaze up at us, recognize us as friends and pass on. It is a wonderful sight, Dagaeoga, and we shall never look upon its like again."

"No," said Robert, as the extraordinary thrill ran through him once more. "Now they have gone into their caves, and I believe with you, Tayoga, that the souls of great warriors truly inhabit the bodies of the bears."

"And since they are snugly in their homes, ready for the long winter sleep, lo! the great snow comes, Dagaeoga!"

A heavy flake fell on Robert's upturned face, and then another and another. The circling clouds, thick and leaden, were beginning to pour down their burden, and the two retreated swiftly to their own dry and well furnished cave. Then they rolled the great stones before the door, and Tayoga said:

"Now, we will imitate our friends, the bears, and take a long winter sleep."

Both were soon slumbering soundly in their blankets and furs, and all that night and all the next day the snow fell on the high mountains in the heart of which they lay. There was no wind, and it came straight down, making an even depth on ridge, slope and valley. It blotted out the mouths of the caves, and it clothed all the forest in deep white. Robert and Tayoga were but two motes, lost in the vast wilderness, which had returned to its primeval state, and the Indians themselves, whether hostile or friendly, sought their villages and lodges and were willing to leave the war trail untrodden until the months of storm and bitter cold had passed.

Robert slept heavily. His labors in preparation for the winter had been severe and unremitting, and his nerves had been keyed very high by the arrival of the bears and the singular quality in the air. Now, nature claimed her toll, and he did not awake until nearly noon, Tayoga having preceded him a half hour. The Onondaga stood at the door of the cave, looking over the stones that closed its lower half. Fresh air poured in at the upper half, but Robert saw there only a whitish veil like a foaming waterfall.

"The time o' day, Sir Tayoga, Knight of the Great Forest," he said lightly and cheerfully.

"There is no sun to tell me," replied the Onondaga. "The face of Areskoui will be hidden long, but I know that at least half the day is gone. The flakes make a thick and heavy white veil, through which

I cannot see, and great as are the snows every winter on the high mountains, this will be the greatest of them all."

"And we've come into our lair. And a mighty fine lair it is, too. I seem to adapt myself to such a place, Tayoga. In truth, I feel like a bear myself. You say that the souls of warriors have gone into the bears about us, and it may be that the soul of a bear has come into me."

"It may be," said Tayoga, gravely. "It is at least a wise thought, since, for a while, we must live like bears."

Robert would have chafed, any other time, at a stay that amounted to imprisonment, but peace and shelter were too welcome now to let him complain. Moreover, there were many little but important household duties to do. They made needles of bone, and threads of sinew and repaired their clothing. Tayoga had stored suitable wood and bone and he turned out arrow after arrow. He also made another bow, and Robert, by assiduous practice, acquired sufficient skill to help in these tasks. They did not drive themselves now, but the hours being filled with useful and interesting labor, they were content to wait.

For three or four days, while the snow still fell, they ate cold food, but when the clouds at last floated away, and the air was free from the flakes, they went outside and by great effort—the snow being four or five feet deep—cleared a small space near the entrance, where they cooked a good dinner from their stores and enjoyed it extravagantly. Meanwhile the days passed. Robert was impatient at times, but never a long while. If the mental weariness of waiting came to him he plunged at once into the tasks of the day.

There was plenty to do, although they had prepared themselves so well before the great snowfall came. They made rude shovels of wood and enlarged the space they had cleared of snow. Here, they fitted stones together, until they had a sort of rough furnace which, crude though it was, helped them greatly with their cooking. They also pulled more brushwood from under the snow, and by its use saved the store they had heaped up for impossible days. Then, by continued use of the bone needles and sinews, they managed to make cloaks for themselves of the bearskins. They were rather shapeless garments, and they had little of beauty save in the rich fur itself, but they were wonderfully warm and that was what they wanted most.

Tayoga, after a while, began slow and painstaking work on a pair of snowshoes, expecting to devote many days to the task.

"The snow is so deep we cannot pass through it," he said, "but I, at least, will pass upon it. I cannot get the best materials, but what I have will serve. I shall not go far, but I want to explore the country about us."

Robert thought it a good plan, and helped as well as he could with the work. They still stayed outdoors as much as possible, but the cold became intense, the temperature going almost to forty degrees below zero, the surface of the snow freezing and the boughs of the big trees about the valley becoming so brittle that they broke with sharp crashes beneath the weight of accumulated snow. Then they paused long enough in the work on the snowshoes to make themselves gloves of buckskin, which were a wonderful help, as they labored in the fresh air. Ear muffs and caps of bearskin followed.

"I feel some reluctance about using bearskin so much," said Robert, "since the bears about us are inhabited by the souls of great warriors and are our friends."

"But the bears that we killed did not belong here," said Tayoga, "and were bears and nothing more. It was right for us to slay them because the bear was sent by Manitou to be a support for the Indian with his flesh and his pelt."

"But how do you know that the bears we killed were just bears and bears only?"

"Because, if they had not been we would not have killed them."

Thus were the qualms of young Lennox quieted and he used his bearskin cap, gloves and cloak without further scruple. The snowshoes were completed and Tayoga announced that he would start early the next morning.

"I may be gone three or four days, Dagaeoga," he said, "but I will surely return. I shall avoid danger, and do you be careful also."

"Don't fear for me," said Robert. "I'm not likely to go farther than the brook, since there's no great sport in breaking your way through snow that comes to your waist, and which, moreover, is covered with a thick sheet of ice. Don't trouble your mind about me, Tayoga, I won't roam from home."

The Onondaga took his weapons, a supply of food, and departed, skimming over the snow with wonderful, flying strokes, while Robert settled down to lonely waiting. It was a hard duty, but he again found solace in work, and at intervals he contemplated the mouths of the bears' caves, now almost hidden by the snow. Tayoga's belief was strong upon him, for the time, and he concluded that the warriors who inhabited the bodies of the bears must be having some long and wonderful dreams. At least, they had plenty of time to dream in, and it was an extraordinary provision of nature that gave them such a tremendous sleep.

Tayoga returned in four days, and Robert, who had more than enough of being alone, welcomed him with hospitable words to a fire and a feast.

"I must first put away my spoils," said the Onondaga, his dark eyes glittering.

"Spoils! What spoils, Tayoga?"

"Powder and lead," he replied, taking a heavy bundle wrapped in deerskin from beneath his bearskin overcoat. "It weighs a full fifty pounds, and it made my return journey very wearisome. Catch it, Dagaeoga!"

Robert caught, and he saw that it was, in truth, powder and lead.

"Now, where did you get this?" he exclaimed. "You couldn't have gone to any settlement!"

"There is no settlement to go to. I made our enemies furnish the powder and lead we need so much, and that is surely the cheapest way. Listen, Dagaeoga. I remembered that to the east of us, about two days' journey, was a long valley sheltered well and warm, in which Indians who fight the Hodenosaunee often camp. I thought it likely they would be there in such a winter as this, and that I might take from them in the night the powder and lead we need so much.

"I was right. The savages were there, and with them a white man, a Frenchman, that Charles Langlade, called the Owl, from whom we fled. They had an abundance of all things, and they were waxing fat, until they could take the war path in the spring. Then, Dagaeoga, I played the fox. At night, when they dreamed of no danger, I entered their biggest lodges, passing as one of them, and came away with the powder and lead."

"It was a great feat, Tayoga, but are you sure none of them will trail you here?"

"The surface of the snow and ice melts a little in the noonday sun, enough to efface all trace of the snowshoes, and my trail is no more than that made by a bird in its flight through the air. Nor can we be followed here while we are guarded by the bears, who sleep, but who, nevertheless, are sentinels."

Tayoga took off his snowshoes, and sank upon a heap of furs in the cave, while Robert brought him food and inspected the great prize of ammunition he had brought. The package contained a dozen huge horns filled with powder, and many small bars of lead, the latter having made the weight which had proved such a severe trial to the Onondaga.

"Here's enough of both lead and powder to last us throughout the winter, whatever may happen," said Robert in a tone of intense satisfaction. "Tayoga, you're certainly a master freebooter. You couldn't have made a more useful capture."

Each, after the invariable custom of hunters and scouts, carried bullet molds, and they were soon at work, melting the lead and casting bullets for their rifles, then pouring the shining pellets in a stream into their pouches. They continued at the task from day to day until all the lead was turned into bullets and then they began work on another pair of snowshoes, these intended for Robert.

Despite the safety and comfort of their home in the rock, both began to chafe now, and time grew tremendously long. They had done nearly everything they could do for themselves, and life had become so easy that there was leisure to think and be restless, because they were far away from great affairs.

"When my snowshoes are finished and I perfect myself in the use of them," said Robert, "I favor an attempt to escape on the ice and snow to the south. We grow rusty, you and I, here, Tayoga. The war may be decided in our absence and I want to see Dave, too. I want to hear him tell how he got through the savage cordon to the lake."

"Have no fear about the war, Dagaeoga," said the Onondaga. "It will not be ended this winter nor the next. Before there is peace between the French king and the British king you will have a chance to make many speeches. Yet, like you, I think we should go. It is not well for us to lie hidden in the ground through a whole winter."

"But when we leave our good home here I shall leave many regrets behind."

He looked around at the cave and its supplies of skins and furs, its stores of wood and food. Fortune had helped their own skill and they had made a marvelous change in the place. Its bleakness and bareness had disappeared. In the cold and bitter wilderness it offered more than comfort, it was luxury itself.

"So shall I," said Tayoga, appreciatively, "but we will heap rocks up to the very top of the door, so that only a little air and nothing else can enter, and leave it as it is. Some day we may want to use it again."

Having decided to go, they became very impatient, but they did not skimp the work on the snowshoes, knowing how much depended on their strength, but that task too, like all the others, came to an end in time. Robert practiced a while and they selected a day of departure. They were to take with them all the powder and bullets, a large supply of food and their heavy bearskin overcoats. They had also made for themselves over-moccasins of fur and extra deerskin leggings. They would be bundled up greatly, but it was absolutely necessary in order to face the great cold, that hovered continuously around thirty to forty degrees below zero. The ear muffs, the caps and the gloves, too, were necessities, but they had the comfort of believing that if the fierce winter presented great difficulties to them, it would also keep their savage enemies in their lodges.

"The line that shut us in in the autumn has thinned out and gone!" exclaimed Robert in sanguine tones, "and we'll have a clear path from here to the lake!"

Then they rolled stones, as they had planned, before the door to their home, closing it wholly except a few square inches at the top, and ascended on their snowshoes to the crest of the ridge.

"Our cave will not be disturbed, at least not this winter," said Tayoga confidently. "The bears that sleep below are, as I told you, the silent sentinels, and they will guard it for us until we come again."

"At least, they brought us good luck," said Robert. Then, with long, gliding strokes they passed over the ridge, and their happy valley was lost to sight. They did not speak again for hours, Tayoga leading the way, and each bending somewhat to his task, which was by no means a light one, owing to the weight they carried, and the extremely mountainous nature of the country. The wilderness was still and intensely cold. The deep snow was covered by a crust of ice, and, despite vigorous exertion and warm clothing, they were none too warm.

By noon Robert's ankle, not thoroughly hardened to the snowshoes, began to chafe, and they stopped to rest in a dense grove, where the searching north wind was turned aside from them. They were traveling by the sun for the south end of Lake George, but as they were in the vast plexus of mountains, where their speed could not be great, even under the best of conditions, they calculated that they would be many days and nights on the way.

They stayed fully an hour in the shelter of the trees, and an hour later came to a frozen lake over which the traveling was easy, but after they had passed it they entered a land of close thickets, in which their progress was extremely slow. At night, the cold was very great, but, as they scooped out a deep hollow in the snow, though they attempted no fire, they were able to keep warm within their bearskins. A second and a third day passed in like fashion, and their progress to the south was unimpeded, though slow. They beheld no signs of human life save their own, but invariably in the night, and often in the day, they heard distant wolves howling.

On the fourth day the temperature rose rapidly and the surface of the snow softened, making their southward march much harder. Their snowshoes clogged so much and the strain upon their ankles grew so great that they decided to go into camp long before sunset, and give themselves a thorough rest. They also scraped away the snow and lighted a fire for the first time, no small task, as the snow was still very deep, and it required much hunting to find the fallen wood. But when the cheerful blaze came they felt repaid for all their trouble. They rejoiced in the glow for an hour or so, and then Tayoga decided that he would go on a short hunting trip along the course of a stream that they could see about a quarter of a mile below.

"It may be that I can rouse up a deer," he said. "They are likely to be in the shelter of the thick bushes along the water's edge, but whether I find them or not I will return shortly after sundown. Do you await me here, Dagaeoga."

"I won't stir. I'm too tired," said Robert.

The Onondaga put on his snowshoes again, and strapped to his back his share of the ammunition and supplies—it had been agreed by the two that neither should ever go anywhere without his half, lest they become separated. Then he departed on smooth, easy strokes, almost like one who skated, and was soon out of sight among the bushes at the edge of the stream. Robert settled back to the warmth and brightness of the fire, and awaited in peace the sound of a shot telling that Tayoga had found the deer.

He had been so weary, and the blaze was so soothing that he sank into a state, not sleep, but nevertheless full of dreams. He saw Willet again, and heard him tell the tale how he had reached the lake and the army with Garay's letter. He saw Colonel Johnson, and the young English officer, Grosvenor, and Colden and Wilton and Carson and all his old friends, and then he heard a crunch on the snow near him. Had Tayoga come back so soon and without his deer? He did not raise his drooping eyelids until he heard the crunch again, and then when he opened them he sprang suddenly to his feet, his heart beating fast with alarm.

A half dozen dark figures rushed upon him. He snatched at his rifle and tried to meet the first of them with a bullet, but the range was too close. He nevertheless managed to get the muzzle in the air and pull the trigger. He remembered even in that terrible moment to do that much and Tayoga would hear the sharp, lashing report. Then the horde was upon him. Someone struck him a stunning blow on the side of the head with the flat of a tomahawk, and he fell unconscious.

When he returned to the world, the twilight had come, the hole in the snow had been enlarged very much, and so had the fire. Seated around it were a dozen Indians, wrapped in thick blankets and armed heavily, and one white man whose attire was a strange compound of savage and civilized. He wore a three-cornered French military hat with a great, drooping plume of green, an immense cloak of fine green cloth, lined with fur, but beneath it he was clothed in buckskin.

The man himself was as picturesque as his attire. He was young, his face was lean and bold, his nose hooked and fierce like that of a Roman leader, his skin, originally fair, now tanned almost to a mahogany color by exposure, his figure of medium height, but obviously very powerful. Robert saw at once that he was a Frenchman and he felt instinctively that it was Langlade. But his head was aching from the blow of the tomahawk, and he waited in a sort of apathy.

"So you've come back to earth," said the Frenchman, who had seen his eyes open—he spoke in good French, which Robert understood perfectly.

"I never had any intention of staying away," replied young Lennox.

The Frenchman laughed.

"At least you show a proper spirit," he said. "I commend you also for managing to fire your rifle, although the bullet hit none of us. It gave the alarm to your comrade and he got clean away. I can make a guess as to who you are."

"My name is Robert Lennox."

"I thought so, and your comrade was Tayoga, the Onondaga who is not unknown to us, a great young warrior, I admit freely. I am sorry we did not take him."

"I don't think you'll get a chance to lay hands on him. He'll be too clever for you."

"I admit that, too. He's gone like the wind on his snowshoes. It seems queer that you and he should be here in the mountain wilderness so far north of your lines, in the very height of a fierce winter."

"It's just as queer that you should be here."

"Perhaps so, from your point of view, though it's lucky that I should have been present with these dark warriors of mine when you were taken. They suffered heavily in the battle by Andiatarocte, and but for me they might now be using you as fuel. Don't wince, you know their ways and I only tell a fact. In truth, I can't make you any promise in regard to your ultimate fate, but, at present, I need you alive more than I need you dead."

"You won't get any military information out of me."

"I don't know. We shall wait and see."

"Do you know the Chevalier de St. Luc?"

"Of course. All Frenchmen and all Canadians know him, or know of him, but he is far from here, and we shall not tell him that we have a young American prisoner. The chevalier is a great soldier and the bravest of men, but he has one fault. He does not hate the English and the Bostonnais enough."

Robert was not bound, but his arms and snowshoes had been taken and the Indians were all about him. There was no earthly chance of escape. With the wisdom of the wise he resigned himself at once to his situation, awaiting a better moment.

"I'm at your command," he said politely to Langlade.

The French leader laughed, partly in appreciation.

"You show intelligence," he said. "You do not resist, when you see that resistance is impossible."

Robert settled himself into a more comfortable position by the fire. His head still ached, but it was growing easier. He knew that it was best to assume a careless and indifferent tone.

"I'm not ready to leave you now," he said, "but I shall go later."

Langlade laughed again, and then directed two of the Indians to hunt more wood. They obeyed. Robert saw that they never questioned his leadership, and he saw anew how the French partisans established themselves so thoroughly in the Indian confidence. The others threw away more snow, making a comparatively large area of cleared ground, and, when the wood was brought, they built a great fire, around which all of them sat and ate heartily from their packs.

Langlade gave Robert food which he forced himself to eat, although he was not hungry. He judged that the French partisan, who could be cruel enough on occasion, had some object in treating him well for the present, and he was not one to disturb such a welcome frame of mind. His weapons and the extra rifle of Garay that they had brought with them, had already been divided among the warriors, who, pleased with the reward, were content to wait.

The night was spent at the captured camp, and in the morning the entire party, Robert included, started on snowshoes almost due north. The young prisoner felt a sinking of the heart, when his face was turned away from his own people, and he began an unknown captivity. He had been certain at first of escape, but it did not seem so sure now. In former wars many prisoners taken on raids into Canada had never been heard of again, and when he reflected in cold blood he knew that the odds were heavy against a successful flight. Yet there was Tayoga. His warning shot had enabled the Onondaga to evade the band, and his comrade would never desert him. All his surpassing skill and tenacity would be devoted to his aid. In that lay his hope.

They pressed on toward the north as fast as they could go, and when night came they were all exhausted, but they ate heavily again and Robert received his share. Langlade continued to treat him kindly, though he still had the feeling that the partisan, if it served him, would be fully as cruel as the Indians. At night, although they built big fires, Langlade invariably posted a strong watch, and Robert noticed also that he usually shared it, or a part of it, from which habit he surmised that the partisan had received the name of the Owl. He had hoped that Tayoga might have a chance to rescue him in the dark, but he saw now that the vigilance was too great.

He hid his intense disappointment and kept as cheerful a face as he could. Langlade, the only white man in the Indian band, was drawn to him somewhat by the mere fact of racial kinship, and the two frequently talked together in the evenings in what was a sort of compulsory friendliness, Robert in this manner picking up scraps of information which when welded together amounted to considerable, being thus confirmed in his belief that Willet with the letter had reached the lake in time. St. Luc with a formidable force had undertaken a swift march on Albany, but the town had been put in a position of defense, and St. Luc's vanguard had been forced to retreat by a large body of rangers after a severe conflict. As the success of the chevalier's daring enterprise had depended wholly on surprise, he had then withdrawn northward.

But Robert could not find out by any kind of questions where St. Luc was, although he learned that Garay had never returned to Albany and that Hendrik Martinus had made an opportune flight. Langlade, who was thoroughly a wilderness rover, talked freely and quite boastfully of the French power, which he deemed all pervading and invincible. Despite the battle at Lake George the fortunes of war had gone so far in favor of France and Canada and against Britain and the Bostonnais. When the great campaign was renewed in the spring more and bigger victories would crown French valor. The Owl grew expansive as he talked to the youth, his prisoner.

"The Marquis de Montcalm is coming to lead all our armies," he said, "and he is a far abler soldier than Dieskau. You really did us a great service when you captured the Saxon. Only a Frenchman is fit to lead Frenchmen, and under a mighty captain we will crush you. The Bostonnais are not the equal of the French in the forest. Save a few like Willet, and Rogers, the English and Americans do not learn the ways of woods warfare, nor do you make friends with the Indians as we do."

"That is true in the main," responded Robert, "but we shall win despite it. Both the English and the English Colonials have the power to survive defeat. Can the French and the Canadians do as well?"

Langlade could not be shaken in his faith. He saw nothing but the most brilliant victories, and not only did he boast of French power, but he gloried even more in the strength of the Indian hordes, that had come and that were coming in ever increasing numbers to the help of France. Only the Hodenosaunee stood aloof from Québec, and he believed the Great League even yet would be brought over to his side.

Robert argued with the Owl, but he made no impression upon him. Meanwhile they continued to march north by west.

CHAPTER VIII.
BEFORE MONTCALM

The Owl, with his warriors and captive, descended in time into the low country in the northwest. They, too, had been on snowshoes, but now they discarded them, since they were entering a region in which little snow had fallen, the severity of the weather abating greatly. Robert was still treated well, though guarded with the utmost care. The Indians, who seemed to be from some tribe about the Great Lakes, did not speak any dialect he knew, and, if they understood English, they did not use it. He was compelled to do all his talking with the Owl who, however, was not at all taciturn. Robert saw early that while a wonderful woodsman and a born partisan leader, he was also a Gascon, vain, boastful and full of words. He tried to learn from him something about his possible fate, but he could obtain no hint, until they had been traveling more than three weeks, and Langlade had been mellowed by an uncommonly good supper of tender game, which the Indians had cooked for him.

"You've been trying to draw that information out of me ever since you were captured," he said. "You were indirect and clever about it, but I noticed it. I, Charles Langlade, have perceptions, you must understand. If I do live in the woods I can read the minds of white men."

"I know you can," said Robert, smilingly. "I observed from the first that you had an acute intellect."

"Your judgment does you credit, my young friend. I did not tell you what I was going to do with you, because I did not know myself. I know more about you than you think I do. One of my warriors was with Tandakora in several of his battles with you and Willet, that mighty hunter whom the Indians call the Great Bear, and Tayoga, the Onondaga, who is probably following on our trail in the hope of rescuing you. I have also heard of you from others. Oh, as I tell you, I, Charles Langlade, take note of all things. You are a prisoner of importance. I would not give you to Tandakora, because he would burn you, and a man does not burn valuable goods. I would not send you to St. Luc, because, being a generous man, he might take some foolish notion to exchange you, or even parole you. I would not give you to the Marquis Duquesne at Quebec, because then I might lose my pawn in the game, and, in any event, the Marquis Duquesne is retiring as Governor General of New France."

"Is that true? I have met him. He seemed to me to be a great man."

"Perhaps he is, but he was too haughty and proud for the powerful men who dwelt at Quebec, and who control New France. I have heard something of your appearance at the capital with the Great Bear and the Onondaga, and of what chanced at Bigot's ball, and elsewhere. Ah, you see, as I told you, I, Charles Langlade, know all things! But to return, the Marquis Duquesne gives way to the Marquis de Vaudreuil. Oh, that was accomplished some time ago, and perhaps you know of it. So, I do not wish to give you to the Marquis de Vaudreuil. I might wait and present you to the Marquis de Montcalm when he comes, but that does not please me, either, and thus I have about decided to present you to the Dove."

"The Dove! Who is the Dove?"

Langlade laughed with intense enjoyment.

"The Dove," he replied, "is a woman, none other than Madame de Langlade herself, a Huron. You English do not marry Indian women often—and yet Colonel William Johnson has taken a Mohawk to wife—but we French know them and value them. Do not think to have an easy and careless jailer when you are put in the hands of the Dove. She will guard you even more zealously than I, Charles Langlade, and you will notice that I have neither given you any opportunity to escape nor your friend, Tayoga, the slightest chance to rescue you."

"It is true, Monsieur Langlade. I've abandoned any such hope on the march, although I may elude you later."

"The Dove, as I told you, will attend to that. But it will be a pretty play of wits, and I don't mind the test. I'm aware that you have intelligence and skill, but the Dove, though a woman, possesses the wit of a great chief, and I'll match her against you."

There was a further abatement of the weather, and they reached a region where there was no snow at all. Warm winds blew from the direction of the Great Lakes and the band traveled fast through a land in which the game almost walked up to their rifles to be killed, such plenty causing the Indians, as usual, now that they were not on the war path, to feast prodigiously before huge fires, Langlade often joining them, and showing that he was an adept in Indian customs.

One evening, just as they were about to light the fire, the warrior who had been posted as sentinel at the edge of the forest gave a signal and a few moments later a tall, spare figure in a black robe with a belt about the waist appeared. Robert's heart gave a great leap. The wearer of the black robe was an elderly man with a thin face, ascetic and high. The captive recognized him at once. It was Father Philibert Drouillard, the priest, whose life had already crossed his more than once, and it was not strange to see him there, as the French priests roamed far through the great wilderness of North America, seeking to save the souls of the savages.

Langlade, when he beheld Father Drouillard, sprang at once to his feet, and Robert also arose quickly. The priest saw young Lennox, but he did not speak to him just yet, accepting the food that the Owl offered him, and sitting down with his weary feet to the fire that had now been lighted.

"You have traveled far, Father?" said Langlade, solicitously.

"From the shores of Lake Huron. I have converts there, and I must see that they do not grow weak in the faith."

"All men, red and white, respect Philibert Drouillard. Why are you alone, Father?"

"A runner from the Christian village came with me until yesterday. Then I sent him back, because I would not keep him too long from his people. I can go the rest of the way alone, as it will be but a few days before I meet a French force."

Then he turned to Robert for the first time.

"And you, my son," he said, "I am sorry it has fared thus with you."

"It has not gone badly, Father," said Robert. "Monsieur de Langlade has treated me well. I have naught to complain of save that I'm a prisoner."

"It is a good lad, Charles Langlade," said the priest to the partisan, "and I am glad he has suffered no harm at your hands. What do you purpose to do with him?"

"It is my present plan to take him to the village in which Madame Langlade, otherwise the Dove, abides. He will be her prisoner until a further plan develops, and you know how well she watches."

A faint smile passed over the thin face of the priest.

"It is true, Charles Langlade," he said. "That which escapes the eyes of the Dove is very small, but I would take the lad with me to Montreal."

"Nay, Father, that cannot be. I am second to nobody in respect for Holy Church, and for you, Father Drouillard, whose good deeds are known to all, and whose bad deeds are none, but those who fight the war must use their judgment in fighting it, and the prisoners are theirs."

Father Drouillard sighed.

"It is so, Charles Langlade," he said, "but, as I have said, the prisoner is a good youth. I have met him before, as I told you, and I would save him. You know not what may happen in the Indian village, if you chance to be away."

"The Dove will have charge of him. She can be trusted."

"And yet I would take him with me to Montreal. He will give his parole that he will not attempt to escape on the way. It is the custom for prisoners to be ransomed. I will send to you from Montreal five golden louis for him."

Langlade shook his head.

"Ten golden louis," said Father Drouillard.

"Nay, Father, it is no use," said the partisan. "I cannot be tempted to exchange him for money."

"Fifteen golden louis, Charles Langlade, though I may have to borrow from the funds of the Church to send them to you."

"I respect your motive, Father, but 'tis impossible. This is a prisoner of great value and I must use him as a pawn in the game of war. He was taken fairly and I cannot give him up."

Again Father Drouillard sighed, and this time heavily.

"I would save you from captivity, Mr. Lennox," he said, "but, as you see, I cannot."

Robert was much moved.

"I thank you, Father Drouillard, for your kind intentions," he said. "It may be that some day I shall have a chance to repay them. Meanwhile, I do not dread the coming hospitality of Madame Langlade."

The priest shook his head sadly.

"It is a great and terrible war," he said, "though I cannot doubt that France will prevail, but I fear for you, my son, a captive in the vast wilderness. Although you are an enemy and a heretic I have only good feeling for you, and I know that the great Chevalier, St. Luc, also regards you with favor."

"Know you anything of St. Luc?" asked Robert eagerly.

"Only that the expedition he was to lead against Albany has turned back and that he has gone to Canada to fight under the banner of Montcalm, when he comes with the great leaders, De Levis, Bourlamaque and the others."

"I thought I might meet him."

"Not here, with Charles Langlade."

The priest spent the night with them and in the morning, after giving them his blessing, captors and captive alike, he departed on his long and solitary journey to Montreal.

"A good man," said Robert, as he watched his tall, thin figure disappear in the surrounding forest.

"Truly spoken," said the Owl. "I am little of a churchman myself, the forest and the war trail please me better, but the priests are a great prop to France in the New World. They carry with them the authority of His Majesty, King Louis."

A week later they reached a small Indian village on Lake Ontario where the Owl at present made his abode, and in the largest lodge of which his patient spouse, the Dove, was awaiting him. She was young, much taller than the average Indian woman, and, in her barbaric fashion, quite handsome. But her face was one of the keenest and most alert Robert had ever seen. All the trained observation of countless ancestors seemed stored in her and now he understood why Langlade had boasted so often and so warmly of her skill as a guard. She regarded him with a cold eye as she listened attentively to her husband's instructions, and, for the remainder of that winter and afterward, she obeyed them with a thoroughness beyond criticism.

The village included perhaps four hundred souls, of whom about a hundred were warriors. Langlade was king and Madame Langlade, otherwise the Dove, was queen, the two ruling with absolute sovereignty, their authority due to their superior intelligence and will and to the service they rendered to the little state, because a state it was, organized completely in all its parts, although composed of only a few hundred human beings. In the bitter weather that came again, Langlade directed the hunting in the adjacent forest and the fishing conducted on the great lake. He also made presents from time to time of gorgeous beads or of huge red or yellow blankets that had been sent from Montreal. Robert could not keep from admiring his diplomacy and tact, and now he understood more thoroughly than ever how the French partisans made themselves such favorites with the wild Indians.

His own position in the village was tentative. Langlade still seemed uncertain what to do with him, and held him meanwhile for a possible reward of great value. He was never allowed to leave the cluster of tepees for the forest, except with the warriors, but he took part in the fishing on the lake, being a willing worker there, because idleness grew terribly irksome, and, when he had nothing to do, he chafed over his long captivity. He slept in a small tepee built against that of Monsieur and Madame Langlade, and from which there was no egress save through theirs.

He was enclosed only within walls of skin, and he believed that he might have broken a way through them, but he felt that the eyes of the Dove were always on him. He even had the impression that she was watching him while he slept, and sometimes he dreamed that she was fanged and clawed like a tigress.

Langlade went away once, being gone a long time, and while he was absent the Dove redoubled her watchfulness. Robert's singular impression that her eyes were always on him was strengthened, and these eyes were increased to the hundred of Argus and more. It became so oppressive that he was always eager to go out with the warriors in their canoes for the fishing. On Lake Ontario he was sure the eyes of the Dove could not reach him, but the work was arduous and often perilous. The great lake was not to be treated lightly. Often it took toll of the Indians who lived around its shores. Winter storms came up suddenly, the waves rolled like those of the sea, freezing spray dashed over them, and it required a supreme exertion of both skill and strength to keep the light canoes from being swamped.

Yet Robert was always happier on water than on land. On shore, confined closely and guarded zealously, his imaginative temperament suffered and he became moody and depressed, but on the lakes, although still a captive, he felt the winds of freedom. When the storms came and the icy blasts swept down upon them he responded, body and soul. Relief and freedom were to be found in the struggle with the elements and he always went back to shore refreshed and stronger of spirit and flesh. He also had a feeling that Tayoga might come by way of the lake, and when he was with the little Indian fleet he invariably watched the watery horizon for a lone canoe, but he never saw any.

The absence of news from his friends, and from the world to which they belonged, was the most terrible burden of all. If the Indians had news they told him none. He seemed to have vanished completely. But, however numerous may have been his moments of despondency, he was not made of the stuff that yields. The flexible steel always rebounded. He took thorough care of his health and strength. In his close little tepee he flexed and tensed his muscles and went through physical exercises every night and morning, but it was on the lake in the fishing, where the Indians grew to recognize his help, that he achieved most. Fighting the winds, the water and the cold, he felt his muscles harden and his chest enlarge, and he would say to himself that when the spring came and he escaped he would be more fit for the life of a free forest runner than he had ever been before. Langlade, when he returned, took notice of his increased size and strength and did not withhold approval.

"I like any prisoner of mine to flourish," he laughed. "The more superior you become the greater will be the reward for me when I dispose of you. You have found the Dove all I promised you she should be, haven't you, Monsieur Lennox?"

"All and more," replied Robert. "Although she may be out of sight I feel that her eyes are always on me, and this is true of the night as well as the day."

"A great woman, the Dove, and a wife to whom I give all credit. If it should come into the king's mind to call me to Versailles and bestow upon me some kind of an accolade perhaps Madame Langlade would not feel at home in the great palace nor at the Grand Trianon, nor even at the Little Trianon, and maybe I wouldn't either. But since no such idea will enter His Majesty's mind, and I have no desire to leave the great forests, the Dove is a perfect wife for me. She is the true wilderness helpmate, accomplished in all the arts of the life I live and love, and with the eye and soul of a warrior. I repeat, young Monsieur Lennox, where could I find a wife more really sublime?"

"Nowhere, Monsieur Langlade. The more I see you two together the more nearly I think you are perfectly matched."

The Owl seemed pleased with the recognition of his marital felicity, and grew gracious, dropping some crumbs of information for Robert. He had been to Montreal and the arrival of the great soldier, the Marquis de Montcalm, with fresh generals and fresh troops from France, was expected daily at Quebec. The English, although their fleets were larger, could not intercept them, and it was now a certainty that the spring campaign would sweep over Albany and almost to New York. He spoke with so much confidence, in truth with such an absolute certainty, that Robert's heart sank and then came back again with a quick rebound.

After a winter that had seemed to the young captive an age, spring came with a glorious blossoming and blooming. The wilderness burst into green and the great lake shining in the sun became peaceful and friendly. Warm winds blew out of the west and the blood flowed more swiftly in human veins. But spring passed and summer came. Then Langlade announced that he would depart with the best of the warriors, and that Robert would go with him, although he refused absolutely to say where or for what purpose.

Robert's joy was dimmed in nowise by his ignorance of his destination. He had not found the remotest chance to escape while in the village, but it might come on the march, and there was also a relief and pleasant excitement in entering the wilderness again. He joyously made ready, the Dove gave her lord and equal, not her master, a Spartan farewell, and the formidable band, Robert in the center, plunged into the forest.

When the great mass of green enclosed them he felt a mighty surge of hope. His imaginative temperament was on fire. A chance for him would surely come. Tayoga might be hidden in the thickets. Action brought renewed courage. Langlade, who was watching him, smiled.

"I read your mind, young Monsieur Lennox," he said. "Have I not told you that I, Charles Langlade, have the perceptions? Do I not see and interpret everything?"

"Then what do you see and interpret now?"

"A great hope in your heart that you will soon bid us farewell. You think that when we are deep in the forest it will not be difficult to elude our watch. And yet you could not escape when we were going through this same forest to the village. Now why do you think it will be easier when you are going through it again, but away?"

"The Dove is not at the end of the march. Her eyes will no longer be upon me."

The Owl laughed deeply and heartily.

"You're a lad of sense," he said, "when you lay such a tribute at the feet of that incomparable woman, that model wife, that true helpmate in every sense of the word. Why should you be anxious to leave us? I could have you adopted into the tribe, and you know the ceremony of adoption is sacred with the Indians. And let me whisper another little fact in your ear which will surely move you. The Dove has a younger sister, so much like her that they are twins in character if not in years. She will soon be of marriageable age, and she shall be reserved for you. Think! Then you will be my brother-in-law and the brother-in-law of the incomparable Dove."

"No! No!" exclaimed Robert hastily.

Now the laughter of the Owl was uncontrollable. His face writhed and his sides shook.

"A lad does not recognize his own good!" he exclaimed, "or is it bashfulness? Nay, don't be afraid, young Monsieur Lennox! Perhaps I could get the Dove to intercede for you!"

Robert was forced to smile.

"I thank you," he said, "but I am far from the marriageable age myself."

"Then the Dove and I are not to have you for a brother-in-law?" said Langlade. "You show little appreciation, young Monsieur Lennox, when it is so easy for you to become a member of such an interesting family."

Robert was confirmed in his belief that there was much of the wild man in the Owl, who in many respects had become more Indian than the Indians. He was a splendid trailer, a great hunter, and the hardships of the forest were nothing to him. He read every sign of the wilderness and yet he retained all that was French also, lightness of manner, gayety, quick wit and a politeness that never failed. It is likely that the courage and tenacity of the French leaders were never shown to better advantage than in the long fight they made for dominion in North America. Despite the fact that he was an enemy, and his belief that Langlade could be ruthless, on occasion, Robert was compelled to like him.

The journey, the destination yet unknown to him, was long, but it was not tedious to the young prisoner. He watched the summer progress and the colors deepen and he was cheered continually by the hope of escape, a fact that Langlade recognized and upon which he commented in a detached manner, from time to time. Now and then the leader himself went ahead with a scout or two and one morning he said to Robert:

"I saw something in the forest last night."

"The forest contains much," said Robert.

"But this was of especial interest to you. It was the trace of a footstep, and I am convinced it was made by your friend Tayoga, the Onondaga. Doubtless he is seeking to effect your escape."

Robert's heart gave a leap, and there was a new light in his eyes, of which the shrewd Owl took notice.

"I have heard of the surpassing skill of the Onondaga," he continued, "but I, Charles Langlade, have skill of my own. It will be some time before we arrive at the place to which we are going, and I lay you a wager that Tayoga does not rescue you."

"I have no money, Monsieur Langlade," said Robert, "and if I had I could not accept a wager upon such a subject."

"Then we'll let it be mental, wholly. My skill is matched against the combined knowledge of Tayoga and yourself. He'll never be able, no matter how dark the night, to get near our camp and communicate with you."

Although Robert hoped and listened often in the dusk for the sound of a signal from Tayoga, Langlade made good his boast. The two were able to establish no communication. It was soon proved that he was in the forest near them, one of the warriors even catching a sufficient glimpse of his form for a shot, which, however, went wild. The Onondaga did not reply, and, despite the impossibility of reaching him, Robert was cheered by the knowledge that he was near. He had a faithful and powerful friend who would help him some day, be it soon or late.

The summer was well advanced when Langlade announced that their journey was done.

"Before night," he said triumphantly, "we will be in the camp of the Marquis de Montcalm, and we will meet the great soldier himself. I, Charles Langlade, told you that it would be so, and it is so."

"What, Montcalm near?" exclaimed Robert, aflame with interest.

"Look at the sky above the tops of those trees in the east and you will see a smudge of smoke, beneath which stand the tents of the French army."

"The French army here! And what is it doing in the wilderness?"

"That, young Monsieur Lennox, rests on the knees of the gods. I have some curiosity on the subject myself."

An hour or two later they came within sight of the French camp, and Robert saw that it was a numerous and powerful force for time and place. The tents stood in rows, and soldiers, both French and Canadian, were everywhere, while many Indian warriors were on the outskirts. A large white marquee near the center he was sure was that of the commander-in-chief, and he was eager to see at once the famous Montcalm, of whom he was hearing so much. But to his intense disappointment, Langlade went into camp with the Indians.

"The Marquis de Montcalm is a great man," he said, "the commander-in-chief of all the forces of His Majesty, King Louis, in North America, and even I, Charles Langlade, will not approach him without ceremony. We will rest in the edge of the forest, and when he hears that I have come he will send for me, because he will want to know many things which none other can tell him. And it may be, young Monsieur Lennox, that, in time, he will wish to see you also."

So Robert waited with as much patience as he could muster, although he slept but little that night, the noises in the great French camp and his own curiosity keeping him awake. What was Montcalm doing so far from the chief seats of the French power in Canada, and did the English and Americans know that he was here?

Curiously enough he had little apprehension for himself, it was rather a feeling of joy that he had returned to the world of great affairs. Soon he would know what had been occurring during the long winter when he was buried in an Indian village, and he might even hear of Willet. Toward dawn he slept a little, and after daylight he was awakened by Langlade who was as assured and talkative as usual.

"It may be, my gallant young prisoner," he said, ruffling and strutting, "that I am about to lose you, but if it is so it will be for value received. I, Charles Langlade, have seen the great Marquis de Montcalm, but it was an equal speaking to an equal. It was last night in his grand marquee, where he sat surrounded by his trusted lieutenants, De Levis, St. Luc, Bourlamaque, Coulon de Villiers and the others. But I was not daunted at all. I repeat that it was an equal speaking to an equal, and the Marquis was pleased to commend me for the work I have already done for France."

"And St. Luc was there?"

"He was. The finest figure of them all. A brave and generous man and a great leader. He stood at the right hand of the Marquis de Montcalm, while I talked and he listened with attention, because the Chevalier de St. Luc is always willing to learn from others. No false pride about him! And the Marquis de Montcalm is like him. I gave the commander-in-chief much excellent advice which he accepted with gratitude, and in return for you, whom he expects to put to use, he has raised me in rank, and has extended my authority over the western tribes. Ah, I knew that you were a prize when I captured you, and I was wise to save you as a pawn."

"How can I be of any value to the Marquis de Montcalm?"

"That is to be seen. He knows his own plans best. You are to come with me at once into his presence."

Robert was immediately in a great stir. He straightened out, and, with his hands, brushed his own clothing, smoothed his hair, intending, with his usual desire for neatness, to make the best possible appearance before the French leader.

After breakfast Langlade took him to the great marquee in which Montcalm sat, as the morning was cool, and when their names had been taken in a young officer announced that they might enter, the officer, to Robert's great surprise, being none other than De Galissonnière, who showed equal amazement at meeting him there. The Frenchman gave him a hearty grasp of the hand in English fashion, but they did not have time to say anything.

Robert, walking by the side of Langlade, entered the great tent with some trepidation, and beheld a swarthy man of middle years, in the uniform of a general of France, giving orders to two officers who stood respectfully at attention. Neither of the officers was St. Luc, nor were they among those whom Robert had seen at Quebec. He surmised, however, that they were De Levis and Bourlamaque, and he learned soon that he was right. Langlade paused until Montcalm was ready to speak to him, and Robert stood in silence at his side. Montcalm finished what he had to say and turned his eyes upon the young prisoner. His countenance was mild, but Robert felt that his gaze was searching.

"And this, Captain Langlade," he said, "is the youth of whom you were speaking?"

So the Owl had been made a captain, and the promotion had been one of his rewards. Robert was not sorry.

"It is the one, sir," replied Langlade, "young Monsieur Robert Lennox. He has been a prisoner in my village all the winter, and he has as friends some of the most powerful people in the British Colonies."

Montcalm continued to gaze at Robert as if he would read his soul.

"Sit down, Mr. Lennox," he said, not unkindly, motioning him to a little stool. Robert took the indicated seat and so quick is youth to warm to courtesy that he felt respect and even liking for the Marquis, official and able enemy though he knew him to be. De Levis and Bourlamaque also were watching him with alert gaze, but they said nothing.

"I hear," continued Montcalm, with a slight smile, "that you have not suffered in Captain Langlade's village, and that you have adapted yourself well to wild life."

"I've had much experience with the wilderness," said Robert. "Most of my years have been passed there, and it was easy for me to live as Captain Langlade lived. I've no complaint to make of his treatment, though I will say that he has guarded me well."

Montcalm laughed.

"It agrees with Captain Langlade's own account," he said. "I suppose that one must be born, or at least pass his youth in it, to get the way of this vast wilderness. We of old Europe, where everything has been ruled and measured for many centuries, can have no conception of it until we see it, and even then we do not understand it. Although with an army about me I feel lost in so much forest. But enough of that. It is of yourself and not of myself that I wish to speak. I have heard good reports of you from one of my own officers, who, though he has been opposed to you many times, nevertheless likes you."

"The Chevalier de St. Luc!"

"Aye, the Chevalier de St. Luc. I know, also, that you have been in the councils of some of the Colonial leaders. You are a friend of Sir William Johnson."

"Colonel William Johnson?"

"No, Sir William Johnson. In reward for the affair at Lake George, in which our Dieskau was unfortunate, he has been made a baronet by the British king."

"I am glad."

"And doubtless Sir William is also. You know him well, I understand, and he was still at the lake when you left on the journey that led to your capture."

Robert was silent.

"I have not asked you to answer," continued Montcalm, "but I assume that it is so. His army, although it was victorious in the battle there, did not advance. There was much disagreement among the governors of the British Colonies. The provinces could not be induced to act together?"

Robert was still silent.

"Again I say I am not asking you to answer, but your silence confirms the truth of our reports."

Robert flushed, and a warm reply trembled on his lips, but he restrained the words. A swift smile passed over the dark face of Montcalm.

"You see, Mr. Lennox," he continued, "I am not asking you to say anything, but there was great disappointment among the British Colonials because there was no advance after the battle at the lake. It has also cooled the enthusiasm of the Iroquois, many of whom have gone home and who perhaps will take no further part in the war as the allies of the English."

Again Robert flushed and again he bit back the hot reply. He looked uneasily at De Levis and Bourlamaque, but their faces expressed nothing. Then Montcalm suddenly changed the subject.

"I am going to make you a very remarkable offer," he said, "and do not think for a moment it is going to imply any change of colors on your part, or the least suspicion of treason, which I could not ask of the gentleman you obviously are. I request of you your parole, your word of honor that you will not take any further part in this war."

"I can't do it! As I have often told Captain Langlade, I intend to escape."

"That is impossible. If you could not do so when you were in Captain Langlade's village, you have no chance at all now that you are surrounded by an army. But since you will not give me your parole it will become necessary to keep you as a prisoner of war, and to send you to a safe place."

"Many of our people in this and former wars with the French have been held prisoners in the Province of Quebec. I know somewhat of the city of Quebec, and it is not wholly an unpleasant place."

"I did not have Quebec, either the province or the city, in mind so far as concerns you, Mr. Lennox. Three of our ships are to return shortly to France, and, not wishing to give us your parole, you are to go to France."

"To France?"

"Yes, to France. Where else? And you should rejoice. It is a fair and glorious land. And I have heard there is a spirit in you, Mr. Lennox, which is almost French, a kindred touch, a Gallic salt and savor, so to speak."

"I'm wholly American and British."

"Perhaps there are others who know you better than you know yourself. I repeat, there is about you a French finish. Why should you deny it? You should be proud of it. We are the oldest of the great civilized nations, and the first in culture. Your stay in France should be very pleasant. You can drink there at the fountain of ancient culture and glory. The wilderness is magnificent in its way, but high civilization is magnificent also in its own and another way. You can see Paris, the city of light, the center of the world, and you can behold the splendid court of His Majesty, King Louis. That should appeal to a young man of taste and discernment."

Robert felt a thrill and his pulses leaped, but the thrill lasted only a moment. It was clearly impossible that he should go even as a prisoner, though a willing one, to France, and he did not see any reason why the Marquis de Montcalm should take any personal interest in his future. But responding invariably to the temperature about him his manner was now as polite as that of the French general.

"You have my thanks, sir," he said, "for the kindly way in which you offer to treat a prisoner, but it is impossible for me to go to France, unless you should choose to send me there by sheer force."

The slight smile passed again over the face of the Marquis de Montcalm.

"I fancied, young sir," he said, "that this would be your answer, and, being what it is, I cannot say that it has lowered you aught in my esteem. For the present, you abide with us."

Robert bowed. Montcalm inspired in him a certain liking, and a decided respect. Then, still under the escort of Langlade, he withdrew.

CHAPTER IX.
THE SIGN OF THE BEAR

Robert returned with Langlade to the partisan's camp at the edge of the forest adjoining that of the main French army, where the Indian warriors had lighted fires and were cooking steaks of the deer. He was disposed to be silent, but Langlade as usual chattered volubly, discoursing of French might and glory, but saying nothing that would indicate to his prisoner the meaning of the present military array in the forest.

Robert did not hear more than half of the Owl's words, because he was absorbed in those of Montcalm, which still lingered in his mind. Why should the Marquis wish to send him to France, and to have him treated, when he was there, more as a guest than as a prisoner? Think as he would he could find no answer to the question, but the Owl evidently had been impressed by his reception from Montcalm, as he treated him now with distinguished courtesy. He also seemed particularly anxious to have the good opinion of the lad who had been so long his prisoner.

"Have I been harsh to you?" he asked with a trace of anxiety in his tone. "Have I not always borne myself toward you as if you were an important prisoner of war? It is true I set the Dove as an invincible sentinel over you, but as a good soldier and loyal son of France I could do no less. Now, I ask you, Monsieur Robert Lennox, have not I, Charles Langlade, conducted myself as a fair and considerate enemy?"

"If I were to escape and be captured again, Captain Langlade, it is my sincere wish that you should be my captor the second time, even as you were the first."

The Owl was gratified, visibly and much, and then he announced a visitor. Robert sprang to his feet as he saw St. Luc approaching, and his heart throbbed as always when he was in the presence of this man. The chevalier was in a splendid uniform of white and silver unstained by the forest. His thick, fair hair was clubbed in a queue and powdered neatly, and a small sword, gold hilted, hung at his belt. He was the finest and most gallant figure that Robert had yet seen in the wilderness, the very spirit and essence of that brave and romantic France with which England and her colonies were fighting a duel to the death. And yet St. Luc always seemed to him too the soul of knightly chivalry, one to whom it was impossible for him to bear any hostility that was not merely official. His own hand went forward to meet the extended hand of the chevalier.

"We seem destined to meet many times, Mr. Lennox," said St. Luc, "in battle, and even under more pleasant conditions. I had heard that you were the prisoner of our great forest ranger, Captain Langlade, and that you would be received by our commander-in-chief, the Marquis de Montcalm."

"He made me a most extraordinary offer, that I go as a prisoner of war to Paris, but almost in the state of a guest."

"And you thought fit to decline, which was unwise in you, though to be expected of a lad of spirit. Sit down, Mr. Lennox, and we can have our little talk in ease and comfort. It may be that I have something to do with the proposition of the Marquis de Montcalm. Why not reconsider it and go to France? England is bound to lose the war in America. We have the energy and the knowledge. The Indian tribes are on our side. Even the powerful Hodenosaunee may come over to us in time, and at the worst it will become neutral. As a prisoner in France you will have no share in defeat, but perhaps that does not appeal to you."

"It does not, but I thank you, Chevalier de St. Luc, for your many kindnesses to me, although I don't understand them. Your solicitude for my welfare cannot but awake my gratitude, but it has been more than once a source of wonderment in my mind."

"Because you are a young and gallant enemy whom I would not see come to harm."

Robert felt, however, that the chevalier was not stating the true reason, and he felt also with equal force that he would keep secret in the face of all questions, direct or indirect, the motives impelling him. St. Luc asked him about his life in the Indian village with Langlade, and then came back presently to Paris and France, which he described more vividly than even Montcalm had done. He seemed to know the very qualities that would appeal most to Robert, and, despite himself, the lad felt his heart leap more than once. Paris appeared in deeper and more glowing colors than ever as the city of light and soul, but he was firm in his resolution not to go there as a prisoner, if choice should be left to him. St. Luc himself became enamored of his own words as he spoke. His eyes glowed, and his tone took on great warmth and enthusiasm. But presently he ceased and when he laughed a little his laugh showed a slight tone of disappointment.

"I do not move you, Mr. Lennox," he said. "I can see by your eye that your will is hardening against my words, and yet I could wish that you would listen to me. You will believe me when I say I mean you only good."

"I am wholly sure of it, Monsieur de St. Luc," said Robert, trying to speak lightly, "but a long while ago I formed a plan to escape, and if I should go to France it would interfere with it seriously. It would not be so easy to leave Paris, and come back to the province of New York, and while I am in North America it is always possible. I informed Captain Langlade that I meant to escape, and now I repeat it to you."

The chevalier laughed.

"Time will tell," he said. "Your ambition to leave is a proper and patriotic motive on your part, and I should be the last to accuse it. But 'tis not easy of accomplishment. I betray no military secret when I say our army marches quickly and you will, of necessity, march with us. Captain Langlade will still keep a vigilant watch over you, and you may be in readiness to depart tomorrow morning."

Robert slept that night in Langlade's little section of the camp, but, before he went to sleep, he spent much time wondering which way they would go when the dawn came. Evidently no attack upon Albany was meant, as they were too far west for such a venture, and he had reason to believe, also, that with the coming of spring the Colonials would be in such posture of defense that Montcalm himself would hesitate at such a task. He made another attempt to draw the information from Langlade, but failed utterly. Garrulous as he was otherwise, the French partisan would give no hint of his general's plans. Yet he and his warriors made obvious preparations for battle, and, before Robert went to sleep, a gigantic figure stalked into the firelight and regarded him with a grim gaze. The young prisoner's back was turned at the moment, but he seemed to feel that fierce look, beating like a wind upon his head, and, turning around, he looked full into the eyes of Tandakora.

The huge Ojibway was more huge than ever. Robert was convinced that he was the largest man he had ever seen, not only the tallest, but the broadest, and the heaviest, and his very lack of clothing—he wore only a belt, breech cloth, leggings and moccasins—seemed to increase his size. His vast shoulders, chest and arms were covered with paint, and the scars of old wounds, the whole giving to him the appearance of some primeval giant, sinister and monstrous. He carried a fine, new rifle of French make and two double barreled pistols; a tomahawk and knife swung from his belt.

Robert, nevertheless, met that full gaze firmly. He shut from his mind what he might have had to suffer from Tandakora had the Ojibway held him a captive in the forest, but here he was not Tandakora's prisoner, and he was in the midst of the French army. Centering all his will and soul into the effort he stared straight into the evil eyes of the Indian, until those of his antagonist were turned away.

"The Owl has a prisoner whom I know," said Tandakora to Langlade.

"Aye, a sprightly lad," replied the partisan. "I took him before the winter came, and I've been holding him at our village on Lake Ontario."

"It was he who, with the Onondaga, Tayoga, and the hunter, Willet, whom we call the Great Bear, carried the letters from Corlear at New York to Onontio at Quebec. The nations of the Hodenosaunee call him Dagaeoga, and he is a danger to us. I would buy him from you. I will send to you for him fifty of the finest buffalo robes taken from the great western plains."

"Not for fifty buffalo robes, Tandakora, no matter how fine they are."

"Ten packs of the finest beaver skins, fifty in each pack."

"It's no use to bid for him, Tandakora. I don't sell captives. Moreover, he has passed out of my hands. I have had my reward for him. His fate rests now with the Chevalier de St. Luc and the Marquis de Montcalm."

The Ojibway's face showed foiled malice. "It is a snake that the Owl warms in his bosom," he said, and strode away. The partisan followed him with observant eyes.

"It is evident that the Ojibway chief bears you no love, young Monsieur Lennox," he said. "Now that you have served the purposes for which I held you I wish you no harm, and so I bid you beware of Tandakora."

"Your advice is good and well meant, and for it I thank you," said Robert; "but I've known Tandakora a long time. My friends and I have met him in several encounters and we've not had the worst of them."

"I judged so by his manner. All the more reason then why you should beware of him. I repeat the warning."

Robert was not bound, and he was permitted to roll himself in a blanket and sleep with his feet to the fire, an Indian on either side of him. Save where a space had been cleared for the French army, the primeval forest, heavy in the foliage of early spring, was all about them, and the wind that sang through the leaves united with the murmuring of a creek, beside which Langlade had pitched his camp.

Slumber was slow in coming to Robert. Too much had occurred for his faculties to slip away at once into oblivion. His interview with Montcalm, his meeting with St. Luc, and the appearance of Tandakora at the camp fire, stirred him mightily. Events were certainly marching, and, while he tried to coax slumber to come, he listened to the noises of the camp and the forest. Where the French tents were spread, men were softly singing songs of their ancient land, and beyond them sentinels in neat uniforms were walking back and forth among trees that had never beheld uniforms before.

The sounds sank gradually, but Robert did not yet sleep. He found a peculiar sort of interest in detaching these murmurs from one another, the stamp of impatient horses, the moving of arms, the last dying, notes of a song, the whisper of the creek's waters, and then, plainly separate from the others, he heard a faint, unmistakable swish, a noise that he knew, that of an arrow flying through the air. Langlade knew it too, and sprang up with an angry cry.

"Now, has some warrior got hold of whiskey to indulge in this madness?" he exclaimed.

The faint swish came a second time, and Robert, who had risen to his feet, saw two arrows standing upright in the earth not twenty feet away. Langlade saw them also and swore.

"They must have come in a wide curve overhead," he said, "or they would not be standing almost straight up in the earth, and that does not seem like the madness of liquor."

He looked suspiciously at the forest, in which Indian sentinels had been posted, but which, nevertheless, was so dark that a cunning form might pass there unseen.

"There is more in this than meets the eye," muttered the partisan, and drawing the arrows from the earth he examined them by the light of the fire. Robert stood by, silent, but his eyes fell on fresh marks with a knife, near the barb on each weapon, and the great pulse in his throat leaped. The yellow flame threw out in distinct relief what the knife had cut there, and he saw on each arrow the rude but unmistakable outline of a bear.

The Owl might not determine the meaning of the picture, but the captive comprehended it at once. It was the pride of Tayoga that he was of the clan of the Bear, of the nation Onondaga, of the great League of the Hodenosaunee, and here upon the arrows was his totem or sign of the Bear. It was a message and Robert knew that it was meant for him. Had ever a man a more faithful comrade? The Onondaga was still following in the hope of making a rescue, and he would follow as long as Robert was living. Once more the young prisoner's hopes of escape rose to the zenith.

"Now what do these marks mean?" said the partisan, looking at the arrows suspiciously.

"It was merely an intoxicated warrior shooting at the moon," replied Robert, innocently, "and the cuts signify nothing."

"I'm not so sure of that. I've lived long enough among the Indians to know they don't fire away good arrows merely for bravado, and these are planted so close together it must be some sort of a signal. It may have been intended for you."

Robert was silent, and the partisan did not ask him any further questions, but, being much disturbed, sent into the forest scouts, who returned presently, unable to find anything.

"It may or it may not have been a message," he said, speaking to Robert, in his usual garrulous fashion, "but I still incline to the opinion that it was, though I may never know what the message meant, but I, Charles Langlade, have not been called the Owl for nothing. If it refers to you then your chance of escape has not increased. I hold you merely for tonight, but I hold you tight and fast. Tomorrow my responsibility ceases, and you march in the middle of Montcalm's army."

Robert made no reply, but he was in wonderful spirits, and his elation endured. His senses, in truth, were so soothed by the visible evidence that his comrade was near that he fell asleep very soon and had no dreams. The French and Indian army began its march early the next morning, and Robert found himself with about a dozen other prisoners, settlers who had been swept up in its advance. They had been surprised in their cabins, or their fields, newly cleared, and could tell him nothing, but he noticed that the march was west.

He believed they were not far from Lake Ontario, and he had no doubt that Montcalm had prepared some fell stroke. His mind settled at last upon Oswego, where the Anglo-American forces had a post supposed to be strong, and he was smitten with a fierce and commanding desire to escape and take a warning. But he was compelled to eat his heart out without result. With French and Indians all about him he had not the remotest chance and, helpless, he was compelled to watch the Marquis de Montcalm march to what he felt was going to be a French triumph.

Swarms of Indian scouts and skirmishers preceded the army and Canadian axmen cut a way for the artillery, but to Robert's great amazement these operations lasted only a short time. Almost before he could realize it they had emerged from the deep woods and he looked again upon the vast, shining reaches of Lake Ontario. Then he learned for the first time that Montcalm's army had come mostly in boats and in detachments, and was now united for attack. As he had surmised, Oswego, which the English and Americans had intended to be a great stronghold and rallying place in the west, was the menaced position.

Robert from a hill saw three forts before the French force, the largest standing upon a plateau of considerable elevation on the east bank of the river, which there flowed into the lake. It was shaped like a star, and the fortifications consisted of trunks of trees, sharpened at the ends, driven deep into the ground, and set as close together as possible. On the west side of the river was another fort of stone and clay, and four hundred yards beyond it was an unfinished stockade, so weak that its own garrison had named it in derision Rascal Fort. Some flat boats and canoes lay in the lake, and it was a man in one of these canoes who had been the first to learn of the approach of Montcalm's army, so slender had been the precautions taken by the officers in command of the forts.

"We have come upon them almost as if we had dropped from the clouds," said Langlade, exultingly, to Robert. "When they thought the Marquis de Montcalm was in Montreal, lo! he was here! It is the French who are the great leaders, the great soldiers and the great nation! Think you we would allow ourselves to be surprised as Oswego has been?"

Robert made no reply. His heart sank like a plummet in a pool. Already he heard the crackling fire of musketry from the Indians who, sheltered in the edge of the forest, were sending bullets against the stout logs of Fort Ontario, but which could offer small resistance to cannon. And while the sharpshooting went on, the French officers were planting the batteries, one of four guns directly on the strand. The work was continued at a great pace all through the night, and when Robert awoke from an uneasy sleep, in the morning, he saw that the French had mounted twenty heavy cannon, which soon poured showers of balls and grape and canister upon the log fort. He also saw St. Luc among the guns directing their fire, while Tandakora's Indians kept up an incessant and joyous yelling.

The defenders of the stockade maintained a fire from rifles and several small cannon, but it did little harm in the attacking army and Robert was soldier enough to know that the log walls could not hold. While St. Luc sent in the fire from the batteries faster and faster, a formidable force of Canadians and Indians led by Rigaud, one of the best of Montcalm's lieutenants, crossed the river, the men wading in the water up to their waists, but holding their rifles over their heads.

Tandakora was in this band, shouting savagely, and so was Langlade, but Robert and the other prisoners, left under guard on the hill, saw everything distinctly. They had no hope whatever that the chief fort, or any of the forts, could hold out. Fragments of the logs were already flying in the air as the stream of cannon balls beat upon them. The garrison made a desperate resistance, but the cramped place was crowded with women—settlers' wives—as well as men, the commander was killed, and at last the white flag was hoisted on all the forts.

Then the Indians, intoxicated with triumph and the strong liquors they had seized, rushed in and began to ply the tomahawk. Montcalm, horrified, used every effort to stop the incipient butchery, and St. Luc, Bourlamaque and, in truth, all of his lieutenants, seconded him gallantly. Tandakora and his men were compelled to return their tomahawks to their belts, and then the French army was drawn around the captives, who numbered hundreds and hundreds.

It was another French and Indian victory like that over Braddock, though it was not marked by the destruction of an army, and Robert's heart sank lower and lower. He knew that it would be appalling news to Boston, to Albany and to New York. The Marquis de Montcalm had justified the reputation that preceded him. He had struck suddenly with lightning swiftness and with terrible effect. Not only this blow, but its guarantee of others to come, filled Robert's heart with fear for the future.

The sun sank upon a rejoicing army. The Indians were still yelling and dancing, and, though they were no longer allowed to sink their tomahawks in the heads of their defenseless foes, they made imaginary strokes with them, and shouted ferociously as they leaped and capered.

Robert was on the strand near the shore of the lake, and wearied by his long day of watching that which he wished least in the world to see, he sat down on a sand heap, and put his head in his hands. Peculiarly sensitive to atmosphere and surroundings, he was, for the moment, almost without hope. But he knew, even when he was in despair, that his courage would come back. It was one of the qualities of a temperament such as his that while he might be in the depths at one hour he would be on the heights at the next.

Several of the Indians, apparently those who had got at the liquor, were careering up and down the sands, showing every sign of the blood madness that often comes in the moment of triumph upon savage minds. Robert raised his face from his hands and looked to see if Tandakora was among them, but he caught no glimpse of the gigantic Ojibway. The French soldiers who were guarding the prisoners gazed curiously at the demoniac figures. They were of the battalions Bearn and Guienne and they had come newly from France. Plunged suddenly into the wilderness, such sights as they now beheld filled them with amazement, and often created a certain apprehension. They were not so sure that their wild allies were just the kind of allies they wanted.

The sun set lower upon the savage scene, casting a dark glow over the ruined forts, the troops, the leaping savages and the huddled prisoners. One of the Indians danced and bounded more wildly than all the rest. He was tall, but slim, apparently youthful, and he wore nothing except breech cloth, leggings and moccasins, his naked body a miracle of savage painting. Robert by and by watched him alone, fascinated by his extraordinary agility and untiring enthusiasm. His figure seemed to shoot up in the air on springs, and, with a glittering tomahawk, he slew and scalped an imaginary foe over and over again, and every time the blade struck in the air he let forth a shout that would have done credit to old Stentor himself. He ranged up and down the beach, and presently, when he was close to Robert, he grew more violent than ever, as if he were worked by some powerful mechanism that would not let him rest. He had all the appearance of one who had gone quite mad, and as he bounded near them, his tomahawk circling about his head, the French guards shrank back, awed, and, at the same time, not wishing to have any conflict with their red allies, who must be handled with the greatest care.

The man paused a moment before the young prisoner, whirled his tomahawk about his head and uttered a ferocious shout. Robert looked straight into the burning eyes, started violently and then became outwardly calm, though every nerve and muscle in him was keyed to the utmost tension. "To the lake!" exclaimed the Indian under his breath and then he danced toward the water.

Robert did not know at first what the words meant, and he waited in indecision, but he saw that the care of the guards, owing to the confusion, the fact that the battle was over, and the rejoicing for victory, was relaxed. It would seem, too, that escape at such a time and place was impossible, and that circumstance increased their inattention.

The youth watched the dancing warrior, who was now moving toward the water, over which the darkness of night had spread. But the lake was groaning with a wind from the north, and several canoes near the beach were bobbing up and down. The dancer paused a moment at the very edge of the water, and looked back at Robert. Then he advanced into the waves themselves.

All the young prisoner's indecision departed in a flash. The signal was complete and he understood. He sprang violently against the French soldier who stood nearest him and knocked him to the ground. Then with three or four bounds he was at the water's edge, leaping into the canoe, just as Tayoga settled himself into place there, and, seizing a paddle, pushed away with powerful shoves.

Robert nearly upset the canoe, but the Onondaga quickly made it regain its balance, and then they were out on the lake under the kindly veil of the night. The fugitive said nothing, he knew it was no time to speak, because Tayoga's powerful back was bending with his mighty efforts and the bullets were pattering in the water behind them. It was luck that the canoe was a large one, partaking more of the nature of a boat, as Robert could remain concealed on the bottom without tipping it over, while the Onondaga continued to put all his nervous power and skill into his strokes. It was equally fortunate, also, that the night had come and that the dusk was thick, as it distracted yet further the hasty aim of the French and Indians on shore. One bullet from a French rifle grazed Robert's shoulder, another was deflected from Tayoga's paddle without striking it from his hand, but in a few minutes they were beyond the range of those who stood on the bank, although lead continued to fall in the water behind them.

"Now you can rise, Dagaeoga," said the Onondaga, "and use the extra paddle that I took the precaution to stow in the boat. Do not think because you are an escaped prisoner that you are to rest in idleness and luxury, doing no work while I do it all."

"God bless you, Tayoga!" exclaimed Robert, in the fullness of his emotion. "I'll work a week without stopping if you say so. I'm so glad to see you that I'll do anything you say, and ask no questions. But I want to tell you you're the most wonderful dancer and jumper in America!"

"I danced and jumped so well, Dagaeoga, because your need made me do so. Necessity gives a wonderful spring to the muscles. Behold how long and strong you sweep with the paddle because the bullets of the enemy impel you."

"Which way are we going, Tayoga? What is your plan?"

"Our aim at this moment, Dagaeoga, is the middle of the lake, because the sons of Onontio and the warriors of Tandakora are all along the beach, and would be waiting for us with rifle and tomahawk should we seek to land. This is but a small boat in which we sit and it could not resist the waves of a great storm, but at present it is far safer for us than any land near by."

"Of course you're right, Tayoga, you always are, but we're in the thick of the darkness now, so you rest awhile and let me do the paddling alone."

"It is a good thought, Dagaeoga, but keep straight in the direction we are going. See that you do not paddle unconsciously in a curve. We shall certainly be pursued, and although our foes cannot see us well in the dark, some out of their number are likely to blunder upon us. If it comes to a battle you will notice that I have an extra rifle and pistol for you lying in the bottom of the canoe, and that I am something more than a supple dancer and leaper."

"You not only think of everything, Tayoga, but you also do it, which is better. I shall take care to keep dead ahead."

Robert in his turn bent forward and plied the paddle. He was not only fresh, but the wonderful thrill of escape gave him a strength far beyond the normal, and the great canoe fairly danced over the waters toward the dusky deeps of the lake, while the Onondaga crouched at the other end of the canoe, rifle in hand, intently watching the heavy pall of dusk behind them.

Their situation was still dangerous in the extreme, but the soul of Tayoga swelled with triumph. Tandakora, the Ojibway, had rejoiced because he had expected a great taking of scalps, but the purer spirit of the Onondaga soared into the heights because he had saved his comrade of a thousand dangers. He still saw faintly through the darkness the campfires of the victorious French and Indian army, and he heard the swish of paddles, but he did not yet discern any pursuing canoe. He detached his eyes for a moment from the bank of dusk in front of him, and looked up at the skies. The clouds and vapors kept him from seeing the great star upon which his patron saint, Tododaho, sat, but he knew that he was there, and that he was watching over him. He could not have achieved so much in the face of uttermost peril and then fail in the lesser danger.

The canoe glided swiftly on toward the wider reaches of the lake, and the Onondaga never relaxed his watchfulness, for an instant. He was poised in the canoe, every nerve and muscle ready to leap in a second into activity, while his ears were strained for the sounds of paddles or oars. Now he relied, as often before, more upon hearing than sight. Presently a sound came, and it was that of oars. A boat parted the wall of dusk and he saw that it contained both French and Indians, eight in all, the warriors uttering a shout as they beheld the fugitive canoe.

"Keep steadily on, Dagaeoga," said the Onondaga. "I have my long barreled rifle, and it will carry much farther than those of the foe. In another minute it will tell them they had best stop, and if they will not obey its voice then I will repeat the command with your rifle."

Robert heard the sharp report of Tayoga's weapon, and then a cry from the pursuing boat, saying the bullet had found its mark.

"They still come, though in a hesitating manner," said Tayoga, "and I must even give them a second notice."

Now Robert heard the crack of the other rifle, and the answering cry, signifying that its bullet, too, had sped home.

"They stop now," said Tayoga. "They heed the double command." He rapidly reloaded the rifles, and Robert, who saw an uncommonly thick bank of dusk ahead, paddled directly into the heart of it. They paused there a few moments and neither saw nor heard any pursuers. Tayoga put down the rifles, now ready again for his deadly aim, and the two kept for a long time a straight course toward the center of the lake.

CHAPTER X.
THE FLIGHT OF THE TWO

Tayoga, into whose hands Robert had entrusted himself with the uttermost faith, at last said stop, and drawing the paddles into the canoe they took long, deep breaths of relief. Around them was a world of waters, silver under the moon and stars now piercing the dusk, and the Onondaga could see the vast star on which sat the mighty chieftain who had gone away four hundred years ago to eternal life.

"O Tododaho," he murmured, "thou hast guarded us well."

"Where do you think we are, Tayoga?" asked Robert.

"Perhaps twenty miles from land," replied the Onondaga, "and the farther the better."

"True, Tayoga. Never before did I see a big lake look so kindly. If it didn't require so much effort I'd like to go to the very center of it and stay there for a week."

"Even as it is, Dagaeoga, we will wait here a while and take the long rest we need."

"And while we're doing nothing but swing in our great canoe, Tayoga, I want to thank you for all you've done for me. I'd been a prisoner much longer than I wished."

"It but repays my debt, Dagaeoga. You will recall that you helped to save me from the hands of Tandakora when he was going to burn me at the stake. My imprisonment was short, but I have been in the forest the whole winter and spring seeking to take you from Langlade."

"All of which goes to show, Tayoga, that we must allow only one of us to be captured at a time. The other must go free in order to rescue the one taken."

Although Robert's tone was light, his feeling was far from frivolous, but he had been at extreme tension so long that he was compelled to seek relief.

"How did you manage it, Tayoga?" he asked.

"In the confusion of the attack on the forts and the rejoicing that followed it was easy," replied the Onondaga. "When so many others were dancing and leaping it attracted no attention for me to dance and leap also, and I selected, without interference, the boat, the extra paddle, weapons and ammunition that I wished. Areskoui and Tododaho did the rest. Do you feel stronger now, Dagaeoga?"

"Aye, I'm still able to handle the paddle. I suppose we'd better seek a landing. We can't stay out in the lake forever. Tayoga, you've taken the part of Providence itself. Now did it occur to you in your infinite wisdom, while you were storing paddles, weapons and ammunition in this boat, to store food also?"

The Onondaga's smile was wide and satisfying.

"I thought of that, too, Dagaeoga," he replied, "because I knew our journey, if we should be so fortunate as to have a journey, would take us out on the lake, and I knew, also, that no matter how many hardships and dangers Dagaeoga might pass through, the time would come when he would be hungry. It is always so with Dagaeoga."

He took a heavy knapsack from the bottom of the canoe and opened it.

"It is a French knapsack," he said, "and it contains both bread and meat, which we will enjoy."

They ate in great content, and their spirits rose to an extraordinary degree, though Tayoga regretted the absence of clothing which his disguise had made necessary. Having been educated with white lads, and having associated with white people so much, he was usually clad as completely as they, either in their fashion or in his own full Indian costume.

"My infinite wisdom was not so infinite that it told me to take a blanket," he said, "and the wind coming down from the Canadian shore is growing cold."

"I'm surprised to hear you speak of such trifles as that, Tayoga, when we've been dealing with affairs of life and death."

"We are cold or we are warm, Dagaeoga, and peril and suffering do not alter it. But lo! the wind is bringing the great mists with it, and we will escape in them."

They turned the canoe toward a point far to the east of the Indian camp and began to paddle, not hastily but with long, slow, easy strokes that sent the canoe over the water at a great rate. The fogs and vapors were thick and close about them, but Tayoga knew the direction. Robert asked him if he had heard of Willet, and the Onondaga said he had not seen him, but he had learned from a Mohawk runner that the Great Bear had reached Waraiyageh with the news of St. Luc's prospective advance, and Tayoga had also contrived to get news through to him that he was lying in the forest, waiting a chance to effect the rescue of Robert.

Toward morning they landed on a shore, clothed in deep and primeval forest, and with reluctance abandoned their canoe.

"It is an Abenaki craft," said Tayoga. "It is made well, it has served us well, and we will treat it well."

Instead of leaving it on the lake to the mercy of storms they drew it into some bushes at the mouth of a small creek, where it would stay securely, and probably serve some day some chance traveler. Then they plunged into the deep forest, but when they saw a smoke Robert remained hidden while Tayoga went on, but with the intention of returning.

The Onondaga was quite sure the smoke indicated the presence of a small village and his quest was for clothes.

"Let Dagaeoga rest in peace here in the thicket," he said, "and when I come back I shall be clad as a man. Have no fears for me. I will not enter the village Until after dark."

He glided away without noise, and Robert, having supreme confidence in him, lay down among the bushes, which were so dense that the keenest eyes could not have seen him ten feet away. His frame was relaxed so thoroughly after his immense exertions and he felt such utter thankfulness at his escape that he soon fell into a deep slumber rather than sleep, and when he awoke the dark had come, bringing with it Tayoga.

"Lo, Dagaeoga," said the Onondaga, in a tone of intense satisfaction, "I have done well. It is not pleasant to me to take the property of others, but in this case what I have seized must have been captured from the English. No watch was kept in the village, as they had heard of their great victory and the warriors were away. I secured three splendid blankets, two of green and one of brown. Since you have a coat, Dagaeoga, you can have one green blanket and I will take the other two, one to wear and the other to sleep in. I also took away more powder and lead, and as I have my bullet molds we can increase our ammunition when we need it. I have added, too, a supply of venison to our beef and bread."

"You're an accomplished burglar, Tayoga, but I think that in this case your patron saint, Tododaho, will forgive you. I'm devoutly glad of the blanket. I feel stiff and sore, after such great exertions, and I find I've grown cold with the coming of the dark."

"It is a relapse," said Tayoga with some anxiety. "The strain on mind and body has been too great. Better wrap yourself in the blanket at once, and lie quiet in the thicket."

Robert was prompt to take his advice, as his body was hot and his sight was wavering. He felt that he was going to be ill and he might get it over all the quicker by surrendering to it at once. He rolled the blanket tightly about himself and lay down on the softest spot he could find. In the night he became delirious and talked continually of Langlade, St. Luc and Montcalm. But Tayoga watched by him continually until late, when he hunted through the forest by moonlight for some powerful herbs known to the Indians. In the morning he beat them and bruised them and cooked them as best he could without utensils, and then dropped the juices into his comrade's mouth, after which he carefully put out the fire, lest it be seen by savage rovers.

Robert was soon very much better. He had a profuse perspiration and came out of his unconscious state, but was quite weak. He was also thoroughly ashamed of himself.

"Nice time for me to be breaking down," he said, "here in the wilderness near an Indian village, hundreds of miles from any of our friends, save those who are captured. I make my apologies, Tayoga."

"They are not needed," said the Onondaga. "You defended me with your life when I was wounded and the wolves sought to eat me, now I repay again. There is nothing for Dagaeoga to do but to keep on perspiring, see that the blanket is still wrapped around him, and tonight I will get something in which to cook the food he needs."

"How will you do that?"

"I will go again to my village. I call it mine because it supplies what we need and I will return with the spoil. Bide you in peace, Dagaeoga. You have called me an accomplished burglar. I am more, I am a great one."

Robert had the utmost confidence in him, and it was justified. When he awoke from a restless slumber, Tayoga stood beside him, holding in his hand a small iron kettle made in Canada, and a great iron spoon.

"They are the best they had in the village," he said. "It is not a large and rich village and so its possessions are not great, but I think these will do. I have also brought with me some very tender meat of a young deer that I found in one of the lodges."

"You're all you claimed to be and more, Tayoga," said Robert earnestly and gratefully.

The Onondaga lighted a fire in a dip, and cutting the deer into tiny bits made a most appetizing soup, which Robert's weak stomach was able to retain and to crave more.

"No," said Tayoga, "enough for tonight, but you shall have twice as much in the morning. Now, go to sleep again."

"I haven't been doing anything but sleep for the last day or two. I want to get up and walk."

"And have your fever come back. Besides, you are not strong enough yet to walk more than a few steps."

Robert knew that he would be forced to obey, and he passed the night partly in dozing, and partly in staring at the sky. In the morning he was very hungry and showed an increase of strength. Tayoga, true to his word, gave him a double portion of the soup, but still forbade sternly any attempt at walking.

"Lie there, Dagaeoga," he said, "and let the wind blow over you, and I'll go farther into the forest to see if friend or enemy be near."

Robert, feeling that he must, lay peacefully on his back after the Onondaga left him. He was free from fever, but he knew that Tayoga was right in forbidding him to walk. It would be several days yet before he could fulfill his old duties, as an active and powerful forest runner. Yet he was very peaceful because the soreness of body that had troubled him was gone and strength was flowing back into his veins. Despite the fact that he was lying on his back alone in the wilderness, with savage foes not far away, he believed that he had very much for which to be grateful. He had been taken almost by a miracle out of the hands of his foes, and, when he was ill and in his weakness might have been devoured by wild beasts or might have starved to death, the most loyal and resourceful of comrades had been by his side to save him.

He saw the great star on which Tayoga's Tododaho lived, and he accepted so much of the Iroquois theology, believing that it was in spirit and essence the same as his own Christian belief, that he almost imagined he could see the great Onondaga chieftain who had gone away four centuries ago. In any event, it was a beneficent star, and he was glad that it shone down on him so brilliantly.

Tayoga before his departure had loaned him one of his blankets and now he lay upon it, with the other wrapped around him, his loaded pistol in his belt and his loaded rifle lying by his side. The fire that the Onondaga had built in the dip not far away had been put out carefully and the ashes had been scattered.

Although it was midsummer, the night, as often happened in that northern latitude, had come on cool, and the warmth of the blankets was not unwelcome. Robert knew that he was only a mote in all that vast wilderness, but the contiguity of the Indian village might cause warriors, either arriving or departing, to pass near him. So he was not surprised when he heard footsteps in the bushes not far away, and then the sound of voices. Instinctively he tried to press his body into the earth, and he also lifted carefully the loaded rifle, but second thought told him he was not likely to be seen.

Warriors presently came so near that they were visible, and to his surprise and alarm he saw the huge figure of Tandakora among them. They were about a dozen in number, walking in the most leisurely manner and once stopped very close to him to talk. Although he raised himself up a little and clutched the rifle more tightly he was still hopeful that they would not see him. The Ojibway chieftain was in full war paint, with a fine new American rifle, and also a small sword swinging from his belt. Both were undoubtedly trophies of Oswego, and it was certain that after carrying the sword for a while as a prize he would discard it. Indians never found much use for swords.

Robert always believed that Tayoga's Tododaho protected him that night, because for a while all the chances were against him. As the warriors stood near talking a frightened deer started up in the thicket, and Tandakora himself brought it down with a lucky bullet, the unfortunate animal falling not thirty yards from the hidden youth. They removed the skin and cut it into portions where it lay, the whole task taking about a half hour, and all the time Robert, lying under the brush, saw them distinctly.

He was in mortal fear lest one of them wander into the dip where Tayoga had built the fire, and see traces of the ashes, but they did not do so. Twice warriors walked in that direction and his heart was in his mouth, but in neither case did the errand take them so far. Tandakora was not alone in bearing Oswego spoils. Nearly all of them had something, a rifle, a pistol or a sword, and two wore officers' laced coats over their painted bodies. The sight filled Robert with rage. Were his people to go on this way indefinitely, sacrificing men and posts in unrelated efforts? Would they allow the French, with inferior numbers, to beat them continuously? He had seen Montcalm and talked with him, and he feared everything from that daring and tenacious leader.

While the Indians prepared the deer the moon and stars came out with uncommon brilliancy, filling the forest with a misty, silver light. Robert now saw Tandakora and his men so clearly that it seemed impossible for them not to see him. Once more he had the instinctive desire to press himself into the earth, but his mind told him that absolute silence was the most necessary thing. As he lay, he could have picked off Tandakora with a bullet from his rifle, and, so far as the border was concerned, he felt that his own life was worth the sacrifice, but he loved his life and the Ojibway might be put out of the way at some other time and place.

Tayoga's Tododaho protected him once more. Two of the Indians wanted water and they started in search of a brook which was never far away in that region. It seemed for a moment or two that they would walk directly into the dip, where scattered ashes lay, but the great Onondaga turned them aside just in time and they found at another point the water they wished. Robert's extreme tension lasted until they were back with the others. Nevertheless their harmless return encouraged him in the belief that the star was working in his behalf.

The Indians were in no hurry. They talked freely over their task of dressing and quartering the deer, and often they were so near that Robert could hear distinctly what they said, but only once or twice did they use a dialect that he could understand, and then they were speaking of the great victory of Oswego, in which they confirmed the inference, drawn from the spoils, that they like Tandakora had taken a part. They were in high good humor, expecting more triumphs, and regarded the new French commander, Montcalm, as a great and invincible leader.

Robert was glad, then, that he was such an insignificant mote in the wilderness and had he the power he would have made himself so small that he would have become invisible, but as that was impossible he still trusted in Tayoga's Tododaho. The Indian chief gave two of the warriors an order, and they started on a course that would have brought them straight to him. The lad gave himself up for lost, but, intending to make a desperate fight for it, despite his weakness, his hand crept to the hammer and trigger of his rifle. Something moved in the thicket, a bear, perhaps, or a lynx, and the two Indians, when they were within twenty feet of him, turned aside to investigate it. Then they went on, and it was quite clear again to Robert that he had been right about the friendly intervention of Tododaho.

Nor was it long until the truth was demonstrated to him once more, and in a conclusive manner. The entire party departed, taking with them the portions of the deer, and they passed so very close to him that their wary eyes, which always watched on all sides, would have been compelled to see him, if Tododaho, or perhaps it was Areskoui, or even Manitou, had not seen fit just at that moment to draw a veil before the moon and stars and make the shadow so deep under the bush where young Lennox lay that he was invisible, although they stepped within fifteen feet of him. They went on in their usual single file, disappearing in the direction of the village, while he lay still and gave thanks.

They had not been gone more than fifteen minutes when there was a faint rustle in the thicket, and Tayoga stood before him.

"I was hid in a clump of weeds not far away and I saw," said the Onondaga. "It was a narrow escape, but you were protected by the great powers of the earth and the air. Else they would have seen you."

"It is so," said Robert, devoutly, "and it makes me all the more glad to see you, Tayoga. I hope your journey, like all the others, has been fruitful."

The Onondaga smiled in the dusk.

"It is a good village to which I go," he replied in his precise fashion. "You will recall that they had in Albany what they call in the English tongue a chemist's shop. It is such that I sought in the village, and I found it in one lodge, the owners of which were absent, and which I could reach at my leisure. Here is a gourd of Indian tea, very strong, made from the essence of the sassafras root. It will purge the impurities from your blood, and, in another day, your appetite will be exceedingly strong. Then your strength will grow so fast that in a short time you will be ready for a long journey. I have also brought a small sack filled with samp."

Robert uttered a little cry of joy. He craved bread, or at least something that would take its place, and samp, a variation of which is known as hominy, was a most acceptable substitute.

"You are, in truth, a most efficient burglar, Tayoga," he said.

"I obtained also information," continued the Onondaga. "While I lay in one of the lodges, hidden under furs, I heard two of the old men talking. They believe since they have taken Oswego that all things are possible for them and the French. Montcalm appears to them the greatest of all leaders and he will take them from one victory to another. Their defeat by Andiatarocte is forgotten, and they plan a great advance toward the south. But they intend first to sweep up all the scouts and bands of the Americans and English. Their first attack will be upon Rogers, him whom we call the Mountain Wolf."

"Rogers! Is he somewhere near us?" exclaimed Robert eagerly.

"Far to the east toward Andiatarocte, but they mean to strike him. The Frenchmen De Courcelles and Jumonville will join with Tandakora, then St. Luc will go too and he will lead a great force against the Mountain Wolf, with whom, I suspect, our friend the Great Bear now is, hoping perhaps, as they hunt through the forest, to discover some traces of us."

"I knew all along, Tayoga, that Dave would seek me and rescue me if you didn't, or if I didn't rescue myself, provided I remained alive, as you see I did."

"The Great Bear is the most faithful of all comrades. He would never desert a friend in the hands of the enemy."

"You think then that we should try to meet the Mountain Wolf and his rangers?"

"Of a certainty. As soon as Dagaeoga is strong enough. Now lie still, while I scout through the forest. If no enemy is near I will heat the tea, and then you must drink, and drink deep."

He made a wide circuit, and, coming back, lighted a little fire on which he warmed the tea in the pot that he had taken from the village on an earlier night. Then, under the insistence of Tayoga, Robert drank a quantity that amounted to three cups, and soon fell into a deep sleep, from which he awoke the next day with an appetite so sharp that he felt able to bite a big piece out of a tree.

"I think I'll go hunt a buffalo, kill him and eat him whole," he said in a large, round voice.

"If so Dagaeoga will have to roam far," said Tayoga sedately. "The buffalo is not found east of the Alleghanies, as you well know."

"Of course I know it, but what are time and distance to a Samson like me? I say I will go forth and slay a buffalo, unless I am fed at once and in enormous quantities."

"Would a haunch of venison and a gallon of samp help Dagaeoga a little?"

"Yes, a little, they'd serve as appetizers for something real and substantial to come."

"Then if you feel so strong and are charged so full of ambition you can help cook breakfast. You have had an easy time, Dagaeoga, but life henceforth will not be all eating and sleeping."

They had a big and pleasant breakfast together and Robert rejoiced in his new vigor. It was wonderful to be so strong after having been so weak, it was like life after death, and he was eager to start at once.

"It is a good thing to have been ill," he said, "because then you know how fine it is to be well."

"But we will not depart before tomorrow," said the Onondaga decisively.

"And why?"

"Because you have lived long enough in the wilderness, Dagaeoga, to know that one must always fight the weather. Look into the west, and you will see a little cloud moving up from the horizon. It does not amount to much at present, but it contains the seed of great things. It has been sent by the Rain God, and it will not do yet for Dagaeoga, despite his new strength, to travel in the rain."

Robert became anxious as he watched the little cloud, which seemed to swell as he looked at it, and which soon assumed an angry hue. He knew that Tayoga had told the truth. Coming out of his fever it would be a terrible risk for him to become drenched.

"We will make a shelter such as we can in the dip where we built the fire," said Tayoga, "and now you can use your new strength as much as you will in wielding a tomahawk."

They cut small saplings with utmost speed and speedily accomplished one of the most difficult tasks of the border, making a rude brush shelter which with the aid of their blankets would protect them from the storm. By the time they had finished, the little cloud which had been at first a mere signal had grown so prodigiously that it covered the whole heavens, and the day became almost as dark as twilight. The lightning began to flash in great, blazing strokes, and the thunder was so nearly continuous that the earth kept up an incessant jarring. Then the rain poured heavily and Robert saw Tayoga's wisdom. Although the shelter and his blanket kept the rain from him he felt cold in the damp, and shivered as if with a chill.

"When the storm stops, which will not be before dark," said Tayoga, "I shall go to the village and get you a heavy buffalo robe. They have some, acquired in trade from the Indians of the western plains, and one of them belongs to you. So, Dagaeoga, I will get it."

"Tayoga, you have taken too much risk for me already. I can make out very well as I am, and suppose we start tonight in search of Rogers and Willet."

"I mean to have my way, because in this case my way is right. We work together as partners, and the partnership becomes ineffective when one member of it cannot endure the hardships of a long march, and perhaps of battle. And has not Dagaeoga said that I am an accomplished burglar? I prove it anew tonight. As soon as the rain ceases I will go to the village, the great storehouse of our supplies."

The Onondaga spoke in a light tone with a whimsical inflection, but Robert saw that he was intensely in earnest, and that it was not worth while for him to say more. The great storm passed on to the southward, the rain sank to a drizzle, but it was very cold in the forest, and Robert's teeth chattered, despite every effort to control his body.

"I go, Dagaeoga," said Tayoga, "and I shall return with the great, warm buffalo robe that belongs to you."

Then he melted without noise into the darkness and Robert was alone. He knew the mission of the Onondaga to be a perilous one, but he did not doubt his success. The cold drizzle fell on the shelter of brush and saplings, and some of it seeped through. Now and then a drop found its way down his neck, and it felt like ice. Physically he was very miserable, and it began to depress his spirit. He hoped that Tayoga would not be long in obtaining the buffalo robe.

The thunder moaned a little far to the south, and then died down entirely. There were one or two stray flashes of lightning and then no more. He sank into a sort of doze that was more like a stupor, from which he was awakened by a dusky figure in the doorway of the little shelter. It was Tayoga, and he bore a heavy dark bundle over his arm.

"I have brought the buffalo robe that belongs to you, Dagaeoga," he said cheerfully. "It was in the lodge of the head chief of the village and I had to wait until he went forth to greet Tandakora, who came with a band of his warriors to claim shelter, food and rest. Then I took what was your own and here it is, one of the finest I have ever seen."

He held up the great buffalo robe, tanned splendidly and rich in fur and the sight of it made Robert's teeth stop chattering. He wrapped it around his body and sufficient warmth came back.

"You're a marvel, Tayoga," he said. "Does the village contain anything else that belongs to us?"

"Nothing that I can think of now. The rain will cease entirely in an hour, and then we will start."

His prediction was right, and they set forth in the dark forest, Robert wearing the great buffalo robe which stored heat and consequent energy in his frame. But the woods were so wet, and it was so difficult to find a good trail that they did not make very great progress, and when dawn came they were only a few miles away. Robert's strength, however, stood the test, and they dared to light a fire and have a warm breakfast. Much refreshed they plunged on anew, hunting for friends who could not be much more than motes in the wilderness. Robert hoped that some chance would enable him to meet Willet, to whom he owed so much, and who stood in the place of a father to him. It did not seem possible that the Great Bear could have fallen in one of the numerous border skirmishes, which must have been fought since his capture. He could not associate death with a man so powerful and vital as Willet.

The day was bright and warm, and he took off the buffalo robe. It was quite a weight to be carried, but he knew he would need it again when night came and particularly if there were other storms. They saw many trails in the afternoon and Tayoga was quite sure they were made by war bands. Nearly all of them led southeast.

"The savages in the west and about the Great Lakes," he said, "have heard of the victory at Oswego, and so they pour out to the French standard, expecting many scalps and great spoils. Whenever the French win a triumph it means more warriors for them."

"And may not some of the bands going to the war stumble on our own trail?"

"It is likely, Dagaeoga. But if it comes to battle see how much better it is that you should be strong and able."

"Yes, I concede now, Tayoga, that it was right for us to wait as long as we did."

The trails grew much more numerous as they advanced. Evidently swarms of warriors were about them and before midday Tayoga halted.

"It will not be wise for us to advance farther," he said. "We must seek some hiding place."

"Hark to that!" exclaimed Robert.

A breeze behind them bore a faint shout to his ear. Tayoga listened intently, and it was repeated once.

"Pursuit!" he said briefly. "They have come by chance upon our trail. It may be Tandakora himself and it is unfortunate. They will never leave us now, unless they are driven back."

"Then we'd better turn back towards the north, as the thickest of the swarms are sure to be to the south of us."

"It is so. Again the longest of roads becomes the safest for us, but we will not make it wholly north, we will bear to the east also. I once left a canoe, hidden in the edge of a lake there, and we may find it."

"What will we do with it if we find it?"

"Tandakora will not be able to follow the trail of a canoe. But now we must press forward with all speed, Dagaeoga. See, there is a smoke in the south and now another answers it in the north. They are talking about us."

Robert saw the familiar signals which always meant peril to them, and he was willing to go forward at the uttermost speed. He had become hardened in a measure to danger, though it seemed to him that he was passing through enough of it to last a lifetime. But his soul rose to meet it.

They used all the customary devices to hide their traces, wading when there was water, walking on stones or logs when they were available, but they knew these stratagems would only delay Tandakora, they could not throw him off the trail entirely. They hoped more from the coming dark, and, when night came, it found them going at great speed. Just at twilight they heard a faint shout again and the faint shout in reply, telling them the pursuit was maintained, but the night fortunately proved to be very dark, and, an hour or two later, they came to a heavy windrow, the result of some old hurricane into which they drew for shelter and rest. They knew that not even the Indian trailers could find them there in such darkness, and for the present they were without apprehension.

"Do you think they will pass us in the night?" asked Robert.

"No," replied Tayoga. "They will wait until the dawn and pick up the trail anew."

"Then we'd better start again about midnight."

"I think so, too."

Meanwhile, lying comfortably among the fallen trees and leaves, they waited in silence.

CHAPTER XI.
THE MYSTIC VOYAGE

The long stay in the windrow served Robert well, more than atoning for the drain made upon his strength by their rapid flight. In three or four hours he was back in his normal state, and he felt proudly that he was now as good as he had ever been. The night, as they had expected, was cold, and he was thankful that he had hung on to the buffalo robe, in which he wrapped himself once more, while Tayoga was snug between two big blankets.

Robert dozed, but he was awakened by something stirring near them, and he sat up with his finger on the trigger of his rifle. The Onondaga was already listening and watching, ready with his weapon. Presently the white youth heard his companion laughing softly, and his own tension relaxed, as he knew Tayoga would not laugh without good cause.

"It is a bear," said Tayoga, "and he has a lair in the windrow, not more than twenty feet away. He has been out very late at night, too late for a good, honest home-keeping bear, but he is back at last, and he smells us."

"And alarmed by the odor he does not know whether to enter his home or not. Well, I hope he'll conclude to take his rest. We eat bear at times, Tayoga, but just now I wouldn't dream of harming one."

"Nor would I, Dagaeoga, and maybe the bear will divine that we are harmless, that is, Tododaho or Areskoui will tell him in some way of which we know nothing that his home is his own to be entered without fear."

"I think I hear him moving now, and also puffing a little."

"You hear aright, Dagaeoga. Tododaho has whispered to him, even as I said, and he is going into his den which I know is snug and warm, in the very thickest part of the windrow. Now he is lying down in it with the logs and branches about him, and soon he will be asleep, dreaming happy dreams of tender roots and wild honey with no stings of bees to torment him."

"You grow quite poetical, Tayoga."

"Although foes are hunting us, I feel the spirit of the forest and of peace strong upon me, Dagaeoga. Moreover, Tododaho, as I told you, has whispered to the animals that we are not to be feared tonight. Hark to the tiny rustling just beyond the log against which we lie!"

"Yes, I hear it, and what do you make of it, Tayoga?"

"Rabbits seeking their nests. They, too, have snuffed about, noticing the man odor, which man himself cannot detect, and once they started away in alarm, but now they are reassured, and they have settled themselves down to sleep in comfort and security."

"Tayoga, you talk well and fluently, but as I have told you before, you talk out of a dictionary."

"But as I learned my English out of a dictionary I cannot talk otherwise. That is why my language is always so much superior to yours, Dagaeoga."

"I'll let it be as you claim it, you boaster, but what noise is that now? I seem to hear the light sound of hoofs."

The Onondaga raised himself to his full height and peered over the dense masses of trunks and boughs, his keen eyes cutting the thick dusk. Then he sank back, and, when he replied, his voice showed distinct pleasure.

"Two deer have come into a little open space, around which the arms of the windrow stretch nearly all the way, and they have crouched there, where they will rest, indifferent to the nearness of the bear. Truly, O Dagaeoga, we have come into the midst of a happy family, and we have been accepted, for the night, as members of it."

"It must be so, Tayoga, because I see a figure much larger than that of the deer approaching. Look to the north and behold that shadow there under the trees."

"I see it, Dagaeoga. It is the great northern moose, a bull. Perhaps he has wandered down from Canada, as they are rare here. They are often quarrelsome, but the bull is going to take his rest, within the shelter of the windrow, and leave its other people at peace. Now he has found a good place, and he will be quiet for the night."

"Suppose you sleep a while, Tayoga. You have done all the watching for a long time, and, as I'm fit and fine now, it's right for me to take up my share of the burden."

"Very well, but do not fail to awaken me in about three hours. We must not be caught here in the morning by the warriors."

He was asleep almost instantly, and Robert sat in a comfortable position with his rifle across his knees. Responsibility brought back to him self-respect and pride. He was now a full partner in the partnership, and will and strength together made his faculties so keen that it would have been difficult for anything about the windrow to have escaped his attention. He heard the light rustlings of other animals coming to comfort and safety, and flutterings as birds settled on upthrust boughs, many of which were still covered with leaves. Once he heard a faint shout deep in the forest, brought by the wind a great distance, and he was sure that it was the cry of their Indian pursuers. Doubtless it was a signal and had connection with the search, but he felt no alarm. Under the cover of darkness Tayoga and he were still motes in the wilderness, and, while the night lasted, Tandakora could not find them.

When he judged that the three hours had passed he awoke the Onondaga and they took their silent way north by east, covering much more distance by dawn. But both were certain that warriors of Tandakora would pick up their traces again that day. They would spread through the forest, and, when one of them struck the trail, a cry would be sufficient to call the others. But they pressed on, still adopting every possible device to throw off their pursuers, and they continued their flight several days, always through an unbroken forest, over hills and across many streams, large and small. It seemed, at times, to Robert that the pursuit must have dropped away, but Tayoga was quite positive that Tandakora still followed. The Ojibway, he said, had divined the identity of the fugitives and every motive would make him follow, even all the way across the Province of New York and beyond, if need be.

They came at last to a lake, large, beautiful, extending many miles through the wilderness, and Tayoga, usually so calm, uttered a little cry of delight, which Robert repeated, but in fuller volume.

"I think lakes are the finest things in the world," he said. "They always stir me."

"And that is why Manitou put so many and such splendid ones in the land of the Hodenosaunee," said Tayoga. "This is Ganoatohale, which you call in your language Oneida, and it is on its shores that I hid the canoe of which I spoke to you. I think we shall find it just as I left it."

"I devoutly hope so. A canoe and paddles would give me much pleasure just now, and Ganoatohale will leave no trail."

They walked northward along the shore of the lake, and they came to a place where many tall reeds grew thick and close in shallow water. Tayoga plunged into the very heart of them and Robert's heart rose with a bound, when he reappeared dragging after him a large and strong canoe, containing two paddles.

"It has rested in quiet waiting for us," he said. "It is a good canoe, and it knew that I would come some time to claim it."

"Before we go upon our voyage," said Robert, "I think we shall have to pay some attention to the question of food. My pouch is about empty."

"And so is mine. We shall have to take the risk, Dagaeoga, and shoot a deer. Tandakora may be so far behind that none of his warriors will hear the shot, but even so we cannot live without eating. We will, however, hunt from the canoe. Since the war began, all human beings have gone away from this lake, and the deer should be plentiful."

They launched the canoe on the deep waters, and the two took up the paddles, sending their little craft northward, with slow, deliberate strokes. They had the luck within the hour to find a deer drinking, and with equal luck Robert slew it at the first shot. They would have taken the body into the canoe, but the burden was too great, and Tayoga cut it up and dressed it with great dispatch, while Robert watched. Then they made room for the four quarters and again paddled northward. Fearing that Tandakora had come much nearer, while they were busy with the deer, they did not dare the wide expanse of the lake, but remained for the present under cover of the overhanging forest on the western shore.

"If we put the lake between Tandakora and ourselves," said Robert, "we ought to be safe."

"It is likely that they, too, have canoes hidden in the reeds," said Tayoga. "Since the French and their allies have spread so far south they would provide for the time when they wanted to go upon the waters of Ganoatohale. It is almost a certainty that we shall be pursued upon the lake."

They continued northward, never leaving the dark shadow cast by the dense leafage, and, as they went slowly, they enjoyed the luxury of the canoe. After so much walking through the wilderness it was a much pleasanter method of traveling. But they did not forget vigilance, continually scanning the waters, and Robert's heart gave a sudden beat as he saw a black dot appear upon the surface of the lake in the south. It was followed in a moment by another, then another and then three more.

"It is the band of Tandakora, beyond a doubt," said Tayoga with conviction. "They had their canoes among the reeds even as we had ours, and now it is well for us that water leaves no trail."

"Shall we hide the canoe again, and take to the woods?"

"I think not, Dagaeoga. They have had no chance to see us yet. We will withdraw among the reeds until night comes, and then under its cover cross Ganoatohale."

Keeping almost against the bank, they moved gently until they came to a vast clump of reeds into which they pushed the canoe, while retaining their seats in it. In the center they paused and waited. From that point they could see upon the lake, while remaining invisible themselves, and they waited.

The six canoes or large boats, they could not tell at the distance which they were, went far out into the lake, circled around for a while, and then bore back toward the western shore, along which they passed, inspecting it carefully, and drawing steadily nearer to Robert and Tayoga.

"Now, let us give thanks to Tododaho, Areskoui and to Manitou himself," said the Onondaga, "that they have been pleased to make the reeds grow in this particular place so thick and so tall."

"Yes," said Robert, "they're fine reeds, beautiful reeds, a greater bulwark to us just now than big oaks could be. Think you, Tayoga, that you recognize the large man in the first boat?"

"Aye, Dagaeoga, I know him, as you do also. How could we mistake our great enemy, Tandakora? It is a formidable fleet, too strong for us to resist, and, like the wise man, we hide when we cannot fight."

Robert's pulses beat so hard they hurt, but he would not show any uneasiness in the presence of Tayoga, and he sat immovable in the canoe. Nearer and nearer came the Indian fleet, partly of canoes and partly of boats, and he counted in them sixteen warriors, all armed heavily. Now he prayed to Manitou, and to his own God who was the same as Manitou, that no thought of pushing among the reeds would enter Tandakora's head. The fleet soon came abreast of them, but his prayers were answered, as Tandakora led ahead, evidently thinking the fugitives would not dare to hide and lie in waiting, but would press on in flight up the western shore.

"I could pick him off from here with a bullet," said Robert, looking at the huge, painted chest of the Ojibway chief.

"But our lives would be the forfeit," the Onondaga whispered back.

"I had no intention of doing it."

"Now they have passed us, and for the while we are safe. They will go on up the lake, until they find no trace of us there, and then Tandakora will come back."

"But how does he know we have a canoe?"

"He does not know it, but he feels sure of it because our trail led straight to the lake, and we would not purposely come up against such a barrier, unless we knew of a way to cross it."

"That sounds like good logic. Of course when they return they'll make a much more thorough search of the lake's edge, and then they'd be likely to find us if we remained here."

"It is so, but perhaps the night will come before Tandakora, and then we'll take flight upon the lake."

They pushed their canoe back to the edge of the reeds, and watched the Indian boats passing in single file northward, becoming smaller and smaller until they almost blended with the water, but both knew they would return, and in that lay their great danger. The afternoon was well advanced, but the sun was very brilliant, and it was hot within the reeds. Great quantities of wild fowl whirred about them and along the edges of the lake.

"No warriors are in hiding near us," said Tayoga, "or the wild fowl would fly away. We can feel sure that we have only Tandakora and his band to fear."

Robert had never watched the sun with more impatience. It was already going down the western arch, but it seemed to him to travel with incredible slowness. Far in the north the Indian boats were mere black dots on the water, but they were turning. Beyond a doubt Tandakora was now coming back.

"Suppose we go slowly south, still keeping in the shadow of the trees," he said. "We can gain at least that much advantage."

Fortunately the scattered fringe of reeds and bushes, growing in the water, extended far to the south, and they were able to keep in their protecting shadow a full hour, although their rate of progress was not more than one-third that of the Indians, who were coming without obstruction in open water. Nevertheless, it was a distinct gain, and, meanwhile, they awaited the coming of the night with the deepest anxiety. They recognized that their fate turned upon a matter of a half hour or so. If only the night would arrive before Tandakora! Robert glanced at the low sun, and, although at all times, it was beautiful, he had never before prayed so earnestly that it would go over the other side of the world, and leave their own side to darkness.

The splendor of the great yellow star deepened as it sank. It poured showers of rays upon the broad surface of the lake, and the silver of the waters turned to orange and gold. Everything there was enlarged and made more vivid, standing out twofold against the burning western background. Nothing beyond the shadow could escape the observation of the Indians in the boats, and they themselves in Robert's intense imagination changed from a line of six light craft into a great fleet.

Nevertheless the sun, lingering as if it preferred their side of the world to any other, was bound to go at last. The deep colors in the water faded. The orange and gold changed back to silver, and the silver, in its turn, gave way to gray, twilight began to draw a heavy veil over the east, and Tayoga said in deep tones:

"Lo, the Sun God has decided that we may escape! He will let the night come before Tandakora!"

Then the sun departed all at once, and the brilliant afterglow soon faded. Night settled down, thick and dark, with the waters, ruffled by a light wind, showing but dimly. The line of Tandakora became invisible, and the two youths felt intense relief.

"Now we will start toward the northeastern end of the lake," said Tayoga. "It will be wiser than to seek the shortest road across, because Tandakora will think naturally that we have gone that way, and he will take it also."

"And it's paddling all night for us," said Robert "Well, I welcome it."

They were interrupted by the whirring of the wild fowl again, though on a much greater scale than before. The twilight was filled with feathered bodies. Tayoga, in an instant, was all attention.

"Something has frightened them," he said.

"Perhaps a bear or a deer," said Robert.

"I think not. They are used to wild animals, and would not be startled at their approach. There is only one being that everything in the forest generally fears."

"Man?"

"Even so, Dagaeoga."

"Perhaps we'd better pull in close to the bank and look."

"It would be wise."

Robert saw that the Onondaga, with his acute instincts, was deeply alarmed, and he too felt that the wild fowl had given warning. They sent the canoe with a few silent strokes through the shallow water almost to the edge of the land, and, as it nearly struck bottom, two dusky figures rising among the bushes threw their weight upon them. The light craft sank almost to the edges with the weight, but did not overturn, and both attackers and attacked fell out of it into the lake.

Robert for a moment saw a dusky face above him, and instinctively he clasped the body of a warrior in his arms. Then the two went down together in the water. The Indian was about to strike at him with a knife, but the lake saved him. As the water rushed into eye, mouth and nostril the two fell apart, but Robert was able to keep his presence of mind in that terrible moment, and, as he came up again, he snatched out his own knife and struck almost blindly.

He felt the blade encounter resistance, and then pass through it. He heard a choked cry and he shuddered violently. All his instincts were for civilization and against the taking of human life, and he had struck merely to save his own, but almost articulate words of thankfulness bubbled to his lips as he saw the dark figure that had hovered so mercilessly over him disappear. Then a second figure took the place of the first and he drew back the fatal blade again, but a soft voice said:

"Do not strike, Dagaeoga. I also have accounted for one of the warriors who attacked us, and no more have yet come. We may thank the wild fowl. Had they not warned us we should have perished."

"And even then we had luck, or your Tododaho is still watching over us. I struck at random, but the blade was guided to its mark."

"And so was mine. What you say is also proved to be true by the fact that the canoe did not overturn, when they threw themselves upon us. The chances were at least ninety-nine out of a hundred that it would do so."

"And our arms and ammunition and our deer?"

"All in the canoe, except the weapons that are in our belts."

"Then, Tayoga, it is quite sure that your Tododaho has been watching over us. But where is the canoe?"

Robert was filled with alarm and horror. They were standing above their knees in the water, and they no longer saw the little craft, which had become a veritable ship of refuge to them. They peered about frantically in the dusk and then Tayoga said:

"There is a strong breeze blowing from the land and waves are beginning to run on the water. They have taken the canoe out into the lake. We must swim in search of it."

"And if we don't find it?"

"Then we drown, but O Dagaeoga, death in the water is better than death in the fires that Tandakora will kindle."

"We might escape into the woods."

"Warriors who have come upon our trail are there, and would fall upon us at once. The attack by the two who failed proves their presence."

"Then, Tayoga, we must take the perilous chance and swim for the canoe."

"It is so, Dagaeoga."

Both were splendid swimmers, even with their clothes on, and, wading out until the water was above their waists, they began to swim with strong and steady strokes toward the middle of the lake, following with exactness the course of the wind. All the time they sought with anxious eyes through the dusk for a darker shadow that might be the canoe. The wind rose rapidly, and now and then the crest of a wave dashed over them. Less expert swimmers would have sunk, but their muscles were hardened by years of forest life—all Robert's strength had come back to him—and an immense vitality made the love of life overwhelming in them. They fought with all the powers of mind and body for the single chance of overtaking the canoe.

"I hope you see it, Tayoga," said Robert.

"Not yet," replied the Onondaga. "The darkness is heavy over the lake, and the mists and vapors, rising from the water, increase it."

"It was a fine canoe, Tayoga, and it holds our rifles, our ammunition, our deer, my buffalo robe, and all our precious belongings. We have to find it."

"It is so, Dagaeoga. We have no other choice. We truly swim for life. One could pray at this time to have all the powers of a great fish. Do you see anything behind us?"

Robert twisted his head and looked over his shoulder.

"I see no pursuit," he replied. "I cannot even see the shore, as the mists and vapors have settled down between. In a sense we're out at sea, Tayoga."

"And Ganoatohale is large. The canoe, too, is afloat upon its bosom and is, as you say, out at sea. We and it must meet or we are lost. Are you weary, Dagaeoga?"

"Not yet. I can still swim for quite a while."

"Then float a little, and we can take the exact course of the wind again. The canoe, of course, will continue to go the way the wind goes."

"Unless it's deflected by currents which do not always follow the wind."

"I do not notice any current, and to follow the wind is our only hope. The mists and vapors will hide the canoe from us until we are very close to it"

"And you may thank Tododaho that they will hide something else also. Unless I make a great mistake, Tayoga, I hear the swish of paddles."

"You make no mistake, Dagaeoga. I too hear paddles, ten, a dozen, or more of them. It is the fleet of Tandakora coming back and it will soon be passing between us and the shore. Truly we may be thankful, as you say, for the mists and vapors which, while they hide the canoe from us, also hide us from our enemies."

"I shall lie flat upon my back and float, and I'll blend with the water."

"It is a wise plan, Dagaeoga. So shall I. Then Tandakora himself would not see us, even if he passed within twenty feet of us."

"He is passing now, and I can see the outlines of their boats."

The two were silent as the fish themselves, sustained by imperceptible strokes, and Robert saw the fleet of Tandakora pass in a ghostly line. They looked unreal, a shadow following shadows, the huge figure of the Ojibway chief in the first boat a shadow itself. Robert's blood chilled, and it was not from the cold of the water. He was in a mystic and unreal world, but a world in which danger pressed in on every side. He felt like one living back in a primeval time. The swish of the paddles was doubled and tripled by his imagination, and the canoes seemed to be almost on him.

The questing eyes of Tandakora and his warriors swept the waters as far as the night, surcharged with mists and vapors, would allow, but they did not see the two human figures, so near them and almost submerged in the lake. The sound of the swishing paddles moved southward, and the line of ghostly canoes melted again, one by one, into the darkness.

"They're gone, Tayoga," whispered Robert in a tone of immense relief.

"So they are, Dagaeoga, and they will seek us long elsewhere. Are you yet weary?"

"I might be at another time, but with my life at stake I can't afford to grow tired. Let us follow the wind once more."

They swam anew with powerful strokes, despite the long time they had been in the water, and no sailors, dying of thirst, ever scanned the sea more eagerly for a sail than they searched through the heavy dusk for their lost canoe. The wind continued to rise, and the waves with it. Foam was often dashed over their heads, the water grew cold to their bodies, now and then they floated on their backs to rest themselves and thus the singular chase, with the wind their only guide, was maintained.

Robert was the first to see a dim shape, but he would not say anything until it grew in substance and solidity. Nevertheless hope flooded his heart, and then he said:

"The wind has guided us aright, Tayoga. Unless some evil spirit has taught my eyes to lie to me that is our canoe straight ahead."

"It has all the appearance of a canoe, Dagaeoga, and since the only canoe on this part of the lake is our canoe, then our canoe it is."

"And none too soon. I'm not yet worn out, but the cold of the water is entering my bones. I can see very clearly now that it's the canoe, our canoe. It stands up like a ship, the strongest canoe, the finest canoe, the friendliest canoe that ever floated on a lake or anywhere else. I can hear it saying to us: 'I have been waiting for you. Why didn't you come sooner?'"

"Truly when Dagaeoga is an old, old man, nearly a hundred, and the angel of death comes for him, he will rise up in his bed and with the rounded words pouring from his lips he will say to the angel: 'Let me make a speech only an hour long and then I will go with you without trouble, else I stay here and refuse to die.'"

"I'm using words to express my gratitude, Tayoga. Look, the canoe is moving slowly toward the center of the lake, but it stays back as much as the wind will let it and keeps beckoning to us. A few more long, swift strokes, Tayoga, and we're beside it."

"Aye, Dagaeoga, and we must be careful how we climb into it. It is no light task to board a canoe in the middle of a lake. Since Tododaho would not let it be overturned, when we fell out of it, we must not overturn it ourselves when we get back into it, else we lose all our arms, ammunition and other supplies."

The canoe was now not more than fifty feet in front of them, moving steadily farther and farther from land before the wind that blew out of the west, but, sitting upright on the waters like a thing of life, bearing its precious freight. The mists and vapors had closed in so much now that their chance of seeing it had been only one in a thousand, and yet that lone chance had happened. The devout soul of Tayoga was filled with gratitude. Even while swimming he looked up at the great star that he could not see beyond the thick veil of cloud, but, knowing it was there, he returned thanks to the mighty Onondaga chieftain who had saved them so often.

"The canoe retreats before us, Dagaeoga," he said, "but it is not to escape us, it is to beckon us on, out of the path of Tandakora's boats which soon may be returning again and which will now come farther out into the lake, thinking that we may possibly have made a dash under the cover of the mists."

"What you predict is already coming true, Tayoga," said Robert, "because I hear the first faint dip of their paddles once more, and they can't be more than two hundred yards behind us."

The regular swishing grew louder and came closer, but the courage of the two youths was still high. They had been drawn on so steadily by the canoe, apparently in a predestined course, and they had been victors over so many dangers, that they were confident the boats of Tandakora would pass once more and leave them unseen.

"They're almost abreast of us now, Tayoga," said Robert.

"Aye, Dagaeoga," said the Onondaga, looking back. "They do not appear through the mist and we hear only the paddles, but we know the threat is there, and we can follow them as well with ear as with eye. They keep straight on, going back toward the north. Nothing tells them we are here, as our canoe beckons to us, nothing guides them to that for which they are looking. Now the sound of their paddles becomes less, now it is faint and now it is gone wholly. They have missed us once more! Let us summon up the last of our strength and overtake the canoe."

They put all their energy into a final effort and presently drew up by the side of the canoe. Tayoga steadied it with his hands while Robert was the first to climb into it. The Onondaga followed and the two lay for a few minutes exhausted on the bottom. Then Tayoga sat up and said in a full voice:

"Lo, Dagaeoga, let us give thanks to Manitou for our wonderful escape, because we have looked into the face of death."

Robert, awed by time and circumstance, shared fully the belief of Tayoga that their escape was a miracle. His nature contained much that was devout and spiritual and he, too, with his impressionable imagination, peopled earth and air almost unconsciously with spirits, good and bad. The good and bad often fought together, and sometimes the good prevailed as they had just done. There lay in the canoe the paddles, which they had lifted out of the water in their surprise at the sudden attack, and beside them were the rifles and everything else they needed.

They were content to let the canoe travel its own course for a long time, and that course was definite and certain, as if guided by the hand of man. The wind always carried it toward the northeast and farther and farther away from the fleet of Tandakora. But they took off their clothing, wrung out as much water as they could, and wrapped themselves in the dry blankets from their packs. Robert's spirits, stimulated by the reaction, bubbled up in a wonderful manner.

"We'll see no more of Tandakora for a long time, at least," he exclaimed, "and now, ho! for our wonderful voyage!"

They drew the wet charges from their pistols and reloaded them, they polished anew their hatchets and knives and then, these tasks done, they still sat for a long time in the canoe, idle and content. Their little boat needed no help or guidance from their hands. That favoring wind always carried it away from their enemies and in the direction in which they wished it to go. And yet the wind did not blow away the mists and vapors, that grew thicker and thicker around them, until they could not see twenty feet away.

Robert's feeling that they were protected, his sense of the spiritual and mystic, grew, and he saw that the mind of Tayoga was under the same spell. The waters of the lake were friendly now. As they lapped around the canoe they made a soothing sound, and the wind that guided and propelled them sang a low but pleasant song.

"We are in the arms of Tododaho," said Tayoga in a reverential tone, "and Hayowentha, the great Mohawk, also looks on and smiles. What need for us to strive when the gods themselves take us in their keeping?"

Hours passed before they spoke again. They had been at the uttermost verge of exhaustion when they climbed into the canoe, and perhaps physical weakness had made their minds more receptive to the belief that they were in hands mightier than their own, but even as strength came back the conviction remained in all its primitive force. Warmth returned to their bodies, wrapped in the blankets, and they felt an immense peace. Midnight passed and the boat bore steadily on with its two silent occupants.

CHAPTER XII.
THE MARVELOUS TRAILER

"Where are we, Tayoga?"

Robert stirred from a doze and the words were involuntary. He looked upon water, covered with mists and vapors, and the driving wind was still behind them.

"I know not, Dagaeoga," replied the Onondaga in devout tones. "I too have dozed for a while, and awoke to find nothing changed. All I know is that we are yet on the bosom of Ganoatohale, and that the west wind has borne us on. I have always loved the west wind, Dagaeoga. Its breath is sweet on my face. It comes from the setting sun, from the greatest of all seas that lies beyond our continent, it blows over the vast unknown plains that are trodden by the buffalo in myriads, it comes across the mighty forests of the great valley, it is loaded with all the odors and perfumes of our immense land, and now it carries us, too, to safety."

"You talk in hexameters, Tayoga, but I think your rhapsody is justified. I also have plenty of cause now to love the west wind. How long do you think it will be until we feel the dawn on our faces?"

"Two hours, perhaps, but we may reach land before then. While I cannot smell the dawn I seem to perceive the odor of the forest. Now it grows stronger, and lo, Dagaeoga, there is another sign! Do you not notice it?"

"No, what is it?"

"The west wind that has served us so well is dying. *Gaoh*, which in our language of the Hodenosaunee is the spirit of the winds, knows that we need it no more. Surely the land is near because *Gaoh* after being a benevolent spirit to us so long would not desert us at the last moment."

"I think you must be right, Tayoga, because now I also notice the strong, keen perfume of the woods, and our west wind has sunk to almost nothing."

"Nay, Dagaeoga, it is more than that. It has died wholly. *Gaoh* tells us that having brought us so near the land we can now fend for ourselves."

The air became absolutely still, the swell ceased, the surface of the lake became as smooth as glass, and, as if swept back by a mighty, unseen hand, the mists and vapors suddenly floated away toward the east. Tayoga and Robert uttered cries of admiration and gratitude, as a high, green shore appeared, veiled but not hidden in the dusk.

"So Tododaho has brought us safely across the waters of Ganoatohale," said the Onondaga.

"Have you any idea of the point to which we have come?" asked Robert.

"No, but it is sufficient that we have come to the shore anywhere. And see, Dagaeoga, the mists and vapors still hang heavily over the western half of the lake, forming an impenetrable wall that shuts us off from Tandakora and his warriors. Truly we are for the time the favorites of the gods."

"Even so, Tayoga, you see, too, that we have come to land just where a little river empties into the lake, and we can go on up it."

They paddled with vigorous arms into the mouth of the stream, and did not stop until the day came. It was a beautiful little river, the massed vegetation growing in walls of green to the very water's edge, the songs of innumerable birds coming out of the cool gloom on either side. Robert was enchanted. His spirits were still at the high key to which they had been raised by the events of the night. Both he and Tayoga had enjoyed many hours of rest in the canoe, and now they were keen and strong for the day's work. So, it was long after dawn when they stopped paddling, and pushed their prow into a little cove.

"And now," said Robert, "I think we can land, dress, and cook some of this precious deer, which we have brought with us in spite of everything."

Their clothing had been dried by the sun, and they resumed it. Then, taking all risks, they lighted a fire, broiled tender steaks and ate like giants who had finished great labors.

"I think," said Tayoga, "that when we proceed a few miles farther it will be better to leave the canoe. It is likely that as we advance the river will become narrower, and we would be an easy target for a shot from the bank."

"I don't like to abandon a canoe which has brought us safely across the lake."

"We will put it away where it can await our coming another time. But I think we can dare the river for some distance yet."

Robert had spoken for the sake of precaution, and he was easily persuaded to continue in the river some miles, as traveling by canoe was pleasant, and after their miraculous escape or rather rescue, as it seemed to them, their spirits, already high, were steadily rising higher. The lone little river of the north, on which they were traveling, presented a spectacle of uncommon beauty. Its waters flowed in a clear, silver stream down to the lake, deeper in tint on the still reaches, and, flashing in the sunlight, where it rushed over the shallows.

All the time they moved between two lofty, green walls, the forest growing so densely on either shore that they could not see back into it more than fifty yards, while the green along its lower edges was dotted with pink and blue and red, where the delicate wild flowers were blooming. The birds in the odorous depths of the foliage sang incessantly, and Robert had never before heard them sing so sweetly.

"I don't think any of our foes can be in ambush along the river," he said. "It's too peaceful and the birds sing with too much enthusiasm. You remember how they warned us of danger once by all going away?"

"True, Dagaeoga, and at any time now they may leave. But, like you, I am willing to take the risk for several hours more. Most of the warriors must be far south of us unless the rangers are in this region, and a special force has been sent to meet them."

They came by and by to a long stretch of rippling shallows, and they were compelled to carry the canoe with its load through the woods and around them, the task, owing to the density of the forest and thicket and the weight of their burden, straining their muscles and drawing perspiration from their faces. But they took consolation from the fact that game was amazingly plentiful. Deer sprang up everywhere, and twice they caught glimpses of bears shambling away. Squirrels chattered over their heads and the little people of the forest rustled all about them.

"It shows that no human being has been through here recently," said Tayoga, "else the game, big and little, would not have been stirring abroad with so much confidence."

"Then as soon as we make the portage we can return to the river with the canoe."

"Dagaeoga grows lazy. Does he not know that to do the hard thing strengthens both mind and body? Has he forgotten what Mynheer Jacobus Huysman told us so often in Albany? Now is a splendid opportunity for Dagaeoga to harden himself a great deal."

"I realize it, Tayoga, but I don't want my mind and body to grow too hard. When one is all steel one ceases to be receptive. Can you see the river through the trees there?"

"I catch the glitter of sunlight on the water."

"I hope it looks like deep water."

"It is sufficient to float the canoe and the lazy Dagaeoga can take to his paddle again."

They put their boat back into the stream, uttering great sighs of relief, and resumed the far more pleasant travel by water, the day remaining golden as if doing its best to please them. They had another long stretch of good water, and they did not stop until they were well into the afternoon. Then Tayoga proposed that they make a fire and cook all of the deer.

"It seems that the risk here is not great," he said, "and we may not have the chance later on."

Robert, who still felt that they were protected and that for a day or two no harm could come to them under any circumstances, was more than willing, and they spent the remainder of the day in their culinary task. After dark he slept three hours, to be followed by Tayoga for the same length of time, and about midnight they started up the stream again, with their food cooked and ready beside them.

Although the Onondaga shared Robert's feeling that they were protected for the time, both exercised all their usual caution, believing thoroughly in the old saying that heaven helps those who help themselves. It was this watchfulness, particularly of ear, that caused them to hear the dip of paddles approaching up the stream. Softly and in silence, they lifted the canoe out of water and hid with it in the greenwood. Then they saw a fleet of eight large canoes go by, all containing warriors, armed heavily and in full war paint.

"Hurons," whispered Tayoga. "They go south for a great taking of scalps, doubtless to join Montcalm, who is surely meditating another sudden and terrible blow."

"And he will strike at our forts by Andiatarocte," rejoined Robert. "I hope we can find Willet and Rogers soon and take the news. All the woods must be full of warriors going south to Montcalm."

"They have French guns, and good ones too, and they are wrapped in French blankets. Onontio does not forget the power of the warriors and draws them to him."

The silent file of war canoes passed on and out of sight, and, for a space, Robert's heart was heavy within him. He felt the call of battle, he ought to be in the south, giving what he could to the defense against the might of Montcalm, but to go now would be merely a dash in the dark. They must continue to seek Willet and Rogers.

When the last Indian canoe was far beyond hearing they relaunched their own and paddled until nearly daybreak, coming to a place where bushes and tall grass grew thick in the shallow water at the edge of the river.

"Here," said Tayoga, "we will leave the canoe. A good hiding place offers itself, and with the dawn it will be time for us to take to the woods."

They concealed with great art the little boat that had served them so well, sinking it in the heart of the densest growth and then drawing back the bushes and weeds so skillfully that the keenest Indian eye would not have noticed that anyone had ever been there.

"I hope," said Robert sincerely, "that we'll have the chance to return here some time or other and use it again."

"That rests in the keeping of Manitou," said the Onondaga, "and now we will take up our packs and go eastward toward Oneadatote."

"But we won't go fast, because my pack, with all this venison in it, is by no means light."

"It is no heavier than mine, Dagaeoga, but, as you say, we will not hasten, lest we pass the Great Bear and the Mountain Wolf in the forest and not know it. But I think we are safe in going toward Oneadatote, as Rogers and his rangers usually operate in the region of George and Champlain."

They traveled two days and two nights and came once more among the high ridges and peaks. They saw many Indian trails and always they watched for another. On the third day Tayoga discovered traces in moss and he said with great satisfaction to his comrade:

"Lo, Dagaeoga, we, too, be wise in our time. The print here speaks to me like the print on the page of a book. It says that the Great Bear has passed this way."

"I can tell that the traces were made by the feet of a white man," said Robert, "but how do you know they are Dave's?"

"I have noticed that the Great Bear's feet are more slender than the average. Also he bears less upon the heel. He poises himself more upon the toe, like the great swordsman we saw him to be that time in Quebec."

"The distinctions are too fine for me, Tayoga, but I don't question your own powers of observation. I accept your statement with gratitude and joy, too, because now we know that Dave is alive, and somewhere in the great northern forest of the Province of New York. I knew he could not be dead, but it's a relief anyhow to have the proof. But as I see no other traces, how is it, do you think, that he happens to be alone?"

"The Great Bear may have been making a little scout by himself. I still think that he is with Rogers and the rangers, and when we follow his trail we are likely to find soon that he has rejoined them."

The traces led north and east until they came to rocky ground, where they were lost, and Tayoga assumed from the fact that they were several days old, otherwise he could have made them out even in the more difficult region. But when the path, despite all his searching, vanished in the air, he began to look higher than the earth. Soon he smiled and said:

"Ah, the Great Bear is as wise as the fox and the serpent combined. He knows that a little chance may lead to great results, and so he neglects none of the little chances."

"I don't understand you," said Robert, puzzled.

The Onondaga bent over a bush and showed where a twig had been cut off.

"See the wound made by his knife," he said, "and look! here is another on a bush farther on. Both wounds are partly healed, showing that the cut of the knife was made several days ago. It occurred to the Great Bear that we might strike his trail some time or other, and when he came to the stony uplift upon which his moccasins would leave no sign, he made traces elsewhere. He knew the chance of our ever seeing them was slight, and he may have made thousands of other traces that we never will see, but the possibility that we would see some one of the many became a probability."

"As you present it, it seems simple, Tayoga, but what an infinity of pains he must have taken!"

"The Great Bear is that kind of a man."

The hard, rocky ground extended several miles and their progress over it was, of necessity, very slow, as Tayoga was compelled to look with extreme care for the signs the hunter might have left. He found the cut twigs five times and twice footprints where softer soil existed between the rocks, making the proofs conclusive to both, and when they emerged into a normal region beyond they picked up his defined and clear trail once more.

"I shall be glad to see the Great Bear," said the Onondaga, "and I think he will be as pleased to know certainly that we are alive as we are to be assured that he is."

"He'd never desert us, and if you hadn't come to the Indian village I think he'd have done so later on."

"The Great Bear is a man such as few men are. Now, his trail leads on, straight and bold. He took no trouble to hide it, which proves that he had friends in this region, and was not afraid to be followed. Here he sat on a fallen log and rested a while."

"How do you know that, Tayoga?"

"See the prints in front of the log. They were made by the heels of his moccasins only. He tilted his feet up until they rested merely on the heels. The Great Bear could not have been in that attitude while standing. Nay, there is more. The Great Bear sat down here not to rest but to think."

"It's just supposition with you, Tayoga."

"It is not supposition at all, Dagaeoga, it is certainty. Look, several little pieces of the bark on the dead log where the Great Bear sat, are picked off. Here are the places from which they were taken, and here are the fragments themselves lying on the ground. The Great Bear must have been thinking very hard and he must have been in great doubt to have had uneasy hands, because, as you and I know, Dagaeoga, his mind and nerves are of the calmest."

"What, then, do you think was on his mind?"

"He was undecided whether to go on towards Oneadatote or to turn back and seek us anew. Here are three or four traces, a short and detached trail leading in the direction from which we have come. Then the traces suddenly turn. He sat down again and thought it over a second time."

"You can't possibly know that he resumed his seat on the log!"

"Oh, yes, I can, Dagaeoga. I wish all that we had to see was as easy, because here is the second place on the log where he picked at the bark. Mighty as the Great Bear is he cannot sit in two places at once. Not Tododaho himself could do that."

"It's conclusive, and I find here at the end of the log his trail, leading on toward the east."

"And he went fast, because the distance between his footprints lengthens. But he did not do so long. He became very slow suddenly. The space between the footprints shortens all at once. He turned aside, too, from his course, and crept through the bushes toward the south."

"How do you know that he crept?"

"Because for many steps he rested his weight wholly on his toes. The traces show it very clearly. The Great Bear was stalking something, and it was not a foe."

"That, at least, is supposition, Tayoga."

"Not supposition, Dagaeoga, and while not absolute certainty it is a great probability. The toeprints lead straight toward the tiny little lake that you see shining through the foliage. It was game and not a foe that the Great Bear was seeking. He wished to shoot a wild fowl.

Look, the edge of the lake here is low, and the tender water grasses grow to a distance of several yards from the shore. It is just the place where wild ducks or wild geese would be found, and the Great Bear secured the one he wanted. If you will look closely, Dagaeoga, you will see the faint trace of blood on the grass. Blood lasts a long time. Manitou has willed that it should be so, because it is the life fluid of his creatures. It was a wild goose that the Great Bear shot."

"And why not a wild duck?"

"Because here are two of the feathers, and even Dagaeoga knows they are the feathers of a goose and not of a duck. It was, too, the fattest goose in the flock."

"Which you have no possible way of knowing, Tayoga."

"But I do, Dagaeoga. It was the fattest goose of the flock, because the fattest goose of the flock was the one that so wise and skillful a hunter as the Great Bear would, as a matter of course, select and kill. Learn, O, Dagaeoga, to trail with your mind as well as with your eye, and ear. The day may come when the white man will equal the red man in intellect, but it is yet far off. The Great Bear was very, very hungry, and we shall soon reach the place where he cleaned and cooked his goose."

"Come, come, Tayoga! You may draw good conclusions from what you see, but there are no prophets nowadays. You don't know anything about the state of Dave's appetite, when he shot that goose, and you can't predict with certainty that we'll soon come to the place where he made it ready for the eating."

"I cannot, Dagaeoga! Why, I am doing it this very instant. Mind! Mind! Did I not tell you to use your mind? O, Dagaeoga, when will you learn the simpler things of life? The Great Bear would not have risked a shot at a wild goose in enemy country, if he had not been very hungry. Otherwise he would have waited until he rejoined the rangers to obtain food. And, having risked his shot, and having obtained his goose, which was the fattest in the flock, he became hungrier than ever. And having risked so much he was willing to risk more in order to complete the task he had undertaken, without which the other risks that he had run would have been all in vain."

"Tayoga, I can almost believe that you have your dictionary with you in your knapsack."

"Not in my knapsack, Dagaeoga, but in my head, where yours also ought to be. Ah, here is where the Great Bear began to make preparations to cook his goose! His trail wanders back and forth. He was looking for fallen wood to build the fire. And there, in the little sink between the hills, was where he built it. Even you, Dagaeoga, can see the ashes and burnt ends of sticks. The Great Bear must have been as hungry as a wolf to have eaten a whole goose, and the fattest goose of the flock, too. How do I know he ate it all? Look in the grass and leaves and you will find enough bones to make the complete frame of a goose, and every bone is picked clean. Wild animals might have gleaned on them, you say? No. Here is the trail of a wolf that came to the dip after the Great Bear had gone, drawn by the savory odors, but he turned back. He never really entered the dip. Why? When he stood at the edge his acute and delicate senses told him no meat was left on the bones, and a wolf neither makes idle exertion, nor takes foolish risk. He went back at once. And if the wolf had not come, there is another reason why I knew the Great Bear ate all the goose. He would not have thrown away any of the bones with flesh still on them. He is too wise a man to waste. He would have taken with him what was left of the goose. Having finished his most excellent dinner, the Great Bear looked for a brook."

"Why a brook?"

"Because he was thirsty. Everyone is thirsty after a heavy meal. He turned to the right, as the ground slopes down in that direction. Even you, Dagaeoga, know that one is more likely to find a brook in a valley than on a hilltop. Here is the brook, a fine, clear little stream with a sandy bottom, and here is where the Great Bear knelt and drank of the cool water. The prints of his strong knees show like carving on a wall. Finding that he was still thirsty he came back for another drink, because the second prints are a little distance from the first.

"Then, after rejoicing over the tender goose and his renewed strength, he suddenly became very cautious. The danger from the warriors, which he had forgotten or overlooked in his hunger, returned in acute form to his mind. He came to the brook a third time, but not to drink. He intended to wade in the stream that he might hide his trail, which, as you well know, Dagaeoga, is the oldest and best of all forest devices for such purposes. How many millions of times must the people of the wilderness have used it!

"Now the Great Bear had two ways to go in the water, up the stream or down the stream, and you and I, Dagaeoga, think he went down the stream, because the current leads on the whole eastward, which was the way in which he wished to go. At least, we will choose that direction and I will take one side of the bank and you the other."

They followed the brook more than a mile with questing eyes, and Tayoga detected the point at which Willet had emerged, plunging anew into the forest.

"Warriors, if they had picked up his trail, could have followed the brook as we did," said Robert.

"Of course," said Tayoga, "but the object of the Great Bear was not so much to hide his flight as to gain time. While we went slowly, looking for the emergence of his trail, he went fast. Now I think he meant to spend the night in the woods alone. The rangers must still have been far away. If they had been near he would not have felt the need of throwing off possible pursuit."

They followed the dim traces several hours, and then Tayoga announced with certainty that the hunter had slept alone in the forest, wrapped in his blanket.

"He crept into this dense clump of bushes," he said, "and lay within their heart, sheltered and hidden by them. You, Dagaeoga, can see where his weight has pressed them down. Why, here is the outline of a human body almost as clear and distinct as if it were drawn with black ink upon white paper! And the Great Bear slept well, too. The bushes are not broken or shoved aside except in the space merely wide enough to contain his frame. Perhaps the goose was so very tender and his nerves and tissues had craved it so much that they were supremely happy when he gave it to them. That is why they rested so well.

"In the morning the Great Bear resumed his journey toward the east. He had no breakfast and doubtless he wished for another goose, but he was refreshed and he was very strong. The traces are fainter than they were, because the Great Bear was so vigorous that his feet almost spurned the earth."

"Don't you think, Tayoga, that he'll soon turn aside again to hunt? So strong a man as Dave won't go long without food, especially when the forest is full of it. We've noticed everywhere that the war has caused the game to increase greatly in numbers."

"It will depend upon the position of the force to which the Great Bear belongs. If it is near he will not seek game, waiting for food until he rejoins the rangers, but if they are distant he will look for a deer or another goose, or maybe a duck. But by following we will see what he did. It cannot be hidden from us. The forest has few secrets from those who are born in it. Ah, what is this? The Great Bear hid in a bush, and he leaped suddenly! Behold the distance between the footprints! He saw something that alarmed him. It may have been a war party passing, and of which he suddenly caught sight. If so we can soon tell."

A hundred yards beyond the clump of bushes they found a broad trail, indicating that at least twenty warriors had gone by, their line of march leading toward the southeast.

"They were in no hurry," said the Onondaga, "as they had no fear of enemies. Their steps are irregular, showing that sometimes they stopped and talked. Doubtless they meant to join Montcalm, but as they can travel much faster than an army they were taking their time about it. We will now return to the bushes in which the Great Bear lay hidden while he watched. The traces of his footsteps in the heart of the clump are much deeper than usual, which proves that he stood there quite a while. It is also another proof that the warriors stopped and talked when they were near him, else he would not have remained in the clump so long. It is likely, too, that the Great Bear followed them when they resumed their journey. Yes, here is his trail leading from the bushes. But it is faint, the Great Bear was stepping lightly and here is where it merges with the trail of the warriors. He could not have been more than three or four hundred yards behind them. The Great Bear was very bold, or else they were very careless. He will not follow them long, as he merely wishes to get a general idea of their course, it being his main object to rejoin the rangers."

"And at this point he turned away from their trail," said Robert, after they had followed it about a mile. "He is now going due east, and his traces lead on so straight that he must have known exactly where he intended to go."

"Stated with much correctness," said Tayoga in his precise school English. "Dagaeoga is taking to heart my assertion that the mind is intended for human use, and he is beginning to think a little. But we shall have to stop soon for a while, because the night comes. We, too, will sleep in the heart of the bushes as the Great Bear did."

"And glad am I to stop," said Robert. "My burden of buffalo robe and deer and arms and ammunition is beginning to weigh on me. A buffalo robe doesn't seem of much use on a warm, summer day, but it is such a fine one and you took so much trouble to get it for me, Tayoga, that I haven't had the heart to abandon it."

"It is well that you have brought it, in spite of its weight," said the Onondaga, "as the night, at this height, is sure to be cold, and the robe will envelop you in its warmth. See, the dark comes fast."

The sun sank behind the forest, and the twilight advanced, the deeper dusk following in its trail, a cold wind began to blow out of the north, and Robert, as Tayoga had predicted, was thankful now that he had retained the buffalo robe, despite its weight. He wrapped it around his body and sat on a blanket in a thicket. Tayoga, by his side, used his two blankets in a similar manner, and they ate of the deer which they had had the forethought to cook, and make ready for all times.

The dusk deepened into the thick dark, and the night grew colder, but they were warm and at ease. Robert was full of courage and hope. The elements and all things had served them so much that he was quite sure they would succeed in everything they undertook. By and by, he stretched himself on the blanket, and clothed from head to foot in the great robe he slept the deep sleep of one who had toiled hard and well. An hour later Tayoga also slept, but in another hour he awoke and sat up, listening with all the marvelous powers of hearing that nature and cultivation had given him.

Something was stirring in the thicket, not any of the wild animals, big or little, but a human being, and Tayoga knew the chances were a hundred to one that it was a hostile human being. He put his ear to the earth and the sound came more clearly. Now his wonderful gifts of intuition and forest reasoning told him what it was. Slowly he rose again, cleared himself of the blankets, and put his rifle upon them.

Then, loosening the pistol in his belt, but drawing his long hunting knife, he crept from the thicket.

Tayoga, despite his thorough white education and his constant association with white comrades, was always an Indian first. Now, as he stole from the thicket in the dark, knife in hand, he was the very quintessence of a great warrior of the clan of the Bear, of the nation Onondaga, of the great League of the Hodenosaunee. He was what his ancestors had been for unnumbered generations, a primeval son of the wilderness, seeking the life of the enemy who came seeking his.

He kept to his hands and knees, and made no sound as he advanced, but at intervals he dropped his ear to the ground, and heard the faint rustling that was drawing nearer. He decided that it was a single warrior who by some chance had struck their trail in the dusk, and who, with minute pains and with slowness but certainty, was following it.

His course took him about thirty yards among the bushes and then through high grass growing luxuriantly in the open. In the grass his eye also helped him, because at a point straight ahead the tall stems were moving slightly in a direction opposed to the wind. He took the knife in his teeth and went on, sure that bold means would be best.

The stalking warrior who in his turn was stalked did not hear him until he was near, and then, startled, he sprang to his feet, knife in hand. Tayoga snatched his own from his teeth and stood erect facing him. The warrior, a Huron, was the heavier though not the taller of the two, and recognizing an enemy, a hated Iroquois, he stared fiercely into the eyes that were so close to his. Then he struck, but, agile as a panther, Tayoga leaped aside, and the next instant his own blade went home. The Huron sank down without a sound, and the Onondaga stood over him, the spirit of his ancestors swelling in fierce triumph.

But the feeling soon died in the heart of Tayoga. His second nature, which was that of his white training and association, prevailed. He was sorry that he had been compelled to take life, and, dragging the heavy body much farther away, he hid it in the bushes. Then, making a circle through the forest to assure himself that no other enemies were near, he went swiftly back to the thicket and lay down again between his blankets. He had a curious feeling that he did not want Robert to know what had happened.

Tayoga remained awake the remainder of the night, and, although he did not stir again from the thicket, he kept a vigilant watch. He would hear any sound within a hundred yards and he would know what it was, but there was none save the rustlings of the little animals, and dawn came, peaceful and clear. Robert moved, threw off the buffalo robe and stood up among the bushes.

"A big sleep and a fine sleep, Tayoga," he said.

"It was a good time for Dagaeoga to sleep," said the Onondaga.

"I was warm, and your Tododaho watched over me."

"Aye, Dagaeoga, Tododaho was watching well last night."

"And you slept well, too, Tayoga?"

"I slept as I should, Dagaeoga. No man can ask more."

"Philosophical and true. It's breakfast now, slices of deer, and water of a brook. Deer is good, Tayoga, but I'm beginning to find I could do without it for quite a long time. I envy Dave the fat goose he had, and I don't wonder that he ate it all at one time. Maybe we could find a juicy goose or duck this morning."

"But we have the deer and the Great Bear had nothing when he sought the goose. We will even make the best of what we have, and take no risk."

"It was merely a happy thought of mine, and I didn't expect it to be accepted. My happiest thoughts are approved by myself alone, and so I'll keep 'em to myself. My second-rate thoughts are for others, over the heads of whom they will not pass."

"Dagaeoga is in a good humor this morning."

"It is because I slept so well last night. Now, having had a sufficiency of the deer I shall seek a brook. I'm pretty sure to find one in the low ground over there."

He started to the right, but Tayoga immediately suggested that he go to the left—the hidden body of the warrior lay in the bushes on the right—and Robert, never dreaming of the reason, tried the left where he found plenty of good water. Tayoga also drank, and with some regret they left the lair in the bushes.

"It was a good house," said Robert. "It lacked only walls, a roof and a floor, and it had an abundance of fresh air. I've known worse homes for the night."

"Take up your buffalo robe again," said the Onondaga, "because when another night comes you will need it as before."

They shouldered their heavy burdens and resumed the trail of the hunter, expecting that it would soon show a divergence from its straight course.

"The rangers seem to be farther away than we thought," said Tayoga, "and the Great Bear must eat. One goose, however pleasant the memory, will not last forever. It is likely that he will turn aside again to one of the little lakes or ponds that are so numerous in this region."

In two hours they found that he had done so, and this time his victim was a duck, as the feathers showed. They saw the ashes where he had cooked it, and as before only the bones were left. Evidently he had lingered there some time, as Tayoga announced a distinctly fresher trail, indicating that they were gaining upon him fast, and they increased their own speed, hoping that they would soon overtake him.

But the traces led on all day, and the next morning, after another night spent in the thickets, Tayoga said that the Great Bear was still far ahead, and it was possible they might not overtake him until they approached the shores of Champlain.

"But if necessary we'll follow him there, won't we, Tayoga?" said Robert.

"To Oneadatote and beyond, if need be," said the Onondaga with confidence.

CHAPTER XIII.
READING THE SIGNS

On the third day the trail of the Great Bear was well among the ranges and Tayoga calculated that they could not be many hours behind him, but all the evidence, as they saw it, showed conclusively that he was going toward Lake Champlain.

"It seems likely to me," said the Onondaga, "that he left the rangers to seek us, and that Rogers meanwhile would move eastward. Having learned in some way or other that he could not find us, he will now follow the rangers wherever they may go."

"And we will follow him wherever he goes," said Robert.

An hour later the Onondaga uttered an exclamation, and pointed to the trail. Another man coming from the south had joined Willet. The traces were quite distinct in the grass, and it was also evident from the character of the footsteps that the stranger was white.

"A wandering hunter or trapper? A chance meeting?" said Robert.

Tayoga shook his head.

"Then a ranger who was out on a scout, and the two are going on together to join Rogers?"

"Wrong in both cases," he said. "I know who joined the Great Bear, as well as if I saw him standing there in the footprints he has made. It was not a wandering hunter and it was not a ranger. You will notice, Dagaeoga, that these traces are uncommonly large. They are not slender like the footprints of the Great Bear, but broad as well as long. Why, I should know anywhere in the world what feet made them. Think, Dagaeoga!"

"I don't seem to recall."

"Willet is a great hunter and scout, among the bravest of men, skillful on the trail, and terrible in battle, but the man who is now with him is all these also. A band attacking the two would have no easy task to conquer them. You have seen both on the trail in the forest and you have seen both in battle. Try hard to think, Dagaeoga!"

"Black Rifle!"

"None other. It is far north for him, but he has come, and he and the Great Bear were glad to see each other. Here they stood and shook hands."

"There is not a possible sign to indicate such a thing."

"Only the certain rules of logic. Once again I bid you use your mind. We see with it oftener than with the eye. White men, when they are good friends and meet after a long absence, always shake hands. So my mind tells me with absolute certainty that the Great Bear and Black Rifle did so. Then they talked together a while. Now the eye tells me, because here are footsteps in a little group that says so, and then they walked on, fearless of attack. It is an easy trail to follow."

He announced in a half hour that they were about to enter an old camp of the two men.

"Any child of the Hodenosaunee could tell that it is so," he said, "because their trails now separate. Black Rifle turns off to the right, and the Great Bear goes to the left. We will follow Black Rifle first. He wandered about apparently in aimless fashion, but he had a purpose nevertheless. He was looking for firewood. We need not follow the trail of the Great Bear, because his object was surely the same. They were so confident of their united strength that they built a fire to cook food and take away the coldness of the night. Although Great Bear had no food it was not necessary for him to hunt, because Black Rifle had enough for both. The fact that the Great Bear did not go away in search of game proves it.

"I think we will find the remains of their fire just beyond the low hill on the crest of which the bushes grow so thick. Once more it is mind and not eye that tells me so, Dagaeoga. They would build a fire near because they had begun to look for firewood, which is always plentiful in the forest, and they would surely choose the dip which lies beyond the hill, because the circling ridge with its frieze of bushes would hide the flames. Although sure of their strength they did not neglect caution."

They passed over the hill, and found the dead embers of the fire.

"After they had built it Black Rifle sat on that side and the Great Bear on this," said Tayoga, "and while they were getting it ready the Great Bear concluded to add something on his own account to the supper."

"What do you mean, Tayoga? Is this mind or eye?"

"A combination of the two. The Great Bear is a wonderful marksman, as we know, and while sitting on the log that he had drawn up before the fire, he shot his game out of the tall oak on our right."

"This is neither eye nor mind, Tayoga, it is just fancy."

"No, Dagaeoga, it is mostly eye, though helped by mind. My conclusion that he was sitting, when he pulled the trigger is mind chiefly. He would not have drawn up the log unless he had been ready to sit down, and everything was complete for the supper. The Great Bear never rests until his work is done, and he is so marvelous with the rifle that it was not necessary for him to rise when he fired. Wilderness life demands so much of the body that the Great Bear never makes needless exertion. There mind works, Dagaeoga, but the rest is all eye. The squirrel was on the curved bough of the oak, the one that projects toward the north."

"You assume a good deal to say that it was a squirrel and surely mind not eye would select the particular bough on which he sat."

"No, Dagaeoga, eye served the whole purpose. All the other branches are almost smothered in leaves, but the curved one is nearly bare. It is only there that the casual glance of the Great Bear, who was not at that time seeking game, would have caught sight of the squirrel. Also, he must have been there, otherwise his body could not have fallen directly beneath it, when the bullet went through his head."

"Now tell me how your eye knows his body fell from the bough."

"Ah, Dagaeoga! Your eye was given to you for use as mine was given to me, then you should use it; in the forest you are lost unless you do. It was my eye that saw the unmistakable sign, the sign from which all the rest followed. Look closely and you will detect a little spot of red on the grass just beneath the bare bough. It was blood from the squirrel."

"You cannot be sure that it was a squirrel. It might have been a pigeon or some other bird."

"That, O, Dagaeoga, would be the easiest of all, even for you, if you could only use your eyes, as I bid you. Almost at your feet lies a slender bone that cannot be anything but the backbone of a squirrel. Beyond it are two other bones, which came from the same body. We know as certainly that it was a squirrel as we know that the Great Bear ate first a wild goose, and then a wild duck. But it is a good camp that those two great men made, and, as the night is coming, we will occupy it."

They relighted the abandoned fire, warmed their food and ate, and Robert was once more devoutly glad that he had kept the heavy buffalo robe. Deep fog came over the mountain soon after dark, and, after a while, a fine cold, and penetrating rain was shed from the heart of it. They kept the fire burning and wrapped, Tayoga in his blankets, and, Robert in the robe, crouched before it. Then they drew the logs that the Great Bear and Black Rifle had left, in such position that they could lean their backs against them, and slept, though not the two at the same time. They agreed that it was wise to keep watch and Robert was sentinel first.

Tayoga, supported by the log, slept soundly, the flames illuminating his bronze face and showing the very highest type of the Indian. Robert sat opposite, his rifle across his knees, but covered by his blanket to protect it from the fine rain, which was not only cold but insidious, trying to insert itself beneath his clothing and chill his body. But he kept himself covered so well that none reached him, and the very wildness of his surroundings increased his sense of intense physical comfort.

He did not stir, except now and then to put a fresh chunk of wood on the fire, and the red blaze between Tayoga and himself was for a time the center of the world. The cold, white fog was rolling up everywhere thick and impenetrable, and the fine rain, like a heavy dew that was distilled from it, fell incessantly. Robert knew that it was moving up the valleys and clothing all the peaks and ridges. He knew, too, that it would hide them from their enemies and his sense of comfort grew with the knowledge. But his conviction that they were safe did not make him relax caution, and, since eye was useless in the fog, he made extreme call upon ear.

It seemed to him that the fog was a splendid conductor of sound. It brought him the rustling of the foliage, the moaning of the light wind through the ravines, and, at last, another sound, sharp, distinct, a discordant note in the natural noises of the wilderness, which were always uniform and harmonious. He heard it a second time, to his right, down the hill, and he was quite sure that it indicated the presence of man, man who in reality was near, but whom the fog took far away. The vapors, however, would lift, then man might come close, and he felt that it was his part to discover who and what he was.

Still wrapped in the buffalo robe, he rose and took a few steps from the fire. Tayoga did not stir, and he was proud that his tread had been without noise. Beyond the rim of firelight, he paused and listening again heard the clank twice, not very loud but coming sharp and definite as before through the vapory air. He parted the bushes very carefully and went down the side of a ravine, the wet boughs and twigs making no noise as they closed up after his passage.

But his progress was very slow, purposely so, as he knew that any mistake or accident might be fatal, and he intended that no fault of his should precipitate such a crisis. Once or twice he thought of going back, deeming his a foolish quest, lost in a wilderness of bushes and blinding fog, but the sharp, clear clank stirred his purpose anew, and he went on down the slope, until he saw a red glow in the heart of the fog. Then he sank down among the bushes and listened with intentness. Presently the faint hum of voices came to his ear, and he was quite sure that many men were not far away.

He resumed his slow advance, but now he was glad the bushes were soaked with water, as they did not crackle or snap with the passage of his body, and the luminous glow in front of him broadened and deepened steadily. Near the bottom of a deep valley he stopped and from his covert saw where great fires had driven the fog away. Around the fires were many warriors, some of them sleeping in their blankets, while others were eating prodigiously, after their manner. Rifles and muskets were stacked in French fashion and the clank, clank that Robert had heard had been made by the warriors as they put up their weapons.

Many were talking freely and seemed to rejoice in the food and fires. It was Robert's surmise that they had arrived but recently and were weary. Their numbers were large, they certainly could not be less than four or five hundred, and his experience was great enough now to tell him that half of them, at least, were Canadian Indians. All were in war paint, and they had an abundance of arms.

Robert's eager eye sought Tandakora, but did not find him. He had no doubt, however, that this great body of warriors was moving against Rogers and his rangers, and that it would soon be joined by the Ojibway chief. Tandakora, anxious for revenge upon the Great Bear and the Mountain Wolf, would be willing to leave Montcalm for a while if he thought that by doing so he could achieve his purpose. His gaze wandered from the warriors to the stacked rifles and muskets, and he saw that many of them were of English or American make, undoubtedly spoil taken at the capture of Oswego. His heart swelled with anger that the border should have its own weapons turned against it by the foe.

It did not take him long to see enough. It was a powerful force, equipped to strike, and now he was more anxious than ever to overtake Willet. The fog was still thick and wet, distilling the fine rain, but he had forgotten discomfort, and, turning back on his path, he sought the dip in which he had left Tayoga sleeping. He felt a certain pride that it had been his fortune to discover the band, and, as he had marked carefully the way by which he had come, it was not a difficult task to retrace his steps.

The Onondaga was still sleeping, his back against the log, but he awoke instantly when Robert touched him gently on the shoulder.

"What is it, Dagaeoga?" he whispered. "You have seen something! Your face tells me so!"

"My face tells you the truth," replied Robert. "There is a valley only a few hundred yards from us, and, in it, are about four hundred warriors, armed for battle. All the signs indicate that they are going eastward in search of our friends."

"You have done well, Dagaeoga. You have used both eye and mind. Was Tandakora there?"

"No, but I'm convinced he soon will be."

"It appears likely. They think, perhaps, they are strong enough to annihilate the rangers."

"Maybe they are, unless the rangers are warned. We ought to move at once."

"But the fog is too thick. We could not tell which way we were going. We must not lose the trail of the Great Bear and Black Rifle, and, if the fog lifts, we can regain it in the morning, going ahead of the war band."

"And then the warriors may pursue us."

"What does it matter, if we keep well ahead of them and overtake the Great Bear and Black Rifle, who are surely going toward the rangers? We will put out the fire, Dagaeoga, and stay here. The fog protects us. Now, you sleep and I will watch."

His calmness was reassuring, and it was true that the fog was an almost certain protection, while it lasted. They smothered the fire carefully, and then, Robert was sufficient master of his nerves, to go to sleep, wrapped in the invaluable buffalo robe. The Onondaga kept vigilant watch. His own ear, too, heard the occasional sound made by human beings in the valley below, but he did not stir from his place. He had absolute confidence in Robert's report, and he would not take any unnecessary risk.

An hour or two before dawn a wind began to rise, and Tayoga knew by feeling rather than sight that the fog was beginning to thin. If the wind held, it would all blow away by sunrise, and the rain with it. He awakened Robert at once.

"I think we would better move now," he said. "We shall soon be able to see our way, and a good start ahead of the war band is important."

They made a northward curve, passing around the valley, in which the camp of the warriors lay, and, when the sun showed its first luminous edge over the horizon, they were several miles ahead. The steady wind had carried all the fog and rain to the southward, but the forest was still wet and dripping.

"And now," said Tayoga, "we must pick up anew the trail of the Great Bear and Black Rifle. We are sure they were continuing east, and by ranging back and forth from north to south and from south to north we can find it."

It was a full two hours before they discovered it, leading up a narrow gorge, and Robert grew anxious lest the war band was already on their own traces, which the warriors were sure to see in time. So they hastened their own pursuit and very soon came to a thicket in which the two redoubtable scouts had passed the night. The trail leading from it was comparatively fresh and Tayoga was hopeful that they might overtake them before the next sunset.

"They do not hurry," he said. "The Great Bear has been telling Black Rifle of us, and now and then it was their thought to go back into the west to make another hunt for us. My certainty about it is based on nothing in the trail. It is just mind once more. It is exactly the idea that a valiant and patient man like the Great Bear would have, and it would appeal too, to the soul of such a great warrior as Black Rifle. But after thinking well upon it, they have decided that the search would be vain for the present, and once more they go on, though the wish to find us puts weights on their feet."

Before noon they came to a place where Black Rifle shot a deer. The useless portions of the body that the two had left behind spoke a language none could fail to understand, and they were sure it was Black Rifle who had fired the shot, because his broader footprints led to the place where the body had fallen.

"It proves," said Tayoga, "that the rangers are still well ahead, else two such wise men as the Great Bear and Black Rifle would not take the trouble to kill a deer here and carry so much weight with them. It is likely that the Mountain Wolf and his men are on the shores of Oneadatote itself."

All that afternoon the trail went upward higher and higher among the ranges and peaks, but the infallible eye of Tayoga never lost it for a moment.

"We will not overtake them today, as I had hoped," he said, "but we shall certainly do so tomorrow before noon."

"And the coming night is going to offer a striking contrast to the one just passed," said Robert. "It will be crystal clear."

"So it will, Dagaeoga, and we will seek a camp among the rocks. It is best to leave no traces for the warriors."

They traveled a long distance on the stony uplift before they stopped for the night, and they did not build any fire, dividing the time into two watches, each kept with great vigilance. But the pursuit which they were so sure was now on did not overtake them, and early in the morning they were once more on the traces of the two hunters.

"It is now sure we shall reach them before noon," said Tayoga, "but in what manner we shall first see them I do not know. The trail has become wonderfully fresh. Ah, they turned suddenly from their course here, and soon they came back to it, at a point not more than ten feet away. We need not follow them on their loop to see where they went. We know without going. They climbed the steep little peak we see on the right, from the crest of which they had a splendid view over an immense stretch of country behind us. They looked in that direction because that was the point from which pursuit or danger would come. The band behind us built a fire, and the Great Bear and Black Rifle saw its smoke. They saw the smoke because they could see nothing else so far behind them. After a good look, they went on at their leisure. They had no fear. It was easy for such as they to leave the band well in the rear, if they wished."

"If they haven't changed greatly since we last saw 'em," said Robert, "they'll go all the more slowly because of the pursuit, and we may catch 'em in a couple of hours. Won't Dave be surprised when he sees us?"

"It will be a pleasant surprise for him. Here, they have stopped again, and one of them climbed the tall elm for another view, while the other stood guard by the trunk. I think, Dagaeoga, that the Great Bear and Black Rifle were beginning to think less of flight than of battle."

"You don't mean that knowing the presence of the band behind us they intended to meet it?"

"Not to stop it, of course, but spirits such as theirs might have a desire to harm it a little, and impede its advance. In any event, Dagaeoga, we shall soon see. Here is where the climber came down, and then the two went on, walking slowly. They walked slowly, because the traces indicate that they turned back often, and looked toward the point at which they had seen the smoke rising. My mind tells me that the Great Bear thought it better to continue straight ahead, but that Black Rifle was anxious to linger, and get a few shots at the enemy. It is so, because the Great Bear, as we know, is naturally cautious and would wish to do what is of the most service in the campaign, while it is always the desire of Black Rifle to injure the enemy as much as he can."

"Your reasoning seems conclusive to me."

"Did I not tell you, Dagaeoga, that you had the beginnings of a mind? Use it sedulously, and it will grow yet more."

"And the time may come when I can talk out of a dictionary as you do, Tayoga."

"Which merely proves, Dagaeoga, that those who learn a language always talk it better than those who are born to it. Ah, they have turned once more, and the trail leads again to the crest of a hill, where they will take another long look backward. It seems that the wishes of Black Rifle are about to prevail. Now we are at the top of the hill, and they stood here several minutes talking and moving about, as the traces show very clearly. But look, Dagaeoga, they saw something very much closer at hand than smoke. Their talk was interrupted with great suddenness, and they took to ambush. They crouched among these bushes, and you and I know they were a very dangerous pair with their rifles ready. Still, Dagaeoga, instead of their taking the battle to the warriors the battle was brought to them."

"You think, then, an encounter occurred?"

"I know it. They did not stay crouched here until the enemy went away, but moved off down the hill, their course on the whole leading away from the lake. The enemy was before them, because they kept among the bushes, always in the densest part of them. Here they knelt. The bent grass stems indicate the pressure of knees. The warriors must have been very close.

"Now the trail divides. Look, Dagaeoga! Black Rifle went to the right and the Great Bear to the left. They formed a plan to flank the enemy and to assail him from two sides. I should judge then that the warriors did not number more than five or six. We will follow the Great Bear, who made the slender traces, and if necessary we will come back and follow also those of Black Rifle. But I think we can read the full account of the contest which most certainly occurred from the evidence that the Great Bear left."

"You feel quite sure then that there was fighting?"

"Yes. It is not an opinion formed from the signs yet seen, but it is drawn from the characters of the Great Bear and Black Rifle. They would not have taken so much care unless there was the certainty of conflict. Here the Great Bear knelt again, and took a long look at his enemy or at least at the place where his enemy was lying. They were coming to close quarters or he would not have knelt and waited. Perhaps he held his fire because Black Rifle was making the wider circuit, and they meant to use their rifles at the same time."

The Onondaga was on his own knees now, examining the faint trail intently, his eyes alight with interest.

"The event will not be delayed long," he said, "because the Great Bear stopped continually, seeking an opportunity for a shot. Here he pulled the trigger."

He picked up a minute piece of the burned wadding of the muzzle-loading rifle.

"The warrior at whom he fired was bound to have been in the thicket beyond the open space," he said, "and it was there that he fell. He fell because at such a critical time the Great Bear would not have fired unless he was sure of his aim. We will look into the thicket"

They found several spots of blood among the bushes and at another point about twenty feet away they saw more.

"Here is where the warrior fell before Black Rifle's bullet," said Tayoga. "He and the Great Bear must have fired almost at the same time. Undoubtedly the warriors retreated at once, carrying their dead with them. Let us see if they did not unite, and leave the thicket at the farthest point from our two friends."

The trail was very clear at the place the Onondaga had indicated, and also many more red spots were there leading away toward the east.

"We will not follow them." said Tayoga, "because they do not interest us any more. They have retreated and they do not longer enter into your campaign and mine, Dagaeoga. We will go back and see where the left wing of our army, that was the Great Bear, reunited with the right wing, that was Black Rifle."

They found the point of junction not far away, and then the deliberate trail led once more toward Champlain, the two pursuing it several hours in silence and both noticing that it was rapidly growing fresher. At length Tayoga stopped on the crest of a ridge and said:

"We no longer need to seek their trail, Dagaeoga, because I will now talk with the Great Bear and Black Rifle."

"Very good, Tayoga. I am anxious to hear what you will say and how you will say it."

A bird sang at Robert's side. It was Tayoga trilling forth a melody, wonderfully clear and penetrating, a melody that carried far up the still valley beyond.

"You will remember, Dagaeoga," he said, "that we have often used this call with the Great Bear. The reply will soon come."

The two listened and Robert's heart beat hard. He owed much to Willet. Their relationship was almost that of son and father, and the two were about to meet after a long parting. He never doubted for a moment that the Onondaga had always read the trail aright, and that Willet was with Black Rifle in the valley below them.

Full and clear rose the song of a bird out of the dense bushes that filled the valley. When it was finished Tayoga sang again, and the reply came as before. The two went rapidly down the slope and the stalwart figures of the hunter and Black Rifle rose to meet them. The four did not say much, but in every case the grasp of the hand was strong and long.

"I went west in search of you, Robert," said the hunter, "but I was compelled to come back, because of the great events that are forward here. I felt, however, that Tayoga was there looking for you and would do all any number of human beings could do."

"He found me and rescued me," said Robert, "and what of yourself, Dave?"

"I'm attached, for the present, to the rangers under Rogers. He's on the shores of Champlain, and he's trying to hold back a big Indian army that means to march south and join Montcalm for an attack on Fort William Henry or Fort Edward."

"And there's a great Indian war band behind you, too, Dave."

"We know it. We saw their smoke. We also had an encounter with some scouting warriors."

"We know that, too, Dave. You ambushed 'em and divided your force, one of you going to the right and the other to the left. Two of their warriors fell before your bullets, and then they fled, carrying their slain with them."

"Correct to every detail. I suppose Tayoga read the signs."

"He did, and he also told me when he rescued me that you had carried the text of the letter we took from Garay to Colonel Johnson in time, and that the force of St. Luc was turned back."

"Yes, the preparations for defense made an attack by him hopeless, and when his vanguard was defeated in the forest he gave up the plan."

They did not stop long, as they knew the great war band behind them was pressing forward, but they felt little fear of it, as they were able to make high speed of their own, despite the weight of their packs, and for several days and nights they traveled over peaks and ridges, stopping only at short intervals for sleep. They had no sign from the band behind them, but they knew it was always there, and that it would probably unite at the lake with the force the rangers were facing.

It was about noon of a gleaming summer day when Robert, from the crest of a ridge, saw once more the vast sheet of water extending a hundred and twenty-five miles north and south, that the Indians called Oneadatote and the white men Champlain, and around which and upon which an adventurous part of his own life had passed. His heart beat high, he felt now that the stage was set again for great events, and that his comrades and he would, as before, have a part in the war that was shaking the Old World as well as the New.

In the afternoon they met rangers and before night they were in the camp of Rogers, which included about three hundred men, and which was pitched in a strong position at the edge of the lake. The Mountain Wolf greeted them with great warmth.

"You're a redoubtable four," he said, "and I could wish that instead of only four I was receiving four hundred like you."

He showed intense anxiety, and soon confided his reasons to Willet.

"You've brought me news," he said, "that a big war band is coming from the west, and my scouts had told me already that a heavy force is to the northward, and what is worst of all, the northern force is commanded by St. Luc. It seems that he did not go south with Montcalm, but drew off an army of both French and Indians for our destruction. He remembers his naval and land defeat by us and naturally he wants revenge. He is helped, too, by the complete command of the lake, that the French now hold. Since we've been pressed southward we've lost Champlain."

"And of course St. Luc is eager to strike," said Willet. "He can recover his lost laurels and serve France at the same time. If we're swept away here, both the French and the Indians will pour down in a flood from Canada upon the Province of New York."

Robert did not hear this talk, as he was seeking in the ranger camp the repose that he needed so badly. He had brought with him some remnants of food and the great buffalo robe that Tayoga had secured for him with so much danger from the Indian village. Now he put down the robe, heaved a mighty sigh of relief and said to the Onondaga:

"I'm proud of myself as a carrier, Tayoga, but I think I've had enough. I'm glad the trail has ended squarely against the deep waters of Lake Champlain."

"And yet, Dagaeoga, it is a fine robe."

"So it is. I should be the last to deny it, but now that we're with the rangers I mean to carry nothing but my arms and ammunition. To appreciate what it is to be without burdens you must have borne them."

The hospitable rangers would not let the two youths do any work for the present, and so they took a luxurious bath in the lake, which they commanded as far as the bullets from their rifles could reach. They rejoiced in the cool waters, after their long flight through the wilderness.

"It's almost worth so many days and nights of danger to have this," said Robert, swimming with strong strokes.

"Aye, Dagaeoga, it is splendid," said the Onondaga, "but see that you do not swim too far. Remember that for the time Oneadatote belongs to Onontio. We had it, but we have lost it."

"Then we'll get it back again," said Robert courageously. "Champlain is too fine a lake to lose forever. Wait until I've had a big sleep. Then my brain will be clear, and I'll tell how it ought to be done."

The two returned to land, dressed, and slept by the campfire.

CHAPTER XIV.
ST. LUC'S REVENGE

When Robert awoke from a long and deep sleep he became aware, at once, that the anxious feeling in the camp still prevailed. Rogers was in close conference with Willet, Black Rifle and several of his own leaders beside a small fire, and, at times, they looked apprehensively toward the north or west, a fact indicating to the lad very clearly whence the danger was expected. Most of the scouts had come in, and, although Robert did not know it, they had reported that the force of St. Luc, advancing in a wide curve, and now including the western band, was very near. It was the burden of their testimony, too, that he now had at least a thousand men, of whom one-third were French or Canadians.

Tayoga was sitting on a high point of the cliff, watching the lake, and Robert joined him. The face of the young Onondaga was very grave.

"You look for an early battle, I suppose," said Robert.

"Yes, Dagaeoga," replied his comrade, "and it will be fought with the odds heavily against us. I think the Mountain Wolf should not have awaited Sharp Sword here, but who am I to give advice to a leader, so able and with so much experience?"

"But we beat St. Luc once in a battle by a lake!"

"Then we had a fleet, and, for the time, at least, we won command of the lake. Now the enemy is supreme on Oneadatote. If we have any canoes on its hundred and twenty-five miles of length they are lone and scattered, and they stay in hiding near its shores."

"Why are you watching its waters now so intently, Tayoga?"

"To see the sentinels of the foe, when they come down from the north. Sharp Sword is too great a general not to use all of his advantages in battle. He will advance by water as well as by land, but, first he will use his eyes, before he permits his hand to strike. Do you see anything far up the lake, Dagaeoga?"

"Only the sunlight on the waters."

"Yes, that is all. I believed, for a moment or two, that I saw a black dot there, but it was only my fancy creating what I expected my sight to behold. Let us look again all around the horizon, where it touches the water, following it as we would a line. Ah, I think I see a dark speck, just a black mote at this distance, and I am still unable to separate fancy from fact, but it may be fact. What do you think, Dagaeoga?"

"My thought has not taken shape yet, Tayoga, but if 'tis fancy then 'tis singularly persistent. I see the black mote too, to the left, toward the western shore of the lake, is it not?"

"Aye, Dagaeoga, that is where it is. If we are both the victims of fancy then our illusions are wonderfully alike. Think you that we would imagine exactly the same thing at exactly the same place?"

"No, I don't! And as I live, Tayoga, the mote is growing larger! It takes on the semblance of reality, and, although very far from us, it's my belief that it's moving this way!"

"Again my fancy is the same as yours and it is not possible that they should continue exactly alike through all changes. That which may have been fancy in the beginning has most certainly turned into fact, and the black mote that we see upon the waters is in all probability a hostile canoe coming to spy upon us."

They watched the dark dot detach itself from the horizon and grow continuously until their eyes told them, beyond the shadow of a doubt, that it was a canoe containing two warriors. It was moving swiftly and presently Rogers and Willet came to look at it. The two warriors brought their light craft on steadily, but stopped well out of rifle shot, where they let their paddles rest and gazed long at the shore.

"It is like being without a right arm to have no force upon the lake," said Rogers.

"It cripples us sorely," said Willet. "Perhaps we'd better swallow our pride, bitter though the medicine may be, and retreat at speed."

"I can't do it," said Rogers. "I'm here to hold back St. Luc, if I can, and moreover, 'tis too late. We'd be surrounded in the forest and probably annihilated."

"I suppose you're right. We'll meet him where we stand, and when the battle is over, whatever may be its fortunes, he'll know that he had a real fight."

They walked away from the lake, and began to arrange their forces to the most advantage, but Robert and Tayoga remained on the cliff. They saw the canoe go back toward the north, melt into the horizon line, and then reappear, but with a whole brood of canoes. All of them advanced rapidly, and they stretched into a line half way across the lake. Many were great war canoes, containing eight or ten men apiece.

"Now the attack by land is at hand," said Tayoga. "Sharp Sword is sure to see that his two forces move forward at the same time. Hark!"

They heard the report of a rifle shot in the forest, then another and another. Willet joined them and said it was the wish of Rogers that they remain where they were, as a small force was needed at that point to prevent a landing by the Indians. A fire from the lake would undoubtedly be opened upon their flank, but if the warriors could be kept in their canoes it could not become very deadly. Black Rifle came also, and he, Willet, Robert, Tayoga and ten of the rangers lying down behind some trees at the edge of the cliff, watched the water.

The Indian fleet hovered a little while out of rifle shot. Meanwhile the firing in the forest grew. Bullets from both sides pattered on leaves and bark, and the shouts of besieged and besiegers mingled, but the members of the force on the cliff kept their eyes resolutely on the water.

"The canoes are moving again," said Tayoga. "They are coming a little nearer. I see Frenchmen in some of them and presently they will try to sweep the bank with their rifles."

"Our bullets will carry as far as theirs," said the hunter.

"True, O, Great Bear, and perhaps with surer aim."

In another moment puffs of white smoke appeared in the fleet, which was swinging forward in a crescent shape, and Robert heard the whine of lead over his head. Then Willet pulled the trigger and a warrior fell from his canoe. Black Rifle's bullet sped as true, and several of the rangers also found their targets. Yet the fleet pressed the attack. Despite their losses, the Indians did not give back, the canoes came closer and closer, many of the warriors dropped into the water behind their vessels and fired from hiding, bullets rained around the little band on the cliff, and presently struck among them. Two of the rangers were slain and two more were wounded. Robert saw the Frenchmen in the fleet encouraging the Indians, and he knew that their enemies were firing at the smoke made by the rifles of the defenders. Although he and his comrades were invisible to the French and Indians in the fleet, the bullets sought them out nevertheless. Wounds were increasing and another of the rangers was killed. Theirs was quickly becoming an extremely hot corner.

But Willet, who commanded at that point, gave no order to retreat. He and all of his men continued to fire as fast as they could reload and take aim. Yet to choose a target became more difficult, as the firing from the fleet made a great cloud of smoke about it, in which the French and Indians were hidden, or, at best, were but wavering phantoms. Robert's excited imagination magnified them fivefold, but he had no thought of shirking the battle, and he crept to the very brink, seeking something at which to fire in the clouds of smoke that were steadily growing larger and blacker.

The foes upon the lake fought mostly in silence, save for the crackle of their rifles, but Robert became conscious presently of a great shouting behind him. In his concentration upon their own combat he had forgotten the main battle; but now he realized that it was being pressed with great fury and upon a half circle from the north and west. He looked back and saw that the forest was filled with smoke pierced by innumerable red flashes; the rattle of the rifles there made a continuous crash, and then he heard a tremendous report, followed by a shout of dismay from the rangers.

"What is it?" he cried. "What is it?"

Willet, who was crouched near him, turned pale, but he replied in a steady voice.

"St. Luc has brought a field piece, a twelve-pounder, I think, and they've opened fire with grape-shot. They'll sweep the whole forest. Who'd have thought it?"

The battle sank for a moment, and then a tremendous yell of triumph came from the Indians. Presently, the cannon crashed again, and its deadly charge of grape took heavy toll of the rangers. Then the lake and the mountains gave back the heavy boom of the gun in many echoes, and it was like the toll of doom. The Indians on both water and shore began to shout in the utmost fury, and Robert detected the note of triumph in the tremendous volume of sound. His heart went down like lead. Rogers crept back to Willet and the two talked together earnestly.

"The cannon changes everything," said the leader of the rangers. "More than twenty of my men are dead, and nearly twice as many are wounded. 'Tis apparent they have plenty of grape, and they are sending it like hail through the forest. The bushes are no shelter, as it cuts through 'em. Dave, old comrade, what do you think?"

"That St. Luc is about to have his revenge for the defeat we gave him at Andiatarocte. The cannon with its grape turns the scale. They come on with uncommon fury! It seems to me I hear a thousand rifles all together."

St. Luc now pressed the attack from every side save the south. The French and Indians in the fleet redoubled their fire. The twelve-pounder was pushed forward, and, as fast as the expert French gunners could reload it, the terrible charges of grape-shot were sent among the rangers. More were slain or wounded. The little band of defenders on the high cliff overlooking the lake at last found their corner too hot for them and were compelled to join the main force. Then the French and Indians in the fleet landed with shouts of triumph and rushed upon the Americans.

Robert caught glimpses of other Frenchmen as he faced the forest. Once an epaulet showed behind a bush and then a breadth of tanned face which he was sure belonged to De Courcelles. And so this man who had sought to make him the victim of a deadly trick was here! And perhaps Jumonville also! A furious rage seized him and he sought eagerly for a shot at the epaulet, but it disappeared. He crept a little farther forward, hoping for another view, and Tayoga noticed his eager, questing gaze.

"What is it, Dagaeoga?" he asked. "Whom do you hate so much?"

"I saw the French Colonel, De Courcelles, and I was seeking to draw a bead on him, but he has gone."

"Perhaps he has, but another takes his place. Look at the clump of bushes directly in front of us and you will see a pale blue sleeve which beyond a doubt holds the arm of a French officer. The arm cannot be far away from the head and body, which I think we will see in time, if we keep on looking."

Both watched the bushes with a concentrated gaze and presently the head and shoulders, following the arm, disclosed themselves. Robert raised his rifle and took aim, but as he looked down the sights he saw the face among the leaves, and a shudder shook him. He lowered his rifle.

"What is it, Dagaeoga?" whispered the Onondaga.

"The man I chose for my target," replied Robert, "was not De Courcelles, nor yet Junonville, but that young De Galissonnière, who was so kind to us in Quebec, and whom we met later among the peaks. I was about to pull trigger, and, if I had done so, I should be sorry all my life."

"Is he still there?"

Robert looked again and De Galissonnière was gone. He felt immense relief. He thought it was war's worst cruelty that it often brought friends face to face in battle.

The French and Indian horde from the lake landed and drove against the rangers on the eastern flank with great violence, firing their rifles and muskets, and then coming on with the tomahawk. The little force of Rogers was in danger of being enveloped on all sides, and would have been exterminated had it not been for his valor and presence of mind, seconded so ably by Willet, Black Rifle and their comrades.

They formed a barrier of living fire, facing in three directions and holding back the shouting horde until the main body of the surviving rangers could gather for retreat. Robert and Tayoga were near Willet, all the best sharpshooters were there, and never had they fought more valiantly than on that day.

Robert crouched among the bushes, peering for the faces of his foes, and firing whenever he could secure a good aim.

"Have you seen Tandakora?" he asked Tayoga.

"No," replied the Onondaga.

"He must be here. He would not miss such a chance."

"He is here."

"But you said you hadn't seen him."

"I have not seen him, but O, Dagaeoga, I have heard him. Did not we observe when we were in the forest that ear was often to be trusted more than eye? Listen to the greatest war shout of them all! You can hear it every minute or two, rising over all the others, superior in volume as it is in ferocity. The voice of the Ojibway is huge, like his figure."

Now, in very truth, Robert did notice the fierce triumphant shout of Tandakora, over and above the yelling of the horde, and it made him shudder again and again. It was the cry of the man-hunting wolf, enlarged many times, and instinct with exultation and ferocity. That terrible cry, rising at regular intervals, dominated the battle in Robert's mind, and he looked eagerly for the colossal form of the chief that he might send his bullet through it, but in vain; the voice was there though his eyes saw nothing at which to aim.

Farther and farther back went the rangers, and the youth's heart was filled with anger and grief. Had they endured so much, had they escaped so many dangers, merely to take part in such a disaster? Unconsciously he began to shout in an effort to encourage those with him, and although he did not know it, it was a reply to the war cries of Tandakora. The smoke and the odors of the burned gunpowder filled his nostrils and throat, and heated his brain. Now and then he would stop his own shouting and listen for the reply of Tandakora. Always it came, the ferocious note of the Ojibway swelling and rising above the warwhoop of the other Indians.

"Dagaeoga looks for Tandakora," said the Onondaga.

"Truly, yes," replied Robert. "Just now it's my greatest wish in life to find him with a bullet. I hear his voice almost continuously, but I can't see him! I think the smoke hides him."

"No, Dagaeoga, it is not the smoke, it is Areskoui. I know it, because the Sun God has whispered it in my ear. You will hear the voice of Tandakora all through the battle, but you will not see him once."

"Why should your Areskoui protect a man like Tandakora, who deserves death, if anyone ever did?"

"He protects him, today merely, not always. It is understood that I shall meet Tandakora in the final reckoning. I told him so, when I was his captive, and he struck me in the face. It was no will of mine that made me say the words, but it was Areskoui directing me to utter them. So, I know, O, my comrade, that Tandakora cannot fall to your rifle now. His time is not today, but it will come as surely as the sun sets behind the peaks."

Tayoga spoke with such intense earnestness that Robert looked at him, and his face, seen through the battle smoke, had all the rapt expression of a prophet's. The white youth felt, for the moment at least, with all the depth of conviction, the words of the red youth would come true. Then the tremendous voice of Tandakora boomed above the firing and yelling, but, as before, his body remained invisible. Tandakora's Indians, many of whom had come with him from the far shores of the Great Lakes, showed all the cunning and courage that made them so redoubtable in forest warfare. Armed with good French muskets and rifles they crept forward among the thickets, and poured in an unceasing fire. Encouraged by the success at Oswego, and by the knowledge that the great St. Luc, the best of all the French leaders, was commanding the whole force, their ferocity rose to the highest pitch and it was fed also by the hope that they would destroy all the hated and dreaded rangers whom they now held in a trap.

Robert had never before seen them attack with so much disregard of wounds, and death. Usually the Indian was a wary fighter, always preferring ambush, and securing every possible advantage for himself, but now they rushed boldly across open spaces, seeking new and nearer coverts. Many fell before the bullets of the rangers but the swarms came on, with undiminished zeal, always pushing the battle, and keeping up a fire so heavy that, despite the bullets that went wild, the rangers steadily diminished in numbers.

"It's a powerful attack," said Robert.

"It's because they feel so sure of victory," said Tayoga, "and it's because they know it's the Mountain Wolf and his men whom they have surrounded. They would rather destroy a hundred rangers than three hundred troops."

"That's so," said Willet, who overheard them in all the crash of the battle. "They won't let the opportunity escape. Back a little, lads! This place is becoming too much exposed."

They withdrew into deeper shelter, but they still fired as fast, as they could reload and pull the trigger. Their bullets, although they rarely missed, seemed to make no impression on the red horde, which always pressed closer, and there was a deadly ring of fire around the rangers, made by hundreds of rifles and muskets.

Robert and Tayoga were still without wounds. Leaves and twigs rained around them, and they heard often the song of the bullets, they saw many of the rangers fall, but happy fortune kept their own bodies untouched. Robert knew that the battle was a losing one, but he was resolved to hold his place with his comrades. Rogers, who had been fighting with undaunted valor and desperation, marshaling his men in vain against numbers greatly superior, made his way once more to the side of Willet and crouched with him in the bushes.

"Dave, my friend," he said, "the battle goes against us."

"So it does," replied the hunter, "but it is no fault of yours or your men. St. Luc, the best of all the French leaders, has forced us into a trap. There is nothing left for us to do now but burst the trap."

"I hate to yield the field."

"But it must be done. It's better to lose a part of the rangers than to lose all. You've had many a narrow escape before. Men will come to your standard and you'll have a new band bigger than ever."

The dark face of the ranger captain brightened a little. But he looked sadly upon his fallen men. He was bleeding himself from two slight wounds, but he paid no attention to them. The need to flee pierced his soul, but he saw that it must be done, else all the rangers would be destroyed, and, while he still hesitated a moment or two, the silver whistle of St. Luc, urging on a fresh and greater attack, rose above all the sounds of combat. Then he knew that he must wait no longer, and he gave the command for ordered flight.

Not more than half of the rangers escaped from that terrible converging attack. St. Luc's triumph was complete. He had won full revenge for his defeat by Andiatarocte, and he pushed the pursuit with so much energy and skill that Rogers bade the surviving rangers scatter in the wilderness to reassemble again, after their fashion, far to the south.

Black Rifle remained with the leader, but Robert, Tayoga and Willet continued their flight together, not stopping until night, when they were safe from pursuit. As the three went southward through the deep forest, they saw many trails that they knew to be those of hostile Indians, and nowhere did they find a sign of a friend. All the wilderness seemed to have become the country of the enemy. When they looked once more from the lofty shores upon the vivid waters of George, they beheld canoes, but as they watched they discovered that they were those of the foe. A terrible fear clutched at their hearts, a fear that Montcalm, like St. Luc, had struck already.

"The tide of battle has flowed south of us," said Tayoga. "All that we find in the forest proclaims it."

"I would you were not right, Tayoga," said the hunter, "but I fear you are."

They came the next day to the trail of a great army, soldiers and cannon. Night overtook them while they were still near the shores of Lake George, following the road, left by the French and Indian host as it had advanced south, and the three, wearied by their long flight, drew back into the dense thickets for rest. The darkness had come on thicker and heavier than usual, and they were glad of it, as they were well hidden in its dusky folds, and they wished to rest without apprehension.

They had food with them which they ate, and then they wrapped their blankets about their bodies, because a wind was coming from the lake, and its touch was damp. Clouds also covered all the skies, and, before long, a thin, drizzling rain fell. They would have been cold, and, in time, wet to the bone, but the blankets were sufficient to protect them.

"Areskoui, after smiling upon us for so long, has now turned his face from us," said Tayoga.

"What else can you expect?" said the valiant Willet. "It is always so in war. You're up and then you're down. We were masters of the peaks for a while, and by our capture of Garay's letter we kept St. Luc from attacking Albany, but the stars never fight for you all the time. We couldn't do anything that would save the rangers from defeat."

The Onondaga looked up. The others could not see his face, but it was reverential, and the cold rain that fell upon it had then no chill for him. Instead it was soothing.

"Tododaho is on his great star beyond the clouds," he said, "and he is looking down on us. We have done wrong or he and Areskoui would not have withdrawn their favor from us, but we have done it unknowingly, and, in time, they will forgive us. As long as the Onondagas are true to him Tododaho will watch over them, although at times he may punish them."

That Tododaho was protecting them even then was proved conclusively to Tayoga before the night was over. A great war party passed within a hundred yards of them, going swiftly southward, but the three, swathed in their blankets, and, hidden in the dark thickets, had no fear. They were merely three motes in the wilderness and the warriors did not dream that they were near. When the last sound of their marching had sunk into nothingness, Tayoga said:

"It was not the will of Tododaho that they should suspect our presence, but I fear that they go to a triumph."

They rose from the thicket early the following morning, and resumed their flight, but it soon came to a halt, when the Onondaga pointed to a trail in the forest, made apparently by about twenty warriors. The hawk eye of Tayoga, however, picked out one trace among them which all three knew was made by a white man.

"I know, too," said the red youth, "the white man who made it."

"Tell us his name," said the hunter, who had full confidence in the wonderful powers of the Onondaga.

"It is the Frenchman, Langlade, who held Dagaeoga a prisoner in his village so long. I know his traces, because I followed them before. His foot is very small, and it has been less than an hour since he passed here. They are ahead of us, directly in our path."

"What do you think we ought to do, Dave?" asked Robert, anxiously. "You know we want to go south as fast as we can."

"We must try to go around Langlade," replied Willet. "It's true, we'll lose time, but it's better to lose time and be late a little than to lose our lives and never get there at all."

"The Great Bear is a very wise man," said Tayoga.

They made at once a sharp curve toward the east, but just when they thought they were passing parallel with Langlade's band, they were fired upon from a thicket, the bullet singing by Robert's ear.

The three took cover in the bushes, and a long and trying combat of sharpshooters took place. Two warriors were slain and both Willet and Tayoga were grazed by the Indian fire, but they were not hurt. Robert once caught sight of Langlade, and he might have dropped the partisan with his bullet, but his heart held his hand. Langlade had shown him many a kindness, during his long captivity and, although he was a fierce enemy now, the lad was not one to forget. As he had spared De Galissonnière, so would he spare Langlade, and, in a moment or two, the Frenchman was gone from his sight.

Another dark and rainy night came, and, protected by it, they crept in silence past the partisan's band soon leaving this new danger far behind them. Tayoga was very grateful, and accepted their escape as a sign.

"While Manitou, who rules all things, has decreed that we must suffer much before victory," he said, "yet, as I see it, he has decreed also that we three shall not fall, else why does he spread so many dangers before us, and then take us safely through them?"

"It looks the same way to me," said Willet. "The dark and rainy night that he sent enabled us to pass by Langlade and his band."

"A second black night following a first," said Tayoga, devoutly. "I do not doubt that it was sent for our benefit by Manitou, who is lord even over Tododaho and Areskoui."

They made good speed near the shores of Andiatarocte and now and then they caught glimpses once more through the heavy green foliage of the lake's glittering waters. But they saw anew the canoes of the French and Indians upon its surface, and they realized with increasing force that Andiatarocte, so vital in the great struggle, belonged, for the time at least, to their enemies. Yet the three themselves were favored. The rain ceased, a warm wind out of the south dried the forest, and their flight became easy. A fat deer stood in their path and fairly asked to be shot, furnishing them all the food they might need for days to come, and they were able to dress and prepare it at their leisure.

"It is clear, as I have already surmised and stated," said Tayoga in his precise language, "that the frown of Manitou is not for us three. The way opens before us, and we shall rejoin our friends."

"If we have any friends left," said the hunter. "I fear greatly, Tayoga, that Montcalm will have struck before we arrive. He has a powerful force with plenty of cannon, and we know he acts with decision and speed."

"He has struck already and he has struck terribly," said Tayoga with great gravity.

"How do you know that?" asked Robert, startled.

"I do not know it because of anything that has been told to me in words," replied the Onondaga, "but O, Dagaeoga, the mind, which is often more potent than eye or ear, as I have told you so many times, is now warning me. We know that our people farther south have been in disagreement. The governors of the provinces have not acted together. Everyone is of his own mind, and no two minds are alike. No effort was made to profit by the great victory last year on the shores of Andiatarocte. Waraiyageh, sore in body and mind, rests at home, so it is not possible that our people have been ready and vigorous."

"While the French and Indians are all that we are not?"

"Even so. Montcalm advances with great speed, and knows precisely what he intends to do. He has had plenty of time to reach our forts below. His force is overwhelming, though more so in preparation and decision, than in numbers. He has had time to strike, and being Montcalm, therefore he has struck. There is no chance of error, O, Dagaeoga and Great Bear, when I tell you a heavy blow has fallen upon us."

"I don't want to believe you, Tayoga," said the hunter, "but I do. The conclusion seems inevitable to me."

"I'm hoping when hope's but faint," said Robert.

They swung again into the great trail, left by the army of Montcalm, or at least a part of it, and the Onondaga and the hunter told its tale with precision.

"Here passed the cannon," said Tayoga. "I judge by the size of the ruts the wheels made that a battery of twelve pounders went this way. What do you say, Great Bear?"

"You're right, of course, Tayoga, and there were eight guns in the battery; a child could tell their number. They had other batteries too."

"And the wooden walls of our forts wouldn't stand much chance against a continuous fire of twelve and eighteen pounders," said Robert.

"No," said Willet. "The forts could be saved only by enterprising and skillful commanders who would drive away the batteries."

"Here went the warriors," said Tayoga. "They were on the outer edges of the great trail, walking lightly, according to their custom. See the traces of the moccasins, scores and scores of them. We will come very soon to a place where the whole army camped for the night. How do I know, O, Dagaeoga? Because numerous trails are coming in from the forest and converging upon one point. They do that because it is time to gather for food and the night's rest. Some of the warriors went into the forest to hunt game, and they found it, too. Look at the drops of blood, still faintly showing on the grass, leading here, and here, and here into the main trail, drops that fell from the deer they had slain. Also they shot birds. Behold feathers hanging on the bushes, blown there by the wind, which proves that the site of their camp is very near, as I said."

"It's just over the hill in that wide, shallow valley," said Willet.

They entered the valley which had been marked by the departed army with signs as clear as the print of a book for the Onondaga and the hunter to read.

"Here at the northern end of the valley is where the warriors cooked and ate the deer they had slain," said Tayoga. "The bones are scattered all about, and we see the ashes of their fires, but they kept mostly to themselves, because few footprints of white men lead to the place they set aside as their own. Just beyond them the cannon were parked. All this is very simple. An Onondaga child eight years old could read what is written in this camp. Here are the impressions made by the cannon wheels, and just beside them the artillery horses were tethered, as the numerous hoofprints show."

"And here, I imagine," said Robert, who had walked on, "the Marquis de Montcalm and his lieutenants spent the night. Tents were pitched for them. You can see the holes left by the pegs."

"Spoken truly, O, Dagaeoga. You are using eye and mind, and lo! you are showing once more the beginnings of wisdom. Four tents were pitched. The rest of the army slept in the open. Montcalm and his lieutenants themselves would have done so, but the setting up of the tents inspired respect in the warriors and even in the troops. The French leaders have mind and they profit by it. They neglect no precaution, no detail to increase their prestige and maintain their authority."

"It is so, Tayoga," said Willet, "and I can wish that our own officers would do the same. The French are marvelously expert in dealing with Indians. They can handle them all, except the Hodenosaunee. But don't you think they held a short council here by this log, after they had eaten their suppers?"

"It cannot be doubted, Great Bear. Montcalm and his captains sat on the log. The Indian chiefs sat in a half circle before it, and they smoked a pipe. See, the traces of the ashes on the grass. They were planning the attack upon the fort. It is bound to be William Henry, because the trail leads in that direction."

"And these marks on the log, Tayoga, show that there was some indecision, at first, and much talking. Two or three of the French officers had their hunting knives in their hands, and they carved nervously at the log, just as a man will often whittle as he argues."

"Well stated, O, Great Bear. After the conference, the chiefs went back in single file to their own part of the camp. Here goes their trail, and you can nearly fancy that all stepped exactly in the footprints of the first."

"The straight, decisive line proves too, Tayoga, that the plan was completed and everything ready for the attack. The chiefs would not have gone away in such a manner if they had not been satisfied."

"Well stated again, Great Bear. The Marquis de Montcalm also went directly back to his tent. See, where the boot heels pressed."

"But you have no way of knowing," said Robert, "that the traces of boot heels indicate the Marquis."

"O, Dagaeoga, after all my teaching, you forget again that mind can see where the eye cannot. Train the mind! Train the mind, and you will get much profit from it. The traces of these boot heels lead directly to the place where the largest tent stood. We know it was the largest, because the holes left by the tent pegs are farthest apart. And we know it belonged to the Marquis de Montcalm, because, always having that keen eye for effect, the French Commander-in-Chief would have no tent but the largest."

"True as Gospel, Tayoga," said the hunter, "and the French officers themselves had a little conference in the tent of the Marquis, after they had finished with the Indian chiefs. Here, within the square made by the pegs, are the prints of many boot heels and they were not all made by the Marquis, since they are of different sizes. Probably they were completing some plans in regard to the artillery, since the warriors would have nothing to do with the big guns. Here are ashes, too, in the corner near one of the pegs. I think it likely that the Marquis smoked a thoughtful pipe after all the others had gone."

"Aye, Dave," said Robert, "and he had much to think about. The officers from Europe find things tremendously changed when they come from their open fields into this mighty wilderness. We know what happened to Braddock, because we saw it, and we had a part in it. I can understand his mistake. How could a soldier from Europe read the signs of the forest, signs that he had never seen before, and foresee the ambush?"

"He couldn't, Robert, lad, but while countries change in character men themselves don't. Braddock was brave, but he should have remembered that he was not in Europe. The Marquis de Montcalm remembers it. He made no mistake at Oswego and he is making none here. He took the Indian chiefs into council, as we have just seen. He placates them, he humors their whims, and he draws out of them their full fighting power to be used for the French cause."

Tayoga ranged about the shallow valley a little, and announced that the whole force had gone on together the morning after the encampment.

"The artillery and the infantry were in close ranks," he said, "and the warriors were on either flank, scouting in the forest, forming a fringe which kept off possible scouts of the English and Americans. There was no chance of a surprise attack which would cut up the forces of Montcalm and impede his advance."

Willet sighed.

"The Marquis, although he may not have known it," he said, "was in no danger from such an enterprise. We have read the signs too well, Tayoga. Our own people have been lying in their forts, weak of will, waiting to defend themselves, while the French and their allies have had all the wilderness to range over, and in which they might do as they pleased. It is easy to see where the advantage lies."

"And we shall soon learn what has happened," said Tayoga, gravely.

The next morning they met an American scout who told them the terrible news of the capture of Fort William Henry, with its entire garrison, by Montcalm, and the slaughter afterward of many of the prisoners by the Indians.

Robert was appalled.

"Is Lake George to remain our only victory?" he exclaimed.

"It's better to have a bad beginning and a good ending than a good beginning and a bad ending," said the scout.

"Remember," said Tayoga, "how Areskoui watched over us, when we were among the peaks. As he watched over us then so later on he will watch over our cause."

"It was only for a moment that I felt despair," said Robert. "It is certain that victory always comes to those who know how to work and wait."

Courage rose anew in their hearts, and once more they sped southward, resolved to make greater efforts than any that had gone before.